CAUTION:
HEROES AT WORK

Grover, posing as Phillip, led the way swinging his two-handed great sword to great effect, to his own surprise and also to the surprise of those that he killed.

Cilla followed in his wake, braining with her club those who had survived Grover's initial onslaught. Together they formed a fighting unit, killing any hapless soldier or knight who came into their path. It seemed they were going to take the field that day.

And then the enemy released his reserve troops. It was a massive wall of steel on the move, a tidal wave of human flesh, unstoppable and unrelenting.

Grover quickly appraised the situation. "This is a disaster."

"You see what happens when you fall for a pretty face," Cilla said.

"I thought we were supposed to win," Grover said, hacking with his sword.

"Me too," Cilla said, bludgeoning someone with her club. "I guess we were wrong."

Ace Books by Kyle Crocco

HEROES, INC.
HEROES WANTED

HEROES WANTED

KYLE CROCCO

ACE BOOKS, NEW YORK

This book is dedicated to the three women who have given me their time and wisdom to help me in my pursuit of writing.

Chris Kridler, my first editor and critic, she never let me down, and always listened to me beyond the time I should have shut up.

Beth Fleisher, my first professional editor and critic, you always remember your first girl.

Laura Anne Gilman, my second professional editor in as many months, thanks for the patience and the on-the-job training, even though I wasn't an English major and didn't read my contract.

But a kingdom that has once been destroyed can never come again into being: nor can the dead ever be brought back to life.

All warfare is based on deception.

—**Sun Tzu,** *The Art of War*

Hoven,
its principalities,
and its rulers

Westerhoven:

1. Ubbergammu
   Sajin
2. Meistertonne
   Richard
3. Vagner
   Bertrand
4. Wunderkinde
   Phillip
5. Dresdel
   Ivan
6. Hoenecker
   Prince Thorn
7. Helmutov
   Dianna
8. Kurtonburg
   Vince and his son Kirk

Sousterhoven:

1. Reichton
   Hans
2. Astertov
   Luke
3. Teuton
   Bertold
4. Auschwitz
   Calvin
5. Gustavus
   David

Hoven

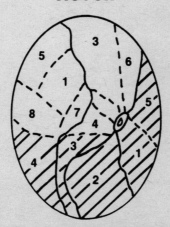

▨ Sousterhoven
▫ Westerhoven

Introduction to a Hero

Cilla: Hi, my name is Cilla.

Argh Representative: And what do you do for a living?

C: You know that, you were at the meeting.

AR: Yes, but you're supposed to tell me.

C: I'm a hero.

AR: What do you think is the greatest problem that heroes have to deal with today?

C: All the idiots you have to work with, like you, for example. If I didn't have to work with so many idiots it would be a better job. Idiots are everywhere. They breed like rabbits.

AR: And when dealing with idiots, what brand of knife do you prefer most?

C: *Argh* brand.

AR: Thank you, Cilla. Whether you are an overrated hero or just pissed off, don't use just a knife, use *Argh* brand, the brand that makes them say "argh."

C: Is it over yet?

AR: Yes, it's over.

C: Then take this

AR: *Argh!*

C::   Hey, it really works.

PART I

How to Ruin a Prophecy on One Betrayal a Day

How to Ruin
a Wizard's Day

. . . another time, another place, on what could have very well been an ordinary day, but wasn't, one man was trying to resolve in his conscience how he could allow his Lord to be killed. His name was Voss, and as he waited in the coolness of the early morning for the sun to break above the treetops, and for Phillip, his Lord, to unravel the mystery of the *Sacred Stone,* he wrestled between his long-standing oath to Phillip and the ties of blood and tradition that made him loyal to the Reichton family, which had forced him into the position he was in now. Betrayal. Betrayal of the very man who had saved him from death.

Of course, it was also true that that man had put him in that position of death, giving him the choice of either jumping off the ledge or becoming his bootlicking slave. But Voss had no insane urge to push Phillip into the reflecting pool and hold his head under until his body stopped writhing, and then go off for a few beers. No, Voss wasn't like that. He was only troubled that he had broken his oath to Phillip no matter how it was made. The very idea of betrayal made his face twitch.

He could have prevented all this from happening. When he had awoken early this morning and had brought Phillip water from a nearby stream, he could have said something like "Oh, by the way, I'm going to betray you today at the reflecting pool, so it might not be a good idea to go," or "I have something on my mind: Is it okay to betray one's Lord and loyalty because of one's former loyalties? I'm just curious." He could have said these things, but to be honest, they didn't occur to him. He had just gazed at Phillip and hoped he would change his mind. But Phillip had awoken eager and didn't have any idea about changing his plans.

So, just as they had planned to, under the cover of darkness, when the city of Hoven was just a dark shadow and the men in their encampment were not yet stirring, they slipped quietly to the *Still Standing Forest* where the reflecting pool was located. Phillip had wanted to come here for a long time, because legend stated

2

that if you looked into the pool you could see the location of the much-sought-after *Sacred Stone*. It was also rumored that you could see your future. But most people who had visited the pool said all you could see was your reflection, or the inscription at the bottom of the pool that read, "This is private property. Get out. That means you." For many, that was omen enough.

They had left the camp without informing any of the other Lords, or even members of their own company, because Phillip was aware that there was still some jealousy on the part of the Lords of Westerhoven about his leadership. He knew that others also sought the *Stone*, especially Prince Thorn, and he didn't want them to know that he was also actively seeking it.

Phillip thought the idea to come out here this morning was solely his own, to see if he could find the *Stone* and if his future was actually as prophesied—that he would unite the Empire of Hoven after three hundred years of factional strife—but really the idea had been Voss's. Voss mentioned that they were close to the pool and he had been the one to suggest they go under the cover of darkness without anyone else knowing. Yet this idea hadn't been Voss's either, but Hans of Reichton's, the admitted foe and rival of Phillip for power in Hoven. Hans had had intermediaries indicate to Voss that he, Voss, was still a citizen of Sousterhoven and it was his duty to help Hans. A duty by ties of blood and tradition, and even of honor. So Voss had betrayed Phillip and had led him to the pool where he would be met by Hans.

The night before they left, Voss had signaled to Hans that they would be going to the pool the next morning before dawn. Just as Hans had predicted, Phillip had come alone, only bringing his swordbearer, Voss. And there, in the cold dawn of a spring morning, Hans waited for the right moment to spring upon Phillip and thus secure his own destiny.

At the very moment when Voss's face twitched with the idea of betrayal, and while he tried to decide if he should cry out to Phillip in warning or maybe say something subtle like "Good day to get betrayed, huh?" Phillip himself was squatting in front of the pool, pulling at the blond whiskers of his beard.

In a land of short men (and women, for that matter) he was tall. And in a land where dark-colored hair was the rule, his hair was blond. And in a land where there were real men, he was a real wo— . . . he was a real man among men. From his youth he had shown no promise at all of ever becoming anything significant, and had been severely beaten and humiliated by his older brothers. His parents saw him as a sure failure and even the court poets had trouble coming up with a good rhyme that didn't produce outright ridicule. But Phillip had overcome the traumas and problems of his youth. From a boy who was short, weak, and stupid he had gone ahead to prove these attributes could be overcome, or at least that they weren't as bad as they looked on paper. From short he had become tall, standing a head above all men. From weak he had become strong, able to defeat any man in a contest of strength or will. And from stupid . . . well, he remained stupid, but he had heart, and determination, and proved that stupid could be an asset, especially in a society where the size of your pride was determined by the length of your sword.

And from his low status in the family, as youngest son, with more competent brothers, he had become the only son, when all the rest had been killed in various battles or quests of honor. And he had gone on to forge a new unit of knights known as the Dude Knights, and with them he had built up the strength to begin unifying Hoven, one principality at a time.

But he thought little of this as he squatted near the edge of the pool, his great sword on the broken and dirty tiles beside him. He was only waiting for the sun to rise.

The light across the lake was becoming brighter and soon the sun would shine a path of light directly to the pool. Behind him, Voss frittered by one of the many columns that flanked the pool and wondered if Hans had gotten the message—if he would come here at all. He was getting angry that he had worried all this time when Hans might just have decided to sleep in this morning instead. He looked at Phillip and wondered what he would look like dead, and made a coughing sound.

Phillip didn't move. His long ponytail of blond hair—his warrior's mane—remained motionless on his back.

Voss gazed at the other marble columns, stained yellow from years of rain, and wondered if Hans was behind them. He then looked at Phillip and coughed again. He couldn't let this happen. He had to warn him. "Ah, O great, and wise, and righteously cool Lord Phillip."

Phillip stirred slightly. "You forgot 'totally chilled.' "

"And totally chilled Lord Phillip," Voss added. He waited, and when Phillip said nothing, he said, "May I have permission to speak?"

"Don't bug me, dude," Phillip said. "Can't you see I'm staring at the pool."

"Yes," Voss said. "But . . . but," and he blurted it out, "maybe we shouldn't have come." And he thought, You fool, I'm betraying you. And then he kept speaking. "You know, we might be missed. The attack is supposed to go on today. Erich might get worried." His words stopped and silence remained. It wasn't good to suggest going back. Because if Hans overheard, he might think he was trying to warn Phillip. But he had an obligation to Phillip, as his swordbearer, to warn him when he was in danger. It occurred to him that he couldn't be loyal to two masters at one time, but since he was young he was willing to give it a try.

"Didn't I say not to bug me? I distinctly recall saying those words. Will you chill out?" Phillip gestured to the pool. "The sun hasn't even risen. The sun has to rise before the location is revealed."

Voss sighed. He had tried. It wasn't his fault now if Phillip died on Han's sword.

Phillip glanced at the water again, slightly annoyed with Voss, who had been acting weird all morning. Probably because he's short, Phillip surmised. I was short once. He turned his full attention to the pool and saw that the surface was still, like glass. He could see the light blue sky clearly reflected in the water, but no pictures of prophecy and no maps to the *Sacred Stone*. But that was all right. It was only a matter of moments before the sun broke from above the trees.

From behind a monument to a long-dead prince, and dressed in iron chain mail and leather breeches, waited Hans of Reichton, the man who had been doomed at birth to rule the broken Empire of Hoven. But he didn't believe in pools of prophecy or in the legend of the *Sacred Stone*. What he did believe in, and strongly, was his own destiny and the curse that was put on his family, and the special curse that said he would die by the hand of a friend once he ruled the empire. And he knew that Phillip was an impediment to his destiny. Phillip too was prophesied to rule Hoven, but where two destinies were the same, only one could come true. And it was going to be his.

Hans was the opposite of Phillip in temperament and in coloring. Where Phillip was light, Hans was dark. His hair was almost black, but was chopped at shoulder length instead of the usual ponytail that most knights had. It was a sign that he had once been captured in battle, and instead of choosing to die, he agreed to be ransomed and now bore that badge of shame. But instead of hiding the fact, he wore his hair short still, and often entered in contests of honor over slights that may have been made about it. In this regard, he wasn't very different from many people in

Hoven, whose only code was honor and family, and if you claimed you were standing for those values and could back it up with a sharp sword and a few friends, then few people were willing to yell insults across the street at you, or find fault with you in public places or publications.

Hans was also different from Phillip in his features. His were sharper, more defined, from a short beak-like nose and thin eyebrows to a pointed chin. Hans was also quite intelligent, though he suffered from some periods of self-doubt. And he found Phillip's lack of social graces insulting. All this and more bothered Hans about Phillip. But what bothered him the most was not that Phillip thought he had the *cojones* to be King of Hoven, and not that Phillip thought he was prophesied to rule, but that Hans of Reichton wasn't even considered a threat in Phillip's mind. That's what bothered him most. That was an insult he could not stand.

So while Phillip waited for the sun to rise, Hans put on his leather gloves and felt the weight of his great sword and knew that this was going to be a good day. Soon, Phillip would be dead, the whole of Westerhoven would be thrown into chaos, and he could take his time in fulfilling his doom.

The sun had finally risen above the trees on the mainland, and Phillip took in a breath and gazed at the pool.

Voss moved up behind him and asked, "Do you see anything?"

Phillip leaned closer, so that his face was only a foot from the surface. "Nothing. Nothing."

"Nothing at all?" Voss asked.

Phillip mumbled no and then said, "Wait. Wait."

"Yes," Voss said.

Phillip pointed at the pool. "I never knew I was this good-looking." He laughed a goofy, hyena-type laugh, which most people found annoying.

Voss cringed from the laugh. "I meant . . ."

"Yeah, I know," Phillip said. "Do you think I'm stupid? You think I'm stupid, don't you?"

Voss was surprised by the assertion. "There's something I have to tell you."

"Later, dude," Phillip said. "Like, I'm busy."

"But I have to . . ."

"Then go behind the bushes," Phillip said. "Didn't I tell you that you don't need to ask for . . ."

"It's not that, it's . . ." Voss started.

Just then, Hans and the five fully armored knights who

accompanied him circled the monument and came into sight, standing at the other side of the pool, their feet making cracking noises on the broken tile.

Phillip looked up suddenly, seeing Hans standing there coolly, dressed boldly in the black and white colors of his principality, holding his great sword in front of him like a wizard's staff.

"So," Hans said. "We meet for the first time."

Phillip turned to Voss. "Didn't I tell you to keep guard?"

"No," Voss said.

"Oh," Phillip muttered. "I thought I did. Well, what's done is done."

Voss backed away from Phillip. "I'm sorry. But I'm related to the Reichton family. My great-great-grandmother's second cousin was married to Hans's great-grandfather's third cousin. So you see, I'm duty bound."

"What! You never said anything about ties to Reichton . . ."

"That's because you always told me to 'shut up, stupid,' " Voss said. "It's always been 'shut up, stupid, shut up, stupid.' Never, 'Here's a free beer, dude,' 'I appreciate you, dude,' 'Go take the night off, dude.' It's always been 'Shine my armor, stupid,' or 'Get me some condoms, stupid.' You know? So are you surprised that I betrayed you?"

Phillip stroked his blond beard. "No," he finally said. "I just thought you would betray me when I wasn't around."

Voss looked confused. "Don't you mean . . ."

Hans stomped his foot on the broken tile and once more there was silence around the reflecting pool. "I hate to break up your intellectual discussion, though it truly fascinates me, but I haven't come here to listen to you bicker."

Phillip and Voss stared at Hans. Meanwhile Hans's knights deployed themselves around the pool, surrounding them. Each had pulled out a great sword.

"Only four men," Phillip sneered. He stood up and held out his own great sword. "I've fought more than that and survived."

"Six men," Voss corrected. "Six men counting Hans."

"Yeah, six, whatever," Phillip said. "So what is it going to be, dude?"

"Don't call me dude," Hans said. "Why can't you speak proper English?"

"What, dude?" Phillip replied.

"Never mind," Hans said.

"So what's it going to be, dude? I will never submit to capture. I'd die before I let my warrior's braid be cut."

Hans shrugged. "Very well. Then I'll kill you."

Phillip blinked and for a moment the reality of his own nonexistence entered his brain. "Surely you're kidding."

Hans shook his head. "I don't joke."

"Really," Phillip said. "That's bogus."

"I can't," Hans explained. "I have no sense of humor. When you're cursed like I am you lose your sense of humor. Everything is just gloom, some things gloomier than others. It is my doom to be ruler of this empire. To do that, you must be dead."

Phillip took a step back from the edge of the pool even though Hans had as yet to move forward. Then he laughed his annoying hyena laugh. "Ha, but there's something you forgot. Man, you really blew it this time. *I'm* supposed to rule Hoven. It was foretold, in prophecy. Ha, you can't fuck with prophecy. So go on, do your worst, dude. I have no worries."

Hans twisted his face distastefully at Phillip's response. He then moved forward slowly. He walked along the edge of the pool, each step carefully placed. As he walked, he spoke as an instructor teaching a young disciple. "Let me tell you something about destiny. You say it is your destiny to rule. It is my destiny to kill you. When there are two destinies that are incompatible, which destiny do you think wins out?"

Phillip was silent. "Is this a trick question?" Vague memories of his school days filtered through his head. "Okay, okay, if I'm meant to be king, and you're meant to kill me . . . Let's see . . . There can only be one king and . . ." Phillip shook his head. "I don't know. You got me."

"I certainly do," Hans said, and stepped forward into striking distance and brought up his great sword. Phillip had little time to respond. His arms were just starting to bring up his own blade to counter when Hans's blade ripped through the skin of his neck, slicing through living muscle, severing the spinal column, and bursting through the other side, so that Phillip's head sprung forward with a jet of blood, a look of anxious puzzlement still set on his features, as his noggin flew through the air.

The head fell into the pool, sank a few feet, and then bobbed to the surface, leaving a trail of blood, like scum, on the water. The rest of the body stood there for a moment and then crumpled appropriately, with a fountain of blood spurting forth at the neck in time with beats of the heart.

"Wipeout, dude," Hans said with mild irony, standing over the corpse.

When the moment of shock was over, Hans examined his blade

and found it notched where it had made contact with bone. He wiped off the excess blood and tissue on Phillip's shirt and then sheathed his blade.

Voss, who had been standing a few feet away, was still stunned. When he saw his Lord's head bob up, he knew that he had finally done the deed, betrayed his own master. There was only one thing left to do.

"So when do I get paid?" Voss asked, stepping forward to present himself, an itchy palm outstretched.

"As agreed," Hans said, and signaled to one of his knights, who brought over a leather pouch. Hans shook the pouch and there was a satisfying jingling sound. Satisfied, he handed the bag over to Voss.

"Thank you," Voss said, gloating over the bag.

"You have served Sousterhoven and the principality of Reichton well. And even Astertov, your home country."

"Thank you," Voss said. "And as agreed, you will allow me to serve you."

"As agreed," Hans said. And then lifted a gloved hand. "As long as you accept the laws and rules that govern Reichton."

"I do," Voss said.

"Then you agree," Hans said.

"I do."

Hans nodded. He lifted the sheathed blade and touched it lightly to each shoulder of Voss and knighted him in the name of Reichton. "You understand as a knight of Reichton that it is treason to have consorted with the enemy."

Voss, who had been thinking about how he could spend the gold in the pouch, looked up in alarm. "Pardon?"

"Sorry, there is no pardon. You entered into the agreement with full knowledge of what you were doing. I commend you for aiding in Phillip's downfall, but you also aided him against us."

"But . . ." Voss said. "I had to . . . I . . ."

"I would kill you myself," Hans said. "But killing a traitor is bad luck and I am already doomed."

"You can't kill . . . Hey," Voss shouted as he saw the five knights approach.

One of them produced a crossbow.

"Wait just a . . ." Voss shouted, and then said no more.

When the sun had fully risen above the island of Hoven, there were two dead bodies lying by the reflecting pool. This scene was taken in by a late-rising wizard, somewhere far west of the actual scene. He turned away from the crystal ball and massaged his aching forehead, caused by a night of too much drinking. He had only two words to sum up his general feelings about life, his often quoted prophecy, the fate of Westerhoven, and his future employment prospects.

"Oh shit."

How to Fake a Prophecy

The wizard was tall and skinny, with long frizzy gray hair that fell down to the small of his back, and which he never seemed to notice when it blew before his eyes or became caught in his mouth. He was gaunt, with sunken-in cheeks and a flat chest, but seemed lively despite his appearance. When asked his age he claimed it to be somewhere over one hundred, but wouldn't specify exactly how much over a hundred, or even if the hundred was supposed to represent years. Many marveled at his longevity and openly wondered what his secret was, thinking it must be something magical that kept him alive. He claimed what kept him alive was the wisdom not to participate in cold-steel fights to the death. Many wondered at these words but few could decipher the riddle in them. Though the people knew of the uses of iron, they knew little of the use of irony.

His name was Beogoat and he claimed to be the younger brother of Beowulf, though no one could see the resemblance. He said the chief difference between the two was that Beowulf was dead and he wasn't.

For as long as anyone could remember he had served at the court of Wunderkinde, performing small feats of magic and generally making sure his paycheck arrived on time. Beogoat was the first to see the potential of the young boy named Phillip, and once that boy had consolidated a few of the scattered principalities, Beogoat had seen fit to make known the prophecy that Phillip would one day unite the Empire of Hoven. Phillip, or one of his heirs. He added the last bit just to play it safe.

It had seemed a good bet at the time, when Phillip's chief rival had been his own ego. Principality after principality had either sworn loyalty to him or been made to submit, until the whole of Westerhoven was united for the first time in centuries. Only Sousterhoven and its individual principalities remained to make unity complete. And then Hans of Reichton appeared on the scene calling upon the other Sousterhoven nations to help him repel Phillip, claiming that, being cursed to make war, it was his doom to bring Phillip to his knees and assume power, only to be killed by his closest friend. No one doubted his claim. The Reichton family, as it was well known, had been cursed for some time. And so some troops were sent to Reichton, not many, but enough for Hans to pose a threat. But Phillip had not been afraid and had been tricked into meeting Hans when he wasn't ready, and so ended his life as stupidly as he had lived it.

Beogoat shook his head sadly, and realized that the Wester-hoven principalities would probably fall apart without a central leader. In that shocking moment of realization, he had made a quick decision, and followed it with a stiff drink. Then two stiff drinks. And then another look at the crystal ball which still displayed the horrid scene.

"What an awful way to wake up," he said to himself. But he was awake now, and once awake there was nothing left to do but get on with it. So he quickly awoke his recalcitrant assistant, aptly named Beoweasel because of his pinched-up face and living habits. And together they went to the island of Hoven, via a little transportation magic Beogoat had picked up.

A few moments later they were standing beside the reflecting pool where Phillip's head still bobbed in the water.

Beogoat hadn't been exactly sure what he was going to do when he arrived, only thinking that the death of Phillip should be kept secret as long as possible.

"But who'll believe he's on vacation?" asked his disciple.

Beogoat rubbed his throbbing skull. "You're right. These people don't even know the concept of vacation. We'll tell them he's on a quest."

Beoweasel walked to the other side of Phillip's body. "But why a quest? He said he would not rest until Hans was dead."

Beogoat rubbed his throbbing skull. "I don't know. Because it was part of the prophecy, damn it. Just stall them. Tell them he's in private counsel. That he needs to make a journey before he can claim victory. Anything."

"I don't like this," Beoweasel said. "I don't think we should be lying. You can go to hell for things like that. And besides, why can't we tell the Lords that Phillip is dead?"

Beogoat brushed the long hair out of his face. "Where did I get you anyway? What's this honesty business? You're my assistant and you do what I say."

"As I said before," Beoweasel recited, "I never wanted to be a wizard. I think magic is distasteful. I only consented because my father was impressed with your ability as an oracle when you predicted two out of three times which way a coin would land."

Beogoat frowned. "Yes, that was how I got you, wasn't it? For some reason I thought you begged to be hired on. Anyway, I don't need this aggravation, damn it." He looked at the bloody corpse of Phillip which lay between them. "Why couldn't he have died later? Things would be much easier if he wasn't dead."

"But he is," Beoweasel said.

"I know that," Beogoat said. "But if they weren't dead . . ."

"But they are," Beogoat stated. "And I think we should tell the Lords now so . . ."

"Quiet or I'll turn you into a frog."

"You wouldn't," Beoweasel said with alarm.

"I might."

"But you told me you don't know how," Beoweasel said.

"Shut up," Beogoat said, "and pull Phillip's head out of the water."

Beoweasel did as he was told and pulled Phillip's dripping head out by its long blond ponytail.

Beogoat paced along the edge of the pool, talking out loud. "If they weren't dead . . ."

"Here's the head," Beoweasel said, holding the dripping head in front of Beogoat.

"Christ, get that out of my face," Beogoat shouted in distaste.

Beoweasel withdrew the head and placed it on Phillip's chest.

"If they weren't dead," Beogoat went on, "then there would be no problem. The union wouldn't break. Hans would be defeated. And you're right, we can't tell the Lords he's on a permanent quest. Damn it, we need them alive."

"But they're dead," Beoweasel said. "How can we bring them back to life?"

"You got me," Beogoat said. And then there was a change in his face. "That's right, we can't bring them back."

"So we tell the Lords."

"No," Beogoat said. "We cover it up. All we need is two people to take their place. So everyone will think Phillip and Voss are alive."

"Impostors?" Beoweasel questioned. "No one would believe them."

"No," Beogoat said. "Not impostors. Just two people to take their place, to look like them, to lead the people, just until Hans is defeated. Then we can have Phillip die. Not before."

Beoweasel was aghast. "I don't like this."

"You don't have to," Beogoat said. "But first we have to dispose of the bodies. And then, then we can get their . . . ah . . . replacements."

So together they gathered the bodies of Phillip and Voss, and once again using a little transportation magic, they spirited them to the *Ice Caves* in the north, so that the bodies would be preserved from decomposition and hidden from untimely exposure, until they were needed again.

And when they finished that distasteful task, Beoweasel turned to his master.

"But where can we find two people to impersonate?"

"Replace," Beogoat admonished.

"Replace," Beoweasel said. "Where can we find two such people in all of Hoven?"

"Nowhere," Beogoat said mischievously.

"I don't understand you," Beoweasel said.

"Sometimes I don't even understand myself," Beogoat admitted. "But enough self-examination. We won't get someone from Hoven. We need two people who aren't from this land, two people who are trained professionals, who know how to handle tasks such as these."

"What kind of people are these?" Beoweasel asked.

Beogoat was silent as he scratched the stubble on his chin. Finally he said, "People who live on the edge of danger for a living."

"What kind of people would do such a thing as that?"

"Heroes," Beogoat said. "Professional heroes."

"Sound more like lunatics to me," Beoweasel said. "I still say it won't work."

"Shut up," Beogoat said. "And pack my travel bag."

How to Ruin a Hero's Day

The torch flickered from an unseen breeze. Faces, tense and frightened, covered with dirt and grime were visible in the orange light. Each face showed a different nationality. But they all had two things in common: a big nose and a fear of death. No one could say which was bigger, but everyone had an opinion and would voice it even if no one else wanted to hear it.

The short one with the dark hair led the way. She was dressed in light cotton clothing, covered by a leather vest and leggings. At her side swung an empty sword sheath. But if one looked to her right hand, one could quickly see that she hadn't just forgotten to bring it when she woke up that morning. The sword was gripped firmly in her hand, like the rag doll she would never admit to carrying in her childhood. The blade shone in the darkness.

She paused for a moment. In the flickering light, her brown eyes bore down on the assembled company, silently regarding them. "Well, come on, you dorks," she said. "We don't have all day. I didn't pay you money just to baby-sit."

The voices of her followers were subdued, but many grumbled that this was not a task for any human being that valued their life. That they should turn back before it was too late—too late for dinner, that is. And maybe the next morning, after a big breakfast, they could rethink the whole deal and maybe just go home.

The woman ignored them. They're just unnerved by all the skulls, she thought. Ever since they had come closer to the lair, they had come upon the skulls and bones of others who had come here—willingly and unwillingly. The foolish followers had thought it was a bad omen. Didn't they know that this evil wizard was just untidy? She glared at them and then pushed on into the darkness.

Behind her followed a huge man, strongly built. He was not dressed for hard work like his leader, but as if he had been detoured from a social function of high standing. His red breeches were of the finest silk, and the yellow blouse of the softest cotton.

Both of these, to his chagrin, were stained, ripped, and soiled beyond almost all recognition.

And if one looked to his waist, one would also see an empty scabbard, not of a mighty broadsword, as one might expect of such a huge and muscular man, but rather one of an exquisite and fine-tooled rapier. This he held in his right hand, rather like a stick to ward off the taunting boys of the village.

He also paused briefly, put a hand to the rough-hewn wall, and not for the first time blurted out his feelings. "I'd rather be surfing."

The woman stopped and looked back at the large man. And if one looked closely (and had read the first book), one could clearly see that this woman wasn't just Indiana Jones in drag, but the renowned hero Cilla, and this man wasn't just a Conan reject, but her sidekick, Grover. And one would also know they didn't have the kind of personalities that worked well together. Even after a few years.

"We're almost there," she hissed.

"This is foolishness," Grover said. "Foolishness. Madness."

"No, it isn't," Cilla said. "We get paid to do this. Who told you such things?"

Grover nodded his head in the direction of the baggage carriers and mountain guides that comprised their following. Five men and women who had followed them beneath the surface of the earth, carrying the extra torches, the rope, and the food supplies they needed to reach the hidden chamber that contained the crypt.

Cilla looked at the followers. "Is that how you guys feel? That this is madness, foolishness?"

A few nodded their heads and there were a couple "yeahs."

"Didn't you see the skulls?" one of them asked.

"Yeah, I saw them," Cilla said. "So what? Losers. They couldn't handle it. We can. I'm your faithful leader. Don't you guys trust me?"

The followers cast down their heads.

"I guess not," Grover said.

Cilla sneered at them and walked forward to the nearest follower, a skinny fellow who wore little but a burlap robe and carried a huge pack. She lifted his chin up and looked directly into his face. "Go, then, if you're afraid."

The servant blinked his eyes and then said, "Really?"

"Yeah," Cilla said.

The servant immediately turned and ran down the way they had come.

Cilla held up her torch and looked at the rest of the followers. "Any more of you afraid? Who want to leave?"

"Cilla," Grover cautioned, "isn't it a bad idea to get rid of our baggage carriers? Bad for labor relations and all that."

Cilla ignored Grover. "There're more servants where they came from." She waved the torch. "Go, go if you want to miss out on a chance to see the Lich destroyed. See if you get credit in the scroll version."

"Fine with me," one woman said, and threw down her pack. "How about you guys?"

"All right with me," said another.

And soon all their packs had been thrown to the irregular stone floor and Cilla and Grover were left standing alone in the cave.

"You have to have firm discipline," Cilla explained. "You just can't get any good, faithful, 'lead me to the end of the earth' servants these days."

"Maybe if you paid them," Grover suggested.

Cilla looked back in shock. "Pay! Pay! When they have the honor of working with me?"

Grover rolled his eyes. "Do you think all this hero stuff is going to your head?"

"No, why?"

Grover shook his head. "And you wonder why we can't get any help these days."

Cilla pointed at the packs on the ground. "I gave them food, didn't I? And shelter. And a chance for adventure. That's all I ever wanted when I was their age."

"Yeah, well, not everybody's like you," Grover said, and then added softly, "Thank the gods for that."

"What was that?"

"Nothing," Grover said.

"Well, come on, then." She turned her back to Grover and made her way down the tunnel, getting ever closer to the chamber.

Grover watched her small form negotiate the rough path, then heaved a sigh and followed.

It wasn't long until they reached the chamber door. It was set in the wall of a rectangular room, carved out of stone. The door was hexagonal in shape and didn't appear to have anything as mundane as a doorknob. Of course, doors to wizards' lairs never did. It was a union rule.

The door was firmly sealed shut. On its surface were inscribed various arcane symbols. Cilla pulled out an ancient manuscript that was crumbling at the edges. On it were symbols similar to those on the door, with the translation to them written on the side. Cilla traced the symbols on the door and then checked them against her manuscript.

"Is it an enchantment to get in?" Grover asked.

"Un-huh," Cilla muttered. And she read the message slowly. "Speak, Stranger, and Bug Off."

"Message seems clear enough to me," Grover said, turning to go back the way he had come.

Cilla threw down the manuscript. "There must be another way." She took her short sword and started digging at the seal around the door. She was working on breaking the seal to the crypt which had hidden and protected the Lich's body for centuries on end, while its spirit had roamed, inhabiting bodies, impersonating persons both famous and inconsequential, and generally putting them into embarrassing situations before they realized they had been possessed. Grover and Cilla had been hired to kill the Lich.

They had traveled many leagues, over various terrains, braving all kinds of weather and low-quality bearers to arrive at the *Hills of Happiness*, where the Lich was rumored to be buried. And it was here they had begun their long, difficult, and often tedious search for the entrance to the right cave which would lead to the lair. It looked as if they would never find the right cave when they stumbled upon the unmistakable signs they were on the right track.

"Bones," Grover said, pointing.

"Those are unmistakable signs we're on the right track," Cilla said cheerfully.

Obviously they had some trouble hiring on people for such a treacherous quest. It had taken all their methods of persuasion just to get their followers to come to the foot of the hills. And now, when they were close to the end of their journey, they had been abandoned to complete the mission alone, just as they had begun it.

Cilla chipped away the last of the seal. "At last," she cried. "Where magic fails, brute force wins over." And she pried open the door, letting it fall to the ground with a loud crash.

There was a sound of rushing air as the room that had been sealed for centuries was finally let open.

The torch, which Grover had been holding while Cilla chipped at the seal, suddenly blew out. And they stood in the dark.

"Well," Grover said. "What now?"

"You know, I hate it when you ask that."

"Should I light a candle or curse the darkness?" Grover asked.

"Just . . ." Cilla started to say, and then stopped.

Because right then, in front of them, they saw a dark-glowing, fiery light. It was like a ball of fire, suspended in the air, with sparks shooting out its sides. It illuminated the interior of the sealed chamber and they could see the Lich's body lying mummified on a slab of stone.

The ball of fire grew brighter, and larger, until it was twice the size it had been before, about the size and volume of a grown man's chest. Like the wheel of a wagon.

Grover glanced at Cilla. "Okay, go ahead, you're the leader. Kill the Lich. I'll wait here like the faithful servant I pretend to be and sing your praises afterward."

"You don't think I'll do it, do you?" Cilla asked Grover.

Grover shrugged. "My mother always told me never to fuck with the supernatural."

"You're just making that up because you're scared."

"No," Grover said. "I'm making it up so I won't have to go in there and get zapped by the Lich, and spend my life in some eternal hell—which by the way I imagine as spending eternity with you."

Cilla scowled. "I'm not afraid." And then she looked at the bright light. It seemed to have grown larger. Within the blue ball of fire were rings of yellow and black. She wiped her brow and looked at Grover again.

Grover motioned her to go in.

Cilla shrugged and made her first step.

But her foot never entered the interior of the chamber. Before she could put her foot down, there was a crack of thunder behind them, and a flare of blue jagged light. And in the light, they could see three or four men dressed in bright outlandish costumes. One of them, a short pudgy man, dressed all in brown leather, with a black cloak thrown over his shoulders, stepped forward.

"Stop," he said, and pointed at Cilla. "We'll take over from here."

"Who are you?" Cilla asked.

"I am he who is the one who has been named before."

"Quite a long name," Grover said. "So what do your friends call you?"

"Skippy," replied the man. He and his crew walked briskly up to the crypt and blocked the entrance. "I have come to take the Lich."

"What?" Cilla cried. She tried to work her way to the entrance but failed to get through. "But we were here first."

Skippy shook his head. "Destiny calls. We have all played our parts and now it is time to play mine."

"Impressive," Grover said. "Did you write that yourself?"

"I made notecards," Skippy said, and held out a few three-by-five cards. "But if you'll kindly step back, I have a job to do."

"But this is our Lich," Cilla said. "Our Lich," she emphasized.

"You aren't with one of those Save the Wizard groups are you?" Skippy asked.

"No," Cilla said.

"Oh," Skippy said. "Just curious." And he turned to go in.

"But what about us?" Cilla cried. "We have come hundreds of leagues, spent weeks looking for this place, and now you come and want to take our Lich. You can't. It's our Lich. It's our Lich, I say. And I'm going in."

Cilla raised her blade and the other three withdrew, but Skippy stayed, and when Cilla drew close he touched her quickly on the shoulder and she stopped dead, paralyzed.

"Can you teach me that trick?" Grover asked.

Skippy shook his head. "Sorry. Trade secret." He paused for a moment and then added, "The spell shouldn't last long."

"Oh well," Grover lamented. "And the Lich?"

"We'll take care of him," Skippy said.

"But . . . but who are you guys?" Grover asked.

"Wizard Collectors," Skippy said, and handed him a card, which simply read *Wizard Collectors*.

And then the three helpers pulled up the hexagonal seal and pulled it in place behind them, leaving them in the darkness of a sealed chamber.

"I hate wizards," Cilla said when she finally broke out of the spell.

Failed Expectations

It didn't occur to Cilla, until she reached the headquarters of Heroes, Inc., that she and Grover had been going on quests and missions for the past three years without any great success. Grover said they were just having a bad year. What Cilla didn't realize until now is that they were having the same bad year three years in a row.

"Boy, I'm bummed," Cilla sighed.

Cilla, who still went by the name of O Great One, when anyone could remember it, remembered that it had all started so well. After their triumph at the cliffs of Jolinstive, succeeding in securing the gonads for Grover, she had finally achieved her lifelong ambition of being a hero. She had been elated. At first. But there was also the nagging feeling in the background, a sense of unhappiness, caused by having what you always wanted in life, and realizing you didn't have anything else to look forward to. But she ignored that feeling and concentrated on the adventures at hand. The first of which had sent them on a rescue mission of two heroes who had been abducted by a nasty villain looking for retribution. She had been made leader of the team that had stormed the keep and rescued the two heroes from their imminent execution. They were already at the chopping block, waiting for the executioner to finish his morning doughnut when she, Grover, and three other hero temps had swung down the castle walls on ropes in a textbook maneuver, and attacked the villain's henchmen, cutting a path to the heroes. Once they reached the heroes they freed them and fled the keep before more henchmen could impede their progress. Once free they eluded all pursuit, and the following morning they were on a ship sailing back to headquarters. Successful.

The heady feeling of success made her forget her early qualms and she convinced herself that it was her destiny to be a great hero. And she eagerly went on a new mission with the feeling that all would go her way. But on the next mission, they made the mistake of killing the wrong man in a heated moment, and the country had ended up in the rule of someone worse who ordered the execution of the man who had contracted their help in the first place. But killing the wrong man could happen to anybody, right? Right. They were bound to make a mistake sometime. Failure built character and all that stuff.

Except at headquarters comments were beginning to be made about her. You were only as good as your last adventure, they said. And her last adventure was a fiasco. So the doubts began to grow again. Until their next adventure. The next adventure was a success. They saved a princess from marrying an evil prince. But Cilla realized that it hadn't been that great of a success. They had gotten to the prince too easily and had killed him off. Very anticlimactic. And on the way back they had been captured by villains, themselves. And had to be rescued. Rescued! After that, mishap seemed to follow mishap, like one ripple after another in a disturbed pool, and their reputation, which was supposed to grow, only diminished. Soon they could only get the most mundane adventures—piddling disputes between peasants and landlords. Stuff that didn't pay well, but which they were relatively successful at, and got a good reputation for among the poorer peoples. But that wasn't what Cilla wanted.

So from a person who had been happy and thought she had all she ever wanted, she changed to being bitter and vaguely dissatisfied all the time. And her partner, Grover, didn't seem to mind, or even fare worse for the experience. He always said look at the bright side, we're not dead, are we? He was always saying look at the bright side. It pissed her off. Especially since he never got depressed or seemed to mind their mishaps. Cilla started to partly blame him. She kept thinking, If only I had a better sidekick, one with brass *cojones*, then we would be successful.

So she had taken to drinking, long naps, and bar fights to alleviate the stress, but not in that order, and sometimes at the same time.

And then the adventure of the Lich came along. It seemed like her long-awaited chance for success. She campaigned for them to be assigned it, and had succeeded. And everything had gone well. They had crossed the mountains, forded the streams, and fought the elements successfully. Guides had shown them through long-faded and forgotten paths. They had consulted elders by small fires in ancient villages. Learned of rumors and pieces of past history about where the Lich resided. Every day they drew closer to his lair. She had become confident once again. It seemed like she was close to the great success she had been waiting for all along. It only took one good adventure to put you on top again.

But after weeks of trial and error, of searching for the right cave, of fighting sickness and disease, mutinies among the followers, and her own belief that maybe she didn't have what it took anymore, they had finally reached the chamber of the Lich, and were about to make the final confrontation, when another wizard, a Wizard Collector at that, had come along and claimed her Lich, pushing her aside and taking away everything she had worked for. She didn't even know what to think or feel afterward. So she thought nothing.

And strangely, or maybe not so strangely, Grover evinced no great emotion. He had taken this adventure as he had taken all their adventures, neither growing too happy when things went well nor becoming angry when things went against them. Unlike Cilla, Grover had come to accept his fate in life. He knew that he was neither greatly talented nor lucky enough to get any more than he had already been born with as a son of a rich and noble family, where his name, Soovo, would promote him, and not himself. As a youth he had chosen dueling as a career when younger boys had beat him up. He thought if he was a good duelist he could challenge them and stop them from harassing him. In time, though, he had grown larger, and stronger, so that no one picked fights with him unless they wanted bruises. And there were a few who wanted bruises. So you could say he took requests but only if they begged for it. He wasn't violent by nature. Just a guy, that's all. And he kept up with his dueling and had improved. His life had seemed preplanned. He would be a respected duelist and live off his father's wealth.

But then disaster had struck, as it usually does, and his brother Ragnar had finagled away his inheritance and his ability to reproduce. But just as quickly as he had regained all that, he also gained a new profession and a new way to live his old life. Something always comes along, Grover thought. So he wasn't disappointed at all with their past adventures. He had no inner need to seek out fame and recognition, having already had some of that as a son of a noble family. He didn't even desire that sort of attention. And to be truthful, he didn't know how to handle it. His only concern was with a meal on the table, wine in the belly, and a woman to cuddle with. And if he got all that by being a sidekick, instead of a duelist, that was fine with him. As long as he didn't have to lead the way into battle, he was content to play lackey to Cilla's whims.

Yes, in almost every way Grover was content.

The two heroes were meant for each other, though they would have said differently. In fact, neither would have thought much of it, since both viewed their relationship as merely temporary. And as long as they never thought about it, they never did anything about it, and so remained partners despite their differences.

When they entered the rec room of Heroes, Inc., that afternoon, fresh from their failed adventure, they were greeted by their peers with strange looks and offhand comments.

"So how'd it go?" asked one blonde woman sidekick. "As bad as usual?"

"Bug off," Cilla said.

Grover noticed one of the more prominent and successful heroes of Heroes, Inc., sit up from a bench, his beefy face grinning crookedly. "So what happened?"

"You wouldn't believe it," Grover replied.

"You're right," he replied. "And it would probably be all lies anyway."

"So how'd you mess up this time?" someone shouted from the back, where they were playing darts.

Cilla rolled her eyes. "Isn't it great to come back to the warm arms of your company, just like an understanding family?"

"Yeah," Grover said.

"Understanding," another hero said. "Who said we understood?"

"No one," Cilla snapped.

"Cool it," Grover said to Cilla.

"Hey, did you get lost this time?" someone else asked.

"I'm getting out of here," Cilla said, and turned to push through the curtain which closed off the room.

"No, don't leave," another shouted. "We want to hear about your adventure. Did you rescue the prisoner and kill the villain, or—the ever popular—rescue the villain and kill the prisoner?"

Cilla glared. "That wasn't my fault. No one told me they were twins."

"But they were fraternal, not identical twins," another shouted.

"Come on," Grover said, putting a hand to Cilla's shoulder. "Let's go."

Cilla shrugged off the touch. "Don't touch me."

"Okay," Grover said, pulling his hands away.

When they came out of the other side of the curtain, Sallu was standing there. She was the assistant to the Mission Master.

"I was looking for you two," she said. "I heard you just got back."

"I don't want to talk about it," Cilla said. "You can read it all in the report. Once we write it, that is."

Sallu looked puzzled and tugged at her lip. "Did you mess up your last adventure?"

"Don't ask," Grover said.

Sallu mused for a moment. "I didn't come here for that. Gallin wants to see you."

"Gallin," Grover said with surprise. Gallin was the Mission Master. "What for?"

"You'll find out when you get there," Sallu said.

"Gallin," Cilla remarked as they walked down the hall. "I don't like the sound of this."

How to Hire a Hero

Gallin looked very much like a bear and it was rumored that he was descended from an odd coupling between a grizzly bear and a human male, but that was just a rumor. Even so, Gallin acted like a bear, huffing and puffing, and sometimes digging into trees with his bare hands in search of honey. But what really made him look like a bear was his hair. He was covered with it, from a black fuzzy beard which went almost up to his eyes, to dark curly hairs which covered most of his body. And he talked like a bear too, grunting most of the time.

He, too, had once been a hero, and was called the One Who Looks Like a Bear by friend and foe alike, but to his close friends he was just known as "bonehead." Years of being a hero had taken their toll—the constant paranoia, incessant exposure to danger, and the publicity tours had all led to his crack-up—and now he couldn't be trusted to go on another mission. So he had been promoted to the post of Mission Master, where he met with prospective contractors and farmed out adventures to the young ambitious heroes who worked under him. The head office was happy to have him, since such an imposing figure inspired confidence in their clients.

But Gallin didn't put too much effort into his job, and sometimes when an adventure needed to be investigated, he let a little checking of the details slide. As yet, this had caused few problems that could be traced back to him. And why should it cause problems, he asked himself, because why would a client lie to him about an adventure? So when this new adventure came across his desk, he didn't ask too many questions. Besides, the guy wanted to ask all the questions himself. If the guy wanted to do the job for him, Gallin didn't mind. It just gave him more time to relax.

Which was what Gallin was doing when Cilla and Grover entered the room. He sat sprawled in the big stuffed chair behind his desk.

The clients sat across from him on the client couch. The one in charge was a strange, wiry old man, and beside him was his short pudgy assistant. The old man alternately smoked a pipe, blowing smoke rings to the ceiling, and drank heavily from a wine decanter which had been brought to him. The pudgy assistant just twiddled his thumbs nervously.

Grover and Cilla took the seats in front of the desk, and Gallin leaned forward to talk.

But before he could grunt a word out, Cilla declared, "It wasn't out fault. Damn wizards screw everything up."

Beogoat spat out his drink and looked sharply at Cilla.

Gallin coughed and then addressed Cilla sternly. "If you would hold back your comments." He then gestured to Beogoat and Beoweasel. "These two men . . ."

"Wizards," Beogoat advised.

"Wizards," Gallin corrected himself. "Came here to hire some heroes."

"You know," Grover said, "it never occurred to me until now that 'wizards' rhymes with 'gizzards.' "

Everyone ignored him.

"Why do they need us?" Cilla asked. "They are wizards after all."

"That'll all be explained," Gallin said. "If you would wait a moment and listen."

"Work for wizards," Cilla muttered, and she looked at Grover, who looked back blankly. "Okay," Cilla said, "we'll listen."

"All right, then," Gallin said, and leaned toward Beogoat, "you've seen them. Are they what you're looking for?"

Beogoat scrutinized Grover and Cilla, his eyes resting on each feature.

"I think so," Beoweasel said. "He's got blond hair like Phillip's and is about the same size. And she is small and dark-haired like Voss was."

Beogoat took another drag from his pipe. "Is this all you have to offer?"

"They're the only two who fit the description . . ."

"What is this?" Cilla asked. "We're heroes, not models."

"Well, *you're* not," Grover said. "I was once."

"Shut up," Cilla said.

Gallin waited until they were finished and went on. "These two are the only ones I can offer. Of course, you don't have to take them . . ."

Beogoat raised his hand. "Not so quick." He stood up and stepped over to Grover and Cilla. He bent close to Grover's face and sniffed curiously, while dripping ashes in Grover's lap.

"Hey," Grover said, and turned to Gallin. "What's all this about anyway?"

Beogoat then moved in front of Cilla. Cilla also looked at Beogoat curiously, and moved away from his touch as he felt her dark hair, which was lying flatly around her head after weeks of travel. "Hmm," Beogoat mused.

"Hey," Cilla said in reply. "Don't touch the hair." Her hand crept to her *Argh* knife. She looked at Gallin. "Yeah, what the hell is this about anyway? Who are these people?"

Beogoat backed away and sat down on Gallin's desk without looking, papers crunching beneath his buttocks.

"Well, what do you think?" Gallin asked again.

Beogoat rubbed his chin, which had perpetual stubble on it. "They'll do. Besides, the magic will make them look like them anyway."

Cilla jumped up. "Like who? I'm not dressing up as some type of goober for any more festivals. Unh-ah. No way." She shook her head violently.

"That goes for me too," Grover said.

Gallin stood up. "Calm down. It's nothing like that. Nothing like it at all. Besides, you were asked by the garrison not to do any more festivals after you beat up all those temple worshippers who thought you guys looked cute."

Beogoat raised his hand to restrain Gallin. "Allow me to speak."

Gallin sank down into his seat with a satisfying thud and stayed there. Cilla also took her seat.

Beogoat waited until the attention was focused on him and then he spoke quickly and softly in a language no one understood, making wild hand gestures. When he was done he asked, "Any questions?"

Grover looked around and then slowly raised his hand.

"Yes," Beogoat said.

"What did you say?"

Beogoat looked puzzled and then hit a belt he was carrying. "Damn translation belt is on the blink. I'm sorry. I'll have to repeat myself. I'm here from another country."

"Hoven," Gallin interjected.

"You know," Beoweasel said from the couch, "I don't even know why you wear that translation belt when these people speak the same language as we do."

"Quiet, Beoweasel," Beogoat said softly. And then addressed

Grover and Cilla. "Yes, we're from Hoven. And because of some political turmoil we've been experiencing for a few years . . ."

"Three hundred years to be exact," Beoweasel interjected.

"Yes," Beogoat said, casting a sharp glance at Beoweasel. "Three hundred years. Anyway, just as the empire was on the brink of being united once again, our leader, Lord Phillip, was killed in an unfortunate accident."

"Hang gliding?" Grover ventured.

"No, ambush," Beogoat said. "Anyway, you can see this is rather an inconvenience to unification. All the Lords are loyal to him, and once they discover he's, ah, had an accident, they'll fight and bicker among themselves."

"So," Cilla said energetically, "you want us to take over the empire ourselves, ousting these petty Lords. Of course, we'll need an army, and some refreshments, because armies eat a lot and . . ."

"No, no, no, no," Beogoat said. "Nothing so drastic."

"That's what you think," Beoweasel muttered.

"No army?" Cilla asked.

"No army," Beogoat said.

"Oh," Cilla said with obvious disappointment, and sank deeper into her seat.

"No," Beogoat repeated. "For you see, before Phillip died, he was to wed the daughter of one of the Hoven Lords. This woman was already with child—Phillip's child, but not yet married to him. If Phillip had married her, then there would be no problem. The Lords would rally around her and his soon-to-be-born child, and we wouldn't be here asking for your help."

Gallin leaned forward. "What he wants you to do is marry the girl."

"Marry," Grover exclaimed. "I don't even know her."

"Not you," Beogoat said. "Phillip."

Cilla grimaced. "A dead guy marrying a live woman. You guys have some pretty sick practices in your country. And what are we supposed to do, be the bridesmaids?"

"No, no, no," Beogoat said, biting down hard on his now-extinguished pipe. "You misunderstand me."

Gallin interjected again. "Grover, he wants you to disguise yourself as Phillip and marry the woman, so you can save the empire. It's a fairly simple hero task if you ask me."

"That's all?" Grover asked.

"Yes," Beogoat lied, nodding his head firmly. "That's all."

Cilla coughed. "Ah, wait a second here. I fail to see where this hero person—me, I mean—fits into all of this. I was just joking about being a bridesmaid."

"You're to be Phillip's personal servant, his swordbearer," Beoweasel said.

"Me," Cilla exclaimed. "A servant. I don't think so. And Grover gets to marry the bride."

"*You* can marry her if you want to," Grover offered.

"You're sick," Cilla said, and then turned back to Gallin and Beogoat. "And I have to sit on my behind while he gets to be hero of the empire?"

"Well, yes," Gallin said. "But in a good way."

"I'll be a servant in a good way," Cilla repeated.

"You'll be a good servant," Grover chided.

Cilla glared at him.

Beogoat interjected. "Allow me to explain. You'll be the servant because you match the description. Grover here looks like Phillip. They could have been brothers. And you, you're about the same size and weight as Voss. It's not meant to be taken as a slight, but we need heroes to replace both of them."

"Oh," Cilla said. "So what does this Voss do anyway?"

"Whatever Phillip asks him to do," Beoweasel explained.

"I think I'm going to like this," Grover said, and leaned forward. "So what am I supposed to do? Marry this girl and then . . . what? What happens after the wedding?"

"You go home," Beogoat said quickly, before Beoweasel could interrupt and ruin everything. "We'll take care of that."

"I don't know," Cilla said. "Why us? Why couldn't you pick just anybody?"

"Because we need heroes," Beogoat said. "Professionals. Someone who can play the part of a hero without acting."

"Okay," Grover said. "So all I have to do is get married. I don't have to talk to anybody or kill anyone?"

"Absolutely not," Beogoat lied again. "You just have to get married."

Grover relaxed in his chair. "I like this adventure."

"You would," Cilla swore. "I don't like it. Not one bit. Servant, huh?"

"Cilla," Gallin grunted. "It's only for a couple of days."

Cilla still looked unhappy.

"You promised us a better adventure. A dragon slaying."

Gallin made an innocent face. "Just do it, and I'll see what I can do when you get back."

Cilla said nothing, kicking the leg of her chair with a booted toe.

Grover nudged her. "Come on, it'll be fun."

"Yes," Beogoat coaxed. "I can show you around all the sights. And as Phillip's servant you'll be revered just like he is. Think of it as a vacation. You get to go to a party, save an empire, and return home heroes."

"We already are heroes," Cilla said.

"You know what I mean," Beogoat said.

Cilla brooded for a moment and then reluctantly replied. "Okay, but just remember, I'm still in charge."

PART II

Is This Damsel Really in Distress?

The Worth of
a Wizard's Advice

Grover and Cilla looked around the colonnaded reflecting pool. Dead leaves and branches lay scattered across the tile and on the surface of the pool. It was early, about midmorning, on a late spring day. A cool breeze blew through the columns and made ripples in the water.

"Whoa," Grover exclaimed, holding his hands to his head.

"Very nice," Cilla said, putting her hands to her hips. "Very nice trick. So where are we?"

Beogoat stroked his gray stubble and arched his eyebrows. "You're in Hoven now."

"That was quick." Grover peered past the columns to see the cool green glade in which the natatorium resided. "So where's the castle?"

Beoweasel appeared from behind one of the columns carrying a load of gear in his arms.

"You're not going to the castle just yet," Beogoat said.

"We're not?" Cilla asked, suspicion evident in her tone. "Why not? I mean, I just want you to know I'm still the hero in charge, even though I'm playing the part of Phillip's servant."

"Of course, of course," Beogoat said. "I have no argument with that."

"Good," Cilla said. "So why aren't we going to the castle?"

"Cilla," Grover warned, "be nice."

Cilla turned to Grover. "What have I always told you?"

"Brush my teeth before and after meals," Grover answered.

"No," Cilla said. "I mean yes, but the other thing, you know. As a hero you need to be direct."

"Oh yeah," Grover said. "That's right. You did say that once. How could I forget?"

Beogoat raised a hand. "No worry, Grover. Cilla is right. This is unexpected. I should have told you before. But since Phillip and Voss have been gone for two days now on what I have said is a quest, it's important that you make an appearance before your men and the other Westerhoven Lords, so they won't think you're dead. Surely Hans has boasted of your, I mean Phillip's, killing by now. You understand."

Grover nodded. "I'm mellow to the effect."

"I'm sure you are," Beogoat said. And he gestured to Beoweasel, who came forward with the clothing and gear. "It's important that you dress in clothing and costume of our nation. So we brought some of Phillip's and Voss's clothing for you."

"But I'm a woman," Cilla pointed out.

"Yes," Beogoat said. "I was aware of that. But with a little disguise magic no one will notice the difference."

"No," Cilla explained. "I mean, I'm a different size. Here and here." She pointed to her hips and bust.

Beogoat coughed and spat on the ground. "Yes, yes."

"It's not a stupid complaint," Cilla said, challenging anyone to say it wasn't so.

Beoweasel handed out the gear, giving Phillip's burgundy cape, black polished boots, black breeches, and white shirt to Grover.

"Nice clothes," Grover said. "I like this guy's style."

"He's dead, Grover," Cilla remarked. And then she looked at her clothes, which were the same as Grover's except smaller in size. "How cute," she said. "They dressed like twins."

Grover and Cilla went off to change into their clothing in private, and when they were done, they came back before Beogoat, who had relit his pipe and was playing tic-tac-toe with his smoke rings. Beoweasel had just placed an *X* in the wrong spot and was promptly defeated before Beogoat took notice of them.

"Awesome," Beogoat said. "If I don't say so myself."

"You did," Beoweasel pointed out.

"I know," Beogoat said dryly. And then he examined Grover and Cilla, his eyes taking in their weapons which they had reattached at their sides.

Beogoat frowned. "You'll have to give me those."

"What?" Cilla cried, putting her hands to her short sword and knife. "Not my weapons. Not my *Argh* knife. I have a contract to use this wherever I go."

"I understand," Beogoat said. "But as Phillip's servant you cannot use them. The make of the weapons is different from here. And besides, Voss uses a club."

"A club," Cilla groaned. "Not a club. Forget it. Forget the whole thing."

"Cilla," Grover said, "it's only for a couple of days, right?"

"Right," Beogoat said carefully. "Sure."

"See," Grover said. "It's only for a day or two."

Cilla looked down at her sword belt and reluctantly pulled it off. Beoweasel came forward to take it. As he reached out for the weapons Cilla pulled them back. "Not so quick." She held them up into the air, took one last look, and then handed them to Beoweasel. "You better be careful with them, or else."

Beogoat then gestured to Grover's waist. "And your rapier also."

"My rapier," Grover said in disbelief. "Not my rapier."

"So who's acting like a child now?" Cilla said.

"I'm not," Grover said, and then addressed Beogoat, clutching at the sheathed rapier. "It's just that I'm a duelist. Going without my rapier is like, like, going somewhere without . . ."

"Your brain," Cilla interjected. "Just give it to him."

Grover's face fell and he sadly handed over the rapier to Beoweasel. Beoweasel took the weapons away and put them in with their clothes, and then came back with a club and a great sword.

"What's this?" Grover asked, looking at the six-foot length of steel.

"Your weapon," Beogoat explained. "All the knights use them. Yours is called *Biff*."

Grover drew back in surprise. "You could cut someone in half with one of these."

"That's the idea," Beogoat said.

Grover felt his stomach roll and then took the weapon. "Well, it's a good thing I don't have to fight anybody."

Beogoat said nothing to this.

Cilla took the wooden club, which had a steel plate molded around the end. She swung it around a few times, feeling its weight. "Well, I guess this could come in handy when I have to keep Grover in line."

"Right," Grover said blandly.

When they were accustomed to their weapons, Beogoat spoke again. "Before I change your appearance, I want to give you some advice about Hoven. These are a warped people. They have a strict allegiance to their families, and never forgive any grievance no matter how long ago it occurred. If it happened to their ancestor it happened to them, and they're still pissed off about it. They have a system of honor, in which they feel it's their right to seek you out and challenge you to a battle to death. But you shouldn't have to worry about that. I already told you Hoven is divided into two principal parts, the Western and the Southern. You're on the Westerhoven side now and are fighting Sousterhoven. As far as being Phillip is concerned, Grover, he isn't too bright. But you won't have to say much. Here's a guidebook to being a knight."

Grover accepted a leather-bound volume where scrawled in gold script it said, "Dude Knights Die Young: A Guide to What's In in Knighthood."

"Read it, live it, learn it," Beogoat said. And then turned to Cilla. "As far as being Voss is concerned, you basically help Phillip out and do what he says. But you guys don't have to worry because I'll be with you the whole time to see you through. Okay?"

Grover and Cilla nodded.

"Now, to change your appearance and your voice. Close your eyes and open your mouth, please."

Grover and Cilla looked at one another and then closed their eyes and opened their mouths. Beogoat took some powder from a small pouch at his waist, first checked to make sure it wasn't tobacco, and then blew it into their faces.

"You can open your eyes now."

Cilla and Grover slowly opened their eyes and then turned to each other.

"But he looks like Grover," Cilla said.

"And Cilla looks the same," Grover remarked.

"Of course you look the same to each other. But to the people of Hoven, who believe in Phillip and Voss, you will appear as Phillip and Voss."

"And to the people who don't?" Cilla asked.

"You'll look like yourselves," Beogoat said.

"And how long does the spell last?" Grover asked.

"Long enough for our purposes," Beogoat said hurriedly. "And now if you'll come with me."

They left the confines of the reflecting pool, walking through the glade, and up a hill, until they broke free from the trees and could see a small walled city standing in the distance, a few dirt roads leading to and from it going in all directions, and on the field before it were large tents, colorful banners, and groups of men milling around.

"What is it, a fair?" Grover asked.

"Of sorts," Beogoat replied carefully.

"Is that where the wedding is to take place?" Grover asked.

"No," Beogoat said. "But your bride is in there. In fact, that is why Phillip came here in the first place. To get her out."

Grover looked back at the field and for the first time noticed that the men were carrying weapons.

How to Fool Friends
and Lead Armies
Without Really Trying

"What! I have to get her out!" Grover exclaimed. "You never said anything about getting her out."

"Ah yes," Beogoat hemmed and hawed. "Ah yes, you're right. It must have slipped my mind."

Cilla perked up and cast her gaze to the city walls. "Save a princess, huh? And I thought this was going to be boring."

"She's not exactly a princess," Beogoat explained.

"She's not?" Grover said. "Then why save her?"

"And you're not exactly a prince," Beogoat said. "So it's all kosher, as us wizards say."

"If I'm not a prince," Grover said, "what am I?"

"You really want to know?" Cilla teased.

"Yeah," Grover said.

"You're an absolute, uncontested . . ."

"Anyway," Beogoat broke in, "Phillip wasn't Prince of Hoven, he just wanted to be."

"A prince wannabe," Cilla remarked.

"You see," Beogoat went on, "nobody is Prince of Hoven. If there were a true Prince of Hoven, then the country wouldn't be divided into thirteen warring principalities, seeking to gain the throne. Isn't that right, Beoweasel?"

"Yup," Beoweasel said.

"Beoweasel here is part of the Meistertonne family and is familiar with the history of the whole empire. Quite a useful fellow except when you need him to do something. But you can't win them all."

Grover hadn't heard a word. "Why didn't you tell me about all this before?"

Beogoat shrugged. "Like I said, must have slipped my mind. But what's the problem? You two are heroes. All you have to do is get Winona out of the city and then you can marry her and you're done."

"Who's Winona?" Cilla asked.

"The bride-to-be," Beogoat explained. "Didn't I tell you that?"

"No," Cilla said.

"Still . . ." Grover protested.

"You're professionals, right?" Beogoat reminded them.

"Of course we are," Cilla spoke up, punching Grover in the shoulder.

"Ow." Grover rubbed his shoulder.

"Don't mind my sidekick," Cilla said. "He sometimes quibbles over little details. But you know how hard it is to find good help these days."

"Help!" Grover exclaimed.

"Ignore him," Cilla said. "So all we have to do is rescue this Winona woman and have lover boy here marry her."

Beogoat nodded. "That's about it."

Cilla put a hand through her short dark hair. She gazed back the ancient city of Hoven, which stood perched on a neighboring hill, looking almost impregnable, with what were probably thirty-foot walls, and hundreds, many thousands of troops waiting inside. "No problem," Cilla said.

"I have a problem," Grover started. "It has to do with death and dying and . . ."

"Men are coming," Beoweasel warned.

They all looked down the hill, to see a score or more of men walking steadily up the grassy slopes, all fully armored and carrying the burgundy and black banner of Wunderkinde.

Leading the band of men was a tall man, but not as tall as Grover. He was lean and dark-haired with an aquiline nose and deep-set moody eyes. His most prominent feature was a fuzzy eyebrow which ran unbroken over both eyes.

Beogoat turned to Grover and Cilla. "Remember your names. The leader is Phillip's best friend. His name is Erich."

"Friend," Grover said. "You didn't say I would have to talk to his friends."

"It is inevitable, I'm afraid," Beogoat said.

"That's easy for you to say," Grover said. "So what should I say to him? What should I do? Is there something special I should say? Only things those two would know?" Grover asked frantically.

Beogoat pursed his mouth. "How would I know things only Phillip and Erich knew?"

"Don't wizards have ways?" Grover asked. "I thought . . ."

"You thought I was a dirty, little-minded eavesdropper, didn't you? Well, I have a mind to tell you," and he pointed a finger in Grover's direction, "that those charges were dropped years ago on lack of evidence. No one calls me a dirty, little-minded eaves-dropper. Nobody."

"I didn't call you a . . ." Grover began to protest.

"Beogoat," Beoweasel hissed in warning.

Erich and his men had come within earshot.

Beogoat was quiet and turned to Grover. "Hail them."

Grover turned to Cilla for support and she just shrugged. "I'm just your servant, remember," she replied.

Grover gulped and dried a sweaty palm on his shirt. He stared down at Erich, who was moving slightly ahead of the rest of the group. "Hail, well-met friend."

Erich did an up-yours gesture with his arm and replied, "Hail, bonehead. What's this well-met stuff? You've been reading books? Where the hell have you been?" He looked sharply at Beogoat. "Consorting with wizards? We were supposed to storm the city two days ago and then you disappear. A scout told us he saw you leave in the direction of the old reflecting pool. But you were nowhere to be found. And then Hans," and he turned to point at the city, "boasted that you were dead, that he left your corpse at the pool, but we looked again and you weren't there. What happened to you? You haven't been drinking again, have you?"

Grover bit his lip. "No. I was away."

"Away," Erich replied. "Where?"

Grover appealed to Beogoat, and Beogoat whispered "a quest" between clenched teeth.

"On a quest," Grover said loudly.

"A quest," Erich said suspiciously. "For what?"

Grover leaned toward the wizard. "He wants to know for what?"

Beogoat hesitated. "I don't know. Make something up."

"And," Erich began, "when did you start consorting with wizards?"

"But I thought," Grover started, meaning he thought Beogoat was Phillip's personal advisor, and that it shouldn't be unusual for them to be seen together. And then he turned to Erich. "Ah, just recently, actually. Since he, ah, gave me some information that will help us, ah, reunify the, ah, empire. That was what the quest was all about. And that's why I had to leave so suddenly. It was a secret."

Erich nodded and then without looking back at his men, he came closer to Grover and gestured for him to do the same, so that they were speaking almost face-to-face. Erich grabbed Grover firmly on both shoulders and asked, "What is this quest? Why haven't you told me? We're supposed to be blood brothers. Am I no longer worthy of your trust? Has someone," and he gave an icy stare at Beogoat, "poisoned you against me?"

Grover realized that Erich felt left out and so squeezed Erich's shoulders in brotherly compassion. "It's not that. I do trust you. Like I always have. But it came up suddenly. I can't really talk more of it now. You understand. There are persons I don't trust." Grover felt Erich stiffen.

"Spies," Erich hissed.

"Ah, yeah," Grover said. "Spies. I can't talk now."

"Whom do you suspect?" Erich demanded. He raised his head up so Grover could see his cool blue eyes.

Grover hesitated and felt a chill he couldn't explain. He shook his head to break the spell. "Later."

Erich waited for a few moments more. "Right. You're right. This is not the time for it, but we must talk later. Privately. There have been new developments."

Grover blanched at the idea of talking to him privately, but knew he should answer positively. "Okay."

"Good," Erich said, and punched Grover in the chest.

Grover felt a sharp pain and gasped, clutching at his chest, while Erich walked back to his men.

"All is well," Erich declared. "Lord Phillip is back and will lead the attack."

Grover's head snapped around and barely gasped, "What?"

But Erich was already leading his contingent of knights back down the hill.

"Way to go," Cilla was saying. "I knew you had a little bloodlust in you. Lead the attack. That's great."

"But I didn't . . ." Grover protested.

"Very good," Beogoat said. "He seemed convinced you were Phillip. I knew my faith in you wasn't misplaced."

"But," Grover protested again, still massaging his chest. But no one was listening.

"Well, that's done," said Beogoat. "Now let's walk to the encampment and get you ready for battle."

For Your Protection

Grover stood in the middle of a green, billowing tent as the whole encampment around him mobilized for the assault. Through the entrance to the tent he could see young men and boys, some dressed in armor, some not, moving to and fro, as banners were raised up to the sky.

A cheer had gone up when Grover entered the encampment and the name Phillip was chanted far and wide. Young man and old took heart as they saw the symbol of their unity stride into camp, his burgundy cape flapping around him.

"Speech, speech," they had cried.

And Grover was reminded of the time when he first stood outside of the Ragged Wyrm, after killing his first villain, and the crowd had called out for noble words. But nothing had changed, and Grover still did not know what to say. But before he could say anything, Erich had run up before him and cupped his hands to his mouth so that all could hear. "Lord Phillip calls us to battle."

A cheer went up from the crowd.

"These guys get excited over battles," Grover remarked.

Cilla smiled and seemed pleased. "I think I'm going to like this place." Her eyes fell approvingly on Erich as he strode forward giving words of encouragement to the various leaders who stood about.

Beogoat just shook his head, chewing on the end of his pipe. "Now you understand what I have to work with."

They moved into Phillip's quarters where they were to get ready for battle. Inside the tent they found two men playing at dice.

"Why, it's Lord Phillip," the first declared. He had long curly brown hair that fell around his shoulders. "Glad to see you back, dude."

The second one stood up, bowed slightly. He had dark hair, cut short on the sides, and a courtly manner. "We awaited your return."

Grover whispered to Beogoat. "Who are these people?"

"Why, we're your cringing sycophants," the first one said.

41

"I have cringing sycophants?" Grover asked. "What do I need with cringing sycophants?"

"Are we fired, then, your lordship?" the second one asked.

Grover turned to Beogoat. Beogoat looked at the two men and said, "You may go now. Lord Phillip will call you when he needs you."

"Okay, whatever," the one with long hair said.

"We will await your pleasure," the second one said. And then they both departed. On the way out the first turned to the second and said, "Was Phillip acting a little weird?" And the second answered, "No more than usual."

"Who are they?" Grover asked when they were gone.

"That was Romeo, your musician, and the other was Bill, your court poet. They record your great deeds and put them to song and music."

"You didn't say anything about cringing sycophants," Grover protested.

"A minor detail," Beogoat said. "I assure you, they will follow your every decree. You have nothing to worry about. No one has doubted so far that you are Phillip. And that's something to be happy about. Frankly I didn't even thing we'd get this far."

Grover looked startled.

"But we did," Beogoat added hastily. "And that's the whole point."

Beoweasel came over with pieces of Phillip's armor in his hands. There were linen undergarments, along with a chain-mail shirt and girdle. There was a wide belt and an odd conch-shaped piece of metal.

"What's this?" Grover asked, gesturing to the metal.

"It's armor. Phillip's armor. You have to wear it."

"What for?" Grover asked. "I thought I was just here for moral support."

"Oh no," Beogoat said. "Phillip always leads his attacks."

"What!" Grover shouted, and he sought out Cilla for help. "Did you hear him?"

"Of course," Cilla said, standing by the entrance to the tent. "I'm not deaf."

"What do you think?" Grover asked.

"I think I like that Erich guy," Cilla said.

"What's that?" Grover asked in exasperation.

Cilla shrugged. "I'm young, I'm attractive, and I make a good salary. We could make a good match. Maybe I'll settle down here and raise a few armies."

"You're weird," Grover said, dismissing Cilla's comments.

Beoweasel handed Grover the linen garments, which he put on after taking off the other clothes. After the linen was on, Beoweasel handed him the mail shirt.

"You know, Cilla," Grover said, tapping the mail with his fist, "we should get some of this stuff and bring it back. How come we never wear armor?"

"Because armor's for wimps," Cilla said.

Next Grover attached the belt firmly around his waist. And then, with Beoweasel's help, he attached the shoulder sheath for his great sword on his back.

"How do I look?" Grover asked when the process was done.

"Great," Beogoat said. "Like a born leader."

Grover nodded to Beoweasel. "And what do you think?"

"You look like Phillip returned," Beoweasel said.

"Yes, but do I look good?" Grover asked.

There was a dead silence and Grover shrugged. It was then that he noticed that his head felt exposed. His throat felt very, very naked above the mail shirt. "Ah, isn't there some sort of protection I'm supposed to wear for my head?"

Beoweasel suddenly found the fabric of the tent very interesting.

"Ah, Beogoat?" Grover asked.

Beogoat squinted and then pulled the pipe fully from his lips. "Phillip doesn't wear a helmet. It's some sort of macho thing."

"Well, Phillip might not," Grover said. "But I will. So where's the helmet?"

"As Phillip's stand-in," Beogoat explained, "you must do everything like him or people will begin to suspect something is wrong. And once people suspect something is wrong, they will begin to doubt, and once they begin to doubt, the magic of your disguise will fail and they will see you're an impostor, and once they find out you're an impostor, they will bring you to the chopping block, or have you drawn and quartered, or broken on the wheel, or some other sort of painful demise. These people don't take deceit very well."

"What!" Grover cried, putting a hand to the soft flesh of his neck.

"But don't worry," Beogoat said. "Once you get Winona, your troubles are over."

Grover shook his head. "Jeez, all I wanted to do was wear a helmet."

Cilla turned away from the entrance. "Erich's coming."

"What could he want?" Grover asked.

"Maybe he's discovered us already," Beogoat said. "I don't know. Do I look like I know all the answers?"

Grover was stunned into silence.

A moment later Erich was pushing aside the tent flap and standing inside. He looked Grover up and down with a scrutiny that was almost unbearable. Finally he said, "Still no helmet. You're as crazy as ever. The men await you. Come on."

"Ah, sure," Grover said. And he followed Erich out of the tent.

Erich paused outside, took a breath of fresh air, and said, "Lovely day for bloodshed."

Grover wasn't actually sure what was a good day for bloodshed but agreed anyway, sighing inwardly.

Erich grinned. "Come on. I bet I'll get more braids than you will today."

"Maybe," Grover said, not knowing what he was talking about.

Erich laughed and led the way past the tents. He talked as they traveled and filled him in on what had happened since he (Phillip) had been gone. "The Hoeneckers almost pulled out, and the Kurtonburgs said they would only wait one more day. But I convinced them to stay."

"Good work," Grover said.

"But the Dresdels are still upset about the wine spilling," Erich added.

Grover was puzzled, so opted to say nothing.

Outside the encampment the men were gathered in long rows, going back for a few acres in either direction. All were dressed in armor, and assembled into contingents based on their principality. They gathered behind one honored man who held up the banner, which flew the colors of their homeland.

Erich bade Grover to stand upon an empty wooden supply wagon, where he was able to see the full extent of the forces he was supposed to command and where they were able to see him. Grover was impressed. There were a few thousand men there. Which were a few thousand more than he had ever commanded. The most he had ever commanded had been one, and that was Cilla, and she had never listened anyway.

"This is what we've been waiting for," Erich whispered to him. "Say something inspirational."

Grover coughed and looked at Erich and then to Cilla, who had followed behind as Phillip's swordbearer was supposed to do. Cilla shrugged as if to say, "It's your problem, not mine."

"Hail, Sousterhoven nations," Grover said.

Erich's eyes opened wide.

There was a murmuring in the crowd.

Grover suddenly realized his mistake. "Or so you will be if you don't follow me," he quickly added.

The murmuring stopped.

"Good morning," Grover went on.

"Hail, Lord Phillip," came their reply.

Grover started to feel a little better. "There have been rumors of my demise, but I must say they were a little optimistic."

There was some laughter.

Grover smiled now. "We all know why we have come here. At least I do, anyway. So, I ask you, why should we spend all our time talking when we know what we should be doing? If you know what I mean."

There were mixed shouts from the crowd.

"So let's go to it, then," Grover said, and attempted to pull out his great sword, *Biff*, from his shoulder sheath, but since he was unused to the sheath, he was only able to pull it out halfway. Cilla came over to help, and together they pulled out the blade. Grover held it out with both hands and lifted it into the air, crying, "To victory."

"To victory," the assembled forces cried back, and then pulled out their own swords.

But Grover's sword didn't stop when he lifted it up. Instead, it went sailing up into the air and then came down heavily, point first, digging into the ground, where it stood quivering.

"Whatever," Grover said, and jumped roughly off the wooden cart.

Erich looked quizzically at Grover. "What's with the sword toss?"

Grover shrugged. "It seemed to fit."

"Well, anyway," Erich said, "that was a good speech. It's the first time you haven't bored the men with the ten reasons why you should be ruler of Hoven."

"Thanks," Grover said.

Erich clapped him heartily on the shoulder and moved off to the Wunderkinde contingent. The other contingents were breaking off also. Ladders and grappling hooks were being brought forward as the armies of Westerhoven readied to assault the ancient city of Hoven. Grover watched this all with the detachment of an observer, until Cilla came up.

"Aren't you supposed to be leading the battle?"

The Doom of Hans

Hans awoke from a fitful sleep, not knowing why. He waited a moment to orient himself, and in that time there was a knocking on the door.

"Who dares to bother me?" he asked.

"Rudolph," came a muffled voice from the other side of the door.

Hans rolled off the cot he had been napping in and threw on a shirt. "I asked not to be disturbed unless there were new developments."

"There have been," Rudolph's muffled reply came.

"Have any more forces left?" Hans asked, pulling on his breeches.

"No," Rudolph said. "And the Hoenecker forces, which seem to be breaking camp, have returned, and there's something else . . ."

"Yes," Hans said.

"This is something you'll have to see for yourself," Rudolph answered.

Hans grunted and went to the door, opening it to see Rudolph patiently waiting there. "What is it?"

"I'm not sure," Rudolph said.

Hans frowned. "I have a feeling this isn't going to make me happy."

"Probably not," Rudolph said.

Hans shook his head, leaving the room. "Have you heard any more jokes?" He always had jokes told to him to alleviate the gloom which always seemed to hang over him.

"Just a short one."

"Tell it to me," Hans said.

"But don't you want to see the new development?"

"Tell it to me as we go," Hans suggested.

"Okay," Rudolph said. And they left the compound to walk up to the battlements, taking the old and crumbling steps very carefully. "What did the eunuch reply when asked why he didn't have any sex?"

"What?" Hans asked.

"For two reasons, the eunuch said. Choice and circumstance. Due to my circumstances I have no choice."

"That wasn't very good," Hans said. "Is that all you have?"

"No, one more," Rudolph said. They were up on the ramparts now. Walking along, passing by the men who patrolled the walls. "Why did the monkey fall out of the tree?"

"Why?" Hans asked.

"Because he was dead," Rudolph answered.

A slight smile crossed Hans's face. "Better," he said. "Now, what is it you wanted me to see?"

"Well," Rudolph started, "it began about midmorning. There was a stirring up in the Westerhoven camp. And we saw someone who looked like Phillip being accompanied by Beogoat and Erich. He then went into Phillip's tent and has been there for some time. And as you can see, it seems that they are preparing for an assault." He pointed where activity seemed to be going on in the encampment.

"That can't be," Hans said. "I cut his head off. You can't recover from a wound like that, even in a few days. It must be someone else."

Rudolph shrugged.

Just then Grover emerged from the tent with Erich and started to walk over to address the men.

"There he is." Rudolph pointed.

Hans stared out and saw the broad back and blond locks of Grover, and from a distance of a few hundred yards, he couldn't tell the difference. "But how?" Hans asked.

Rudolph shrugged. "Remember what the witch said?"

"The three things that will stop my prophecy from coming true," Hans replied. "It can't be."

"A hero will return from death," Rudolph repeated.

Hans lowered his head. "I'm doomed. Doomed," he moaned.

"Surely you can defeat him," Rudolph said.

"What does it matter, for I am doomed," Hans said, his gloom returning. He looked at his hands with which he had strangled his own brother. Then he turned to Rudolph. "You are my friend, aren't you?"

"Yes," Rudolph said. "I'm here for you."

"I thought so," Hans said, and shoved Rudolph over the wall. There was a short agonizing scream and then a satisfying thud.

Hans looked over the wall and saw Rudolph's crumpled body on the ground. "I had to do it," he whispered. "I had to do it because I'm doomed. You might have betrayed me."

And then he looked to a startled knight who had watched the whole thing. "Tell the men to get ready for battle. Phillip seems to have conquered death and is back to lead the Westerhoven forces against us."

The knight bowed and quickly moved off.

Hans just stared at his hands and then went off to find the Lady Winona.

Excerpts from
the Battle at Large

Bill and Romeo, the cringing sycophants, never got close enough to the battle to see anything, and only caught a few glimpses from where they watched in the relative safety of a kitchen wagon, where they had easy access to some cheap wine. But even so, they put their heads together and came up with music and verse to celebrate the triumphant and often fictitious events of the day.

And here is a sampling of some of that verse:

> The walls were tall and that's not all
> There were bad guys on every spire.
> But Phillip was cool as was the rule
> To dudedom he did aspire.
>
> Because he had the balls, he climbed the walls
> And fought for his fair nation.
> The fighting was tough, things got rough
> But this dude took no vacation.
>
> His knights were fierce, their swords did pierce
> The armor of those who opposed them.
> Then things got bad, Hans got mad
> And . . .

"What rhymes with 'them'?" Bill asked.

Romeo stopped in mid-drink. "I don't know. Skip to a new verse."

"Okay," Bill said.

Meanwhile, Grover had to deal with more pressing issues than what rhymed with "them." He had to lead the charge of men up over the walls and into the city of Hoven.

"Are we following some sort of plan?" Grover asked Erich as they ran toward the walls.

"Yes, don't you remember?" Erich replied. "We're doing exactly what you decided at the war meeting."

"Oh," Grover said. "And what was that?"

Erich answered as if he were used to his leader forgetting things. "You wanted to storm the city and meet Hans in one-on-one combat and show him as the coward and dog that he is. And to save Winona."

"Oh," Grover said. "Is that a good plan?"

"You're the leader," Erich said. "How could you make a bad plan?"

Grover shrugged.

They separated as they reached the walls. All around them, other contingents were rushing forward. Ladders were thrown up. Grappling hooks were tossed over. Knights rushed forward to climb to the top. Cilla and Grover watched as the Sousterhoven defenders pushed the ladders back and cut the ropes from the grappling hooks. Knights fell to the ground, not to get up again. Others scrambled to throw up the ladders once more, or to pull away the wounded knights.

"This doesn't look too safe," Grover commented. He saw another knight fall to the ground and not get up. "Or very healthy."

"You can't back down now," Cilla said. "You have to go up. Because you're Phillip. You don't have the luxury to be a coward."

"As if I ever did," Grover sighed. "Maybe we should trade places."

"I wish we could," Cilla said. "But this is your job, so go." And she pushed Grover to one of the ladders.

"Damn," Grover said.

Another group of soldiers rushed by and threw up a ladder. A young lad with a bright cherubic face cried out, "Your ladder, my lord."

"Go on," Cilla said.

"Can't I just wait until they break in and open the city gates?" Grover asked.

Cilla shook her head.

Grover groaned and went to the ladder. It was bad enough that he had to wear armor, but now he had to climb about thirty feet, straight up. With his luck the ladder would probably break before the enemy had a chance to push him back to the ground. Grover paused and looked up at the wall, and it seemed clear. All around him men were either scaling ladders or shooting a covering fire of arrows at the defenders.

"What are you waiting for?" Cilla asked behind him.

Grover glared back and began climbing the ladder. If I ever get out of this alive, he thought, I'm going to quit being a hero.

Cilla followed directly behind.

Grover clutched the ladder the whole way and grimly kept an eye on the top of the wall, waiting for the defenders to push him off. He knew they were just waiting until there were enough men to make it worthwhile. That's why they hadn't pushed yet. He got halfway and still nothing happened. He kept climbing. About three-fourths of the way up he could see the top of the wall. If he fell now, he was bound to hurt something. But there was nothing to do but go on. When he was almost at the top he saw his first defender.

"It's Phillip, Phillip," the defender cried as he ran away.

"What are they afraid of?" Grover asked when he reached the top of the ramparts.

"I don't know. Could be your looks," Cilla said. "Being that I never saw Phillip's face, I can't be sure."

They moved along the battlements to let the other soldiers up. All around them, Westerhoven soldiers were reaching the top of the walls. Sousterhoven knights and troops were pulling back from the walls now and making a stand in the city. Back on the field lay scores of Westerhoven knights who had died trying to get up, and scores more were scattered on the ramparts where they had fought to maintain their position until other knights could come up. There were Sousterhoven dead also, but not as many.

"Well, we're here," Grover said.

"Yes, we are," Cilla said, hefting her club. "Now let's go kick some butt."

"Hey, I got something," Romeo said a little later.

"Let me hear it," Bill replied, who was still trying to find something that rhymed with "them." By now, they had seen the Westerhoven forces go over the walls and could hear sounds of fighting from within.

Romeo strummed a few chords of his lute. "Okay, this is a little ditty about an anonymous knight fighting for the glory of Phillip."

"Good," Bill said. "That always sounds good when you throw in something about the common man."

Romeo grinned and started to play.

"And then the anonymous knight, fighting for the glory of Phillip . . ."

"Wait," Bill said. "Maybe you shouldn't make that part so overt. Make it more subtle."

"Okay," Romeo said. He thought for a moment and started to strum again. "You have to remember this is in four-part harmony."

"Okay," Bill said.

And here is what Romeo sang:

"The brave knight fought for Phillip
Fought for Phillip did he
And when he died all he cried
Was be all you can be—in the army reserves."

Romeo stopped playing. "What do you think?"

"Needs work," Bill said. "Here, drink this for inspiration." And he passed over a wine bottle.

Grover and Cilla made it to the streets with little trouble. Wherever they went, the knights of Westerhoven rallied around him and fought the Sousterhoven forces. Grover didn't even have to swing his blade. Knights gladly threw themselves in the path of a Sousterhoven blade so that Phillip wouldn't have to exert himself.

"Pretty neat," Grover whispered to Cilla.

"Pretty stupid," Cilla said, who was getting upset that she wasn't able to hit anybody. Whenever a Sousterhoven knight seemed to be about to break through their line, another Westerhoven knight would come in and Cilla was pushed aside.

Since Grover didn't have to fight, he had time to observe the difference in battle styles. The knights of Hoven didn't fight at all like the duelists of Jolinstive. Instead of standing apart and using their weapons with skill and speed, the knights would wade into the thick of battle, waving their giant swords, cutting a path through the lines. There was no finesse, no stopping to consider strategy. The knights would continue to trade blows until one had fallen. And if the loser happened to be alive, the victor would take his blade, hold it over the throat of his opponent, and ask if he surrendered. If he did, which Grover found amazing enough, he would walk back over to the Westerhoven camp and stay there. They wouldn't fight back or stab someone in the back. They would simply return to the camp and wait, talking with their friends. But if they refused to surrender, and some did refuse, the victor would push his sword into the throat of the defeated one and take his life. In some senses it was more civil, but on the whole it seemed much more barbaric. Especially when a knight would get in a particularly good blow and decapitate his opponent. The other knights would cry, "Wipeout," and raise a cheer.

The battle went on and Grover and his forces kept moving continually forward until their last defenders died and the last Sousterhoven troops had retreated further into the city. For the first time since they had arrived, Grover and Cilla found themselves alone. They heard fighting going on, but they couldn't see it, since they were on the other side of buildings, unable to get to it.

The battle had gone on for hours and it seemed to them that they were winning. The Sousterhoven troops seemed to fall back wherever they went. Grover realized this was partly due to his being Phillip. This battle wouldn't have been possible without him. And he started to feel good about coming here. Until Cilla brought him back to the situation at hand.

"We're lost," she said.

"We can't be," Grover said. "Can't we just walk back the way we came?"

Cilla shrugged. "Tell me truthfully, does any of this look familiar to you?"

Grover looked at the ancient stone buildings that seemed to grow out of the earth around him. They had fought up and down the streets all day and Grover had never thought to look for a landmark. None of it looked familiar, or more accurately, all of it looked the same.

"I guess not," Grover replied.

Cilla seemed to think for a moment and then said, "I hear something. Must be more of our troops."

"Guess we could ask them," Grover said.

Cilla walked down a wide, extremely clean alley. Grover followed, great sword in his hands. The alley opened up into a courtyard, where they could see some saddled horses.

"Horses," Cilla said.

"But our troops didn't have any horses," Grover pointed out.

"I know," Cilla said.

And just then they saw some Sousterhoven troops emerge from a side door of the building close to them. Several armored men exited the door and walked out of sight into the courtyard. One of the men was dressed in black and white and seemed to be the leader.

"What is the report?" the leader asked.

"The Westerhoven troops have pushed back our troops and

seem to be winning on all sides. There's just too many of them," a lieutenant reported.

"I see," the leader said. "And what of Phillip?"

"Wherever he goes our lines fall back."

The leader shook his head.

Cilla turned back to Grover. "That's Hans. I bet it is."

"Great," Grover said. "Maybe we should run away now."

"I think we should surprise-attack them," Cilla said.

"There must be at least ten knights that we can't see," Grover said. "Besides, we're here to save Winona."

"Wimp," Cilla said.

Back in the courtyard, the lieutenant was asking, "What are your orders?"

"There's nothing to be gained by staying. Tell the troops to keep fighting. I will get Winona, and the troops will fight a delaying action until we can get out."

The lieutenant nodded and walked out of their view.

"Let's get him," Cilla said, and started forward with her club.

"No," Grover said, and held back on Cilla, clutching at her sleeve.

"Let go," Cilla cried out.

Grover's heart leaped up to his throat. Cilla's cry had been too loud. Grover peered down the alley to see Hans turning in the courtyard. The game was up. Grover let go of Cilla and grabbed his sword in both hands.

While We Gathered Our Wits About Us

Grover opened his eyes to see Cilla's oval face hovering above him. Her dark eyes looked concerned as she brought the flat of her hand down to slap his face vigorously.

"What, what," Grover shouted, feeling the sting on his face. He lifted up his body with a sudden motion and saw that he was lying in an empty alley. "What the hell?" And then he turned to Cilla. "I was having the most horrible dream and you were in it. We were hired to go to this terrible place called Hoven, where I was supposed to pretend to be some guy named Phillip and then . . ."

"Wake up," Cilla said, taking the opportunity to slap his face again. "It wasn't a dream."

"Ouch," Grover said, rubbing his face. "You were mean to me in my dream too."

"Well, you were probably telling lies again," Cilla said.

"I wasn't," Grover lied defensively. "And you were still mean."

Cilla shook her head but didn't say anything.

Grover rubbed the back of his head where it felt bruised and looked at the armor on his body, and the burgundy clothing that Cilla wore. It was real. "What happened?" he asked when he finally adjusted to the fact that this was all really happening.

Cilla held out a hand to help Grover up. Grover took it and managed to rise to his feet.

"You fainted in fear," Cilla explained.

"Did not."

"Did so," Cilla said.

"No way," Grover replied.

"Then what do you call the little catnap you took?"

Grover looked at the street which had been his most recent bed. "It was exhaustion," Grover said. "I must have fainted from exhaustion. From running around carrying all this heavy armor. You would too if you had to carry all this metal on your body."

"Un-huh," Cilla replied doubtfully. "Sure."

"Well, don't believe me, then," Grover said. He looked up the alley to see the courtyard was empty. "So where's Hans?"

"He took off," Cilla said. "And I think he's going to get Winona."

"So he's gone," Grover said. "Hmm, that's too bad."

"That's right," Cilla said. "He's gone. And he might take your bride, and that would sort of screw up our mission. So, if you don't mind, I think it's time we left and went looking for her."

"But where?" Grover asked. "Do you think they still keep maidens in towers these days?"

"I don't know," Cilla said. "But I guess we'll find out."

Do Damsels Really Want to Be Saved?

Winona wasn't a pretty girl by any means and only looked okay on the best of days. Her hair, which was blonde, did not shine like gold, but rather looked like limp, wet straw. And her face was not one of an angel descended to the earth, but was all rounded and sort of lumpy, like an unbaked dough sculpture. And her nose, which could have been perky, was only like a knob at the end of a door. And her eyebrows were not thin and graceful, but seemed just a little off kilter, no matter how she plucked them.

Her only saving grace was her eyes, which were a most startling shade of green, and if you looked at them you could almost forget how ordinary the rest of her face appeared.

No, she wasn't pretty at all, and had been made aware of that condition all of her life, because every time she went to a ball or a tourney, she heard rude comments made by taller, more slender, attractive daughters from the other principalities. Didn't she just look all dumpy and squat is what they said. And in fact, some people did call her "dumpling" because of this, or maybe because it was one of her favorite foods, which had contributed amply to her chubby figure. Yes, she was well aware of the fact she wasn't pretty, but she also knew she had one thing all those pretty girls did not have, and that was the unalterable fact she was a direct descendant of the last Queen of Hoven, and was thus a much better political match than any of them would ever make.

This, too, she was aware of from a very early age and she used it to her advantage whenever she possibly could. Though she may not have been born beautiful—and beauty fades anyway—she had been born with a brain—and that doesn't fade—and had learned how to use it to make the most of an opportunity. She just wasn't going to wait until she was married off as some political salve to protect her father's eastern farmlands, she was going to marry so that she would never have to suffer insults again. And she was going to marry someone she could control.

So she had diligently worked at writing letters of love and had sent them to the most promising men in each principality. Soon she had become the center of attention and had more suitors than any of the pretty girls who had made fun of her. And she had vied one suitor off another, never making a definitive choice, just waiting for the right one to come her way. And then one night it had all come to an end. She had drunk too much at a ball in Wunderkinde and had somehow ended up in the bed of Phillip. A month later her fears had come true and she knew she was to bear Phillip's child. Phillip's child! She didn't even like Phillip. Now all her plans were ruined, because pregnancy was as good as a marriage vow. Now she was expected to marry him. And she almost did too, until she managed to escape the week before the wedding was to take place.

She couldn't marry Phillip because he would never let her have her way. Not only that, Phillip only wanted to marry her so he could have a better claim to the Hoven throne. Once married, she would be cast aside. It was a total ruination of all she had planned for, besides the fact that she detested him to the core. So she escaped and went south to meet with Hans. If she was captured by Hans, then Phillip could not marry her. It seemed like a good plan at the time. But then things went wrong again.

She had reached the city well enough and had met up with Hans, who had come with a large force of men. But she hadn't counted on Phillip coming so soon, and he had brought his Dude Knights. There had been a skirmish outside the gates, with Hans eventually withdrawing into the city and closing the gates. More troops had been called for by both sides, and soon she was in a siege situation. And now she had been placed in a tower for safety, with nothing to do, and only her handmaiden, Erika, for company. And if that wasn't bad enough, Erika happened to like Phillip and wanted nothing more than to talk about him all day.

"Isn't he brave?" Erika would croon. "Isn't he handsome?" she would ask.

"Isn't he stupid?" Winona would reply. "Isn't he a total bore and scoundrel?" she would add.

And so time passed, but slowly. And when she heard Phillip had died she had rejoiced.

"I'm so happy," Winona said.

But her handmaiden only wept. "I'm so sorry for you. You must feel terrible."

"Yes, terrible," Winona agreed. "Terrible it didn't happen sooner."

Erika's response was to raise a hand to her mouth in astonishment. "You cannot mean that, you must be in shock."

"Yes, yes, that's it," Winona said. And threw one of her bonnets out the window of the tower. "Will you go fetch that for me?"

But Erika did not jump out the window as Winona hoped she would. So Winona had to endure her company. Hans had said she would be able to depart this very day. He had come to her and had asked her to get ready. She had been excited and had her handmaiden pack all her things. But an hour later the walls of the city had been stormed by the Westerhoven troops.

"Can you believe it?" Winona asked aloud. "All this just because of me." And inside her heart she felt glad.

But Erika only said, "Surely they are attacking to defeat Hans and not just to save you."

"Shut up," Winona said. "You're just a stupid handmaiden, and you have no idea what you're talking about." Then she turned back to watch the skirmish in the street.

And all along, her handmaiden would ask, "Have you seen Phillip? Is he here? Will we be saved?" For she believed that Phillip was still alive.

And all along, Winona ignored her and bit her already-too-short nails, and wondered when Hans would come to save her.

Hans never reached Winona's tower as he had planned. After leaving the courtyard with his fiercest knights he had ridden straight for the tower. But the way was blocked by Westerhoven forces—a contingent led by Erich—and after a short scuffle, it was obvious they would not break through. There were too many Westerhoven knights, and even though they had the superiority of horses, they did not have enough men to break through. So Hans had turned around and retreated, calling the rest of his forces with him as he went, to leave Winona and the battle behind for another day.

Winona didn't know of this and so waited in the vain hope that Hans would arrive. Suddenly she heard sounds on the steps and grew excited, believing that Hans had come to save her. She turned to look at the door and was disappointed with the outcome.

With an outward crash, the door to Winona's room fell to the floor and standing in the door frame was Phillip and his sword-bearer, Voss.

"It had to be the last tower," Grover whined, wiping the sweat off his forehead.

"Stop whining," Cilla said.

"Phillip," Erika cried. "Are you here to save us?"

Grover looked at Erika, who was the very picture of loveliness that damsels were supposed to be, and also the exact type of girl Winona detested. Grover was charmed and immediately took her for Winona. "Are you Winona?" he asked.

"Is that some sort of sick joke?" Winona asked from across the room.

"What?" Grover asked, looking away from Erika to see a dumpy-looking girl, sitting by the window, with a cross look on her face.

"Did you come here to insult me too?" Winona asked.

"What, no," Grover said in confusion. "I didn't come here to insult anybody."

"I'm not Winona," Erika said. "She is."

Grover glanced back at the dumpy girl, and a look of disappointment crossed his face. "Just great."

Winona stood up and went to the window. "If you came to save me, think again. I will not marry you."

"You won't?" Grover asked. He looked at Cilla, who returned his quizzical expression.

"Do I have to tell you everything twice?" Winona asked. "I knew you were dumb but I didn't think you were deaf."

"Hey, just a moment," Grover cried. "No one calls me stu—"

"Just get her," Cilla said. "And let's go."

"I'll jump," Winona said, lifting one leg up to the window.

"But I thought she wanted to be saved," Grover said.

"You're such a fool," Winona said. "Don't think I won't do it."

"She's crazy," Erika cried.

"You got that right, sister," Cilla said.

"You have to stop her," Erika pleaded. "She hasn't been in her right mind since she heard of your death."

"Not true," Winona said. "I was happy to hear of your death."

"She was?" Grover asked.

"You see," Erika said. "She's crazy. You must stop her."

"But what can I do?" Grover asked. He took a step forward. Winona edged more of her body out the window.

Erika turned to Voss. "You're her brother. You try to talk to her."

Cilla looked surprised.

Grover arched his eyebrows at Cilla. "You're her brother. Now, that's interesting."

"Shut up," Cilla said. And then she gazed down at Erika, who was on her knees trembling. "The situations I get in," Cilla muttered. She looked over at Winona. "Just get away from that window."

"You can't order me around," Winona said. "You're no longer my brother. Once you were captured and served this vermin, you renounced your allegiance to Astertov and to me. I spit on you."

"I guess she told you," Grover remarked.

Cilla frowned. "Damn sisters. Some things never change."

"Do something," Erika cried.

"If you don't leave, I'll jump," Winona threatened.

"Go ahead, then, jump," Grover said on impulse, not thinking she would do it.

"Okay," Winona said, and thrust her whole body forward.

Cilla saw what was happening and ran forward, as did Grover when he realized Winona was actually doing it. They got there just in time. As Winona's body was fully out the window, they caught at the edge of her dress, stopping her from falling.

Grover grunted. "God, she's heavy."

"It's all those dumplings," Erika said from behind them. "I told her to go on a diet. But would she listen to me? Noooo."

Outside the window Winona screeched. "Let me go. Let me go. I'll die before I ever marry you."

"Sick woman," Cilla remarked. "There's more necrophiliacs here than an undead convention."

Together they pulled Winona back in the tower, where Winona promptly spit in Grover's face.

As the spit dripped off his cheeks Grover turned to Cilla. "Do you think Beogoat isn't telling us everything?"

What Beogoat
Isn't Telling Us

Westerhoven claimed victory that day, chasing the Sousterhoven forces all the way to the lake, where they were allowed to cross unmolested over to the Reichton border. The captured knights were allowed to leave after paying a ransom, or after promising to send the ransom money. The wounded were treated and the dead were moved to where they could be buried. Night had already fallen by the time the troops returned to camp, where a drunken Romeo and an inebriated Bill were able to watch.

"I guess we're still employed," Romeo observed.

"We better go greet our lordship, then," Bill said. "And tell him of the poems and songs we have written to his greatness."

"And then ask for a raise," Romeo suggested.

"Right," Bill nodded.

And together they stumbled over to Phillip's tent to tell their lordship what they had done in his honor.

Grover, Cilla, Beogoat, and Beoweasel were already there. They had finally gained some peace, after the representatives of the Lords of Westerhoven, or the actual Lords themselves, had come to pay a visit and praise Phillip for his victory. Of the actual Lords, only three were in attendance: Prince Thorn of Hoenecker, Richard of Meistertonne, and Young Dianna from Helmutov. They each paid homage and once again swore loyalty. None of them seemed suspicious in the least, and only one—Lord Richard—had asked directly about the nature of his absence, and nodded his head grimly when he heard that it was a secret quest.

"I see," Richard finally said. "And that's all?"

"Why, yes," Grover said.

Richard nodded and had then exited the tent.

"Was that guy uptight or what?" Cilla asked when he left. "I thought I was going to have to knife him."

"He's always been that way," Beogoat said. "Right, Beoweasel?"

"If you mean wise," Beoweasel said, "then yes. Richard is no fool."

"Beoweasel used to be part of the Meistertonne family," Beogoat explained. "Before he came to work for me."

Just then Romeo, carrying his lute, and Bill, carrying his sheaf of notes, burst into the tent.

"Hey," Romeo said.

"Greetings," Bill said.

"We wrote some poems and music for you," Romeo explained.

The room was silent. Grover turned to Beogoat to rectify the situation. Beogoat coughed. "Bug off, guys. Phillip is busy."

Romeo looked affronted. "Yeah, and since when did you speak for Phillip? Just like you wizard dudes. You come in and take our place, and it's out the door with us."

Beogoat gestured to Grover. "What do you say, Lord Phillip?"

It took a moment for Grover to realize it was his decision, and when he did, he said, "You guys will have to leave for a while."

"Oh, okay," Romeo said. "Totally bogus."

Bill bowed from the waist and then asked, "When will you next require our services?"

Grover shrugged. "I'll call you."

"Very well, then," Bill said, and turned to leave.

Romeo took one last look and then put his arm around Bill, loudly asking, "Why do we always have to leave? I thought we were supposed to hang around him all the time and placate him."

"I don't know," Bill said. "I don't know."

And then they were gone.

Grover sat down. "How long will I have to put up with them?"

"Not very long," Beogoat replied.

"Good," Grover said. "The less people I have to see, the better I feel. I feel like I'm going to be exposed any minute."

"Well, you weren't," Beogoat said. "So how did it go in there? I haven't heard anything. I assume you defeated Hans."

"Ah no," Grover said, glaring at Cilla to keep her mouth shut about the little episode they had back in the city.

"You didn't?" Beogoat said. "I was sort of hoping you would have killed him."

"He escaped," Cilla explained. "But we did manage to save Winona. That's what you wanted, right?"

"Yeah, sure," Beogoat said. "And you say Hans got away?"

"Yes," Grover said. "He got away. That wasn't our job anyway."

"Of course," Beogoat said, pulling out his pipe and chewing on the end. "You're right. Saving your devoted bride Winona was the whole point."

"Ah, Beogoat," Cilla said, "we wanted to ask you about that."

"About what?" Beogoat asked carefully.

"Yeah," Grover chimed in. "She didn't actually seem as devoted as you said she was. I thought she wanted to marry Phillip?"

"She does," Beogoat said.

"She said she would rather die than marry Phillip," Grover went on. "We had to stop her from jumping out of a tower."

"Hmm," Beogoat said. "I meant, she does, but she doesn't know it yet."

"It seems like she won't ever know it," Cilla said.

Beogoat scowled and turned to Beoweasel. "Beoweasel, doesn't the Lady Winona desire to marry Phillip?"

"Whatever you say," Beoweasel replied.

"You see?" Beogoat said. "There you go. You must have been misinformed."

"We heard her scream it," Grover said. "We saw her try to jump from the tower. Is there something you're not telling us?"

"Yes," Cilla said. "So far we've had to fight a battle we weren't supposed to be in and save a bride who was supposed to be waiting for us and who wanted to marry Phillip and not be forced into it. I have a feeling that you're not being straight with us."

"Hmm," Beogoat said. "You have a point. I didn't want to trouble you with the minor details."

"Minor details," Grover screeched. "Those are just a bit bigger than minor details."

"Yes," Cilla said. "What exactly haven't you been telling us?"

"Nothing, nothing," Beogoat replied hastily. "I'm surprised that you're so upset. What's the problem? You saved the Lady Winona. All you have to do is marry her now."

"We're just concerned," Cilla said, "that there are more minor details you have forgotten to tell us."

"Nothing more," Beogoat said. "All you have to do is have Grover here marry Winona. Everything should be smooth sailing from now on." And he gestured with his hand using a flat motion to demonstrate smooth sailing.

"Are you sure?" Cilla asked. She gazed at him skeptically. "I don't want any more surprises."

Beogoat shrugged. "None that I know of. Honestly."

Cilla stared at him for a few moments more and then lowered her gaze. "Well, all right, then."

"So what happens now?" Grover asked.

"Well," Beogoat said, "we travel back to Castle Wunderkinde, where the wedding will take place."

"And how long will that take?" Grover asked.

"A few days," Beogoat said. "If the weather is good."

"What?" Grover cried. "I thought we were only supposed to be here a few days?"

Beogoat shrugged, pulling a hair from his mouth. "I must have miscalculated the time needed. It's only a few more days."

"I thought you said no more surprises?" Cilla said.

"Were you surprised?" Beogoat asked. But before Cilla could answer he turned to Beoweasel. "We must go now. I'm sure you're tired from all the fighting. And so am I. If you have nothing more to say, I'll be going." And he gestured to Beoweasel. "Come on."

"But," Grover said.

"Hey," Cilla cried.

But Beogoat and Beoweasel had already left, and Cilla and Grover were left alone in the tent.

After a few moments Cilla turned to Grover. "Well, what are you looking at?"

"Don't you mean, what are you looking at, *my lord*?" Grover suggested.

"No," Cilla said, and promptly looked away. "God, I hate wizards."

PART III
How to Hatch a Plot

How to Abduct a Wizard

You watch from the crowded streets of Wunderkinde town as Phillip returns triumphant with his bride Winona, fresh from the battle. At his right side rides his best friend and lieutenant, Erich, and to his left rides the court wizard, Beogoat. Behind Phillip rides his faithful swordbearer, Voss. They all look larger than life astride their mighty steeds, dressed in their finest clothes and their brightest armor. Trailing behind are the Dude Knights, smiling and laughing as they parade through the town. People are gathered at every corner, and hang from every window, to see them come back. And at the very end of the group is the Lady Winona, accompanied by her handmaiden, Erika. They have an honor guard all their own.

As the company passes off from the town and files into the great castle of Wunderkinde, you follow along unobserved. It is easy to mix in with the company. Nobody seems to notice you. But when you reach the gate to the castle, it closes in front of you and you aren't able to pass within.

You spend hours waiting outside the castle until darkness falls. With the darkness comes one of the cold spring rains. But even though the rain chills you to the bone, it also covers your movements as you scale the rough stone wall. Various rooms are lit, and you can see the lighted windows like a checkered pattern against the darkness.

You know that Beogoat resides in one of the four towers. You see that the highest one is lit fairly bright, so you decide to climb this one. Scaling the tower is difficult, and the rain doesn't make it any easier. You slip and fall, scratching yourself, sometimes almost losing grip totally, but somehow you make it to the top. There you pull open the window without the occupant noticing, and reach in with one soggy hand to pull aside the heavy green curtains.

Inside you see a floor piled thick with intricately woven rugs, one thrown atop the other. In one corner of the room is a small cot,

67

with black satin sheets tangled up all about it. A heavy quilt lies beside it on the floor. Not too far from the bed is a table, texts and papers littering the surface. A human skull lies on top of a dark wooden box which has silver inlaid runes upon it.

Looking from wall to wall, you can see the many shelves that have been placed there, filled with all manner of objects mundane and fanciful. Books, thickly bound, falling apart. Scrolls open and torn. Stuffed animals, bones, a deck of cards. Even mugs, plates of half-eaten food, a Rubik's Cube, and even some old back issues of *Dragon* magazine. And lying right in front of the shelves is a well-thumbed copy of *Heroes, Inc.*

And in the midst of all this clutter, standing in front of the sputtering fireplace, is a tall wiry old man, his hair gray, his face covered with a sparse gray stubble. He is wearing a thin brown robe, loosely sashed at the waist. Clenched in his teeth you see a carved meerschaum pipe, with rainbow-colored smoke rising to the ceiling.

Yes, you have found the right room. This is Beogoat. And if you listen carefully, over the sigh of the wind and the crackling of the fire, you will be able to hear what he is muttering.

Beogoat paced back and forth across his thickly carpeted floor, his bare toes digging into the fabric whenever he chose to stop. Behind him, on his desk, a blank book lay open and a quill pen stood poised over the page, of its own volition, inscribing words in a dark Indian ink.

"Let me see," he muttered. "It was the first time I had met Marilyn, and not soon after, we went off to my place to have sex. She was really great in bed."

Beogoat paused, and something told him to look at the pen scribbling all on its own. Blue smoke emitting from his pipe, he crossed over to the desk, looking for the lines he had just spoken.

Written on the page was, "And then after I first beheld the vision of loveliness named Lady Marilyn, how I swoon when I say that name. It wasn't long before I proposed marriage. She was radiant when I asked."

"That's not what I said," wailed Beogoat at the magic pen. "What are you doing?"

The pen did not move.

Beogoat frowned. He looked at the word "marriage" on the page, obviously a replacement for the word "sex." On impulse he said, "She said she wouldn't go down on me unless I was a priest. What a bitch."

The pen scribbled on the page with long florid strokes. "She would not let me hold her hand unless I had cleansed myself from sin. What a wily one she was."

"What the . . ." Beogoat said, and reached out for the pen. He gave it close examination and noticed that the inscribed label said, "Courtier style."

"I knew it," Beogoat said. "Beoweasel purchased the wrong magic pen." He sighed. "Oh well, I guess I'll have to write my sexual memoirs another night." He placed the pen back on the page where it resumed its waiting position.

Beogoat puffed on his pipe and thought for a minute. "Okay, we'll start on Chapter Seven. We'll title it 'Helping Friends.' " Beogoat meditated, gathering his thoughts about him, while outside he could hear the wind rush by and the rain slap hard against the walls of the tower. "Okay, okay. I think I got it."

The pen was poised and ready.

"It was Merlyn who first told me never to get involved in the affairs of man. Or was that Gandalf? Gandalf said never be a meddling wizard. Or was that Belgareth? I can't seem to get them straight in my mind. Anyway, we were all frat brothers. I can still remember that time Gandalf and I dropped acid at Berkeley. Or was that with Jerry G.? I can't remember. Let me see . . ."

His ruminations were halted by a heavy knocking at the door. Beogoat looked with irritation at the thick wooden door.

"Bug off," he said. "I told you I don't want to be disturbed."

There was silence. The pen scribbled some more. Beogoat thought he had achieved peace when he heard some shuffling and then a muffled voice spoke.

"What was that?" Beogoat inquired. He looked at the door again and wondered who could be bothering him at such a time. He thought of telling them to go away, but they would probably be only more insistent. It was better just to get it over with. "Who is it?" Beogoat asked.

"The Avon lady," a gruff voice responded.

"The Avon lady," Beogoat said with surprise. He looked through the peephole in the door and saw a lone man standing there. He was balding, dressed in leathers, with a black cloak thrown over him.

"Who's the Avon lady?" Beogoat asked, opening the door. And then he saw—too late—it wasn't just one man standing there, but four men. One of them pulled out a card that said *Wizard Collectors*. "You've missed some payments on some magic scrolls," the leader said.

"But," Beogoat protested.

"You're coming with us," another one said, hefting a club.

Cilla Does Her Part

Cilla opened the door to see an unfamiliar face. "Yes?" she said. "What is it?"

"You must come quickly," the guard said.

"What for?" Cilla asked. "What is it?"

"You'll be told when you get there. It is of the utmost importance."

Cilla frowned. "It is?"

"Just act normal," the guard said. And when he saw Cilla turn to look back in her room, he added, "And don't bring anything."

"Okay," Cilla said.

The guard gestured for her to follow and Cilla walked out, pulling her door closed behind her. "What's this all about?" she asked again.

The guard started walking and said in a low voice, "There's been an emergency meeting. He wants to meet you."

"Phillip? Erich?" Cilla asked.

The guard gave her a sharp look. "This isn't a joking matter."

"Sorry," Cilla said. And after a moment, "What does he want to see me about?"

"Can't say," the guard answered.

"What's your name again?" Cilla asked.

The guard looked at her, surprised. "You know I can't tell you that. It's bad enough we had to meet face-to-face. But this was the only way."

"Sorry," Cilla said.

The guard kept walking quickly and whenever they passed someone in the hall he greeted them in a normal tone of voice, but didn't stop to talk. A few people also called out greetings to Voss, but Cilla did little more than acknowledge the person with a glance. They descended two flights of stairs, walked down a dark, barely used corridor until they reached a locked door. The guard pulled a key from his pocket and inserted it into the lock.

"Where are we going?" Cilla asked.

"This your first time here?" the guard asked.

Cilla made a noncommittal sound which the man interpreted as positive.

"I'm not surprised," he said. "Very few have been to all the rooms. But it's safer that way."

Cilla didn't ask why it was safer that way.

On the other side of the door was a small storage room. It was filled with old furniture. Before going in the guard took a lantern which lay on the floor and lighted it. He then closed the door. Once closed he walked over to where an old desk was. He moved the desk aside and tapped on the wall. The guard then put the lantern down and pushed on the hard surface.

"Must be stuck," the guard explained, and he pushed harder. Slowly a crack appeared in the wall. And a passage was slowly revealed.

"Come on," he said when it was fully open.

Cilla followed as the guard led the way down a narrow, foul-smelling corridor. "This leads out of the castle," he said.

They walked for some distance until they came to some steps and emerged to the surface. The guard turned down the lantern and then there was a sound of a heavy board being grated against stone. There was light, and rain came down.

"We're out," he whispered.

Cilla followed him out into the wetness. They had emerged under the overhang of a bridge a short distance from the castle. She could see the walls and the lights from the castle windows. Waiting beneath the bridge was a man in a black cloak. She couldn't see his face because it was turned away from her.

"I brought him," the guard said, pointing to her.

The man in the black cloak turned and Cilla saw that his face was obscured by the mask of a demon. He also had a red scarf around his neck. Behind the man with the scarf stood four others.

"Very good," said the man in the red scarf. He turned to Cilla.

"Sorry about the meeting place," he said.

Cilla shivered from the cold rain but said nothing.

"Should I wait?" the guard asked.

"Yes, because I have something to tell you," the man in the scarf said.

"New orders?" he asked.

"No," the man in the scarf replied. "Your business with us is done. Your face has been seen. We can't afford that."

"But you told me to . . . Those were your orders," the guard cried.

"Yes, and you also swore to obey them," the man in the scarf replied.

The guard turned to run. There was an abrupt twanging sound. The guard's torso twisted unnaturally. He fell to the muddy bank of the stream, gasping.

"Finish him," the man in the scarf said.

Two of the other fellows dressed in masks and black cloaks came up pulling knives out and bent down to the guard. "No," the guard gurgled as they sliced his throat. But that was all, for his body was turned over so his face was in the mud.

"Put this on him," the man in the scarf said. He took off his scarf and handed it to one of the men who had slit the guard's throat. The scarf was then tied around the guard's wrist.

When that business was done the leader spoke to Cilla again. "Come here," he said.

Cilla stared at him. As she saw it, she only had three choices: One was to run away, two was to attack them, and three was to come closer. If she ran away she probably would be doing herself more harm than good, because Voss obviously knew these people and her behavior would be out of character. Attacking them, which is what she wanted to do, would probably serve no purpose until she found out who they were and what they wanted. So since she couldn't run, and it wasn't wise to attack, especially since she didn't have a weapon, she saw that her only response was to come forward cautiously.

"This is what I need you to do," the leader started to say.

Cilla looked up into the mask. Something struck her as familiar about the man. For one thing he was tall. Most men in this land weren't tall.

The leader continued. "You must tell me the location of the *Sacred Stone*. I know, I know, you don't know it, but you must try to get the information from Phillip."

Cilla nodded.

"Does he suspect at all?" he asked.

"He tells me very little," Cilla said.

The man did not say anything for a moment. "Do what you can."

"How will I notify you?" Cilla asked.

"The usual way," he said.

Cilla nodded, though she had no idea what the usual way was. The man turned to one of the others. "Do you have the key?"

One of the black-cloaked figures brought up the key the guide had used to unlock the door.

"You can find your way back?"

Cilla nodded, taking the key.

"Good," he said. "And now that Phillip is to wed again, we will go back to our original plan. Will you be ready?"

"Of course," Cilla said.

"Then go," the man said. "And be discreet about it."

"I always am," Cilla said, backing toward the door.

What was it about that voice? She went down into the passage, stopped to turn up the lantern, and walked back. If only she could figure out why she thought that voice was familiar, then she could figure out what the hell she just agreed to.

More Things
My Wizard Never Told Me

Having followed Cilla to her rendezvous, you are once again caught out in the rain. The leader dismisses the rest of the group and each member takes off in a different direction. You decide to follow the leader. He leads you back to the castle through another secret entrance. You follow him through a dank tunnel, similar to the one you were in before, but this time you emerge in a crypt. Everywhere you can see the brass plates with the names of the deceased written on them. The leader walks by them with a small lantern, paying them no mind. You would like to see the names of who lies buried within these vaults, but feel you might miss out on something if you don't keep following the leader.

From the crypt you emerge into a church. Here the leader pauses and takes off the cloak and mask. Underneath he is wearing the normal dress of a noble son, all fine clothes in the national colors of burgundy and black. He is also very dry, unlike you, who is shivering from the coldness of the rain.

You go up closer to get a look at him, but he turns away, stuffing the cloak and mask into a sack he carries with him, and hurries up the hall. It is even later now, and there is no one in the halls, as he mounts two flights of stairs, walks down two hallways, and stops at a door. But he does not stop to knock, only to unlock it.

You follow him quickly in and see the rich decorations of the room within. The four-poster bed is made of the finest mahogany, and the whitest cotton sheets cover it. There is a small writing table with ink and papers on it. In one corner lie the man's armor and weapons, all polished and well cared for. And on one wall you see a mirror, in which this fellow stops to look.

You can see his full features now. He is tall, dark, thin, with deep-inset eyes and a long distinctive eyebrow that crosses both eyes. You recognize this man from the parade. He is Phillip's best friend and lieutenant, Erich.

You gasp and quickly put a hand over your mouth. It is obvious that Erich wasn't wearing a black cloak and a demon's mask just to plan Phillip's secret bachelor party. No, you begin to suspect that something much worse is going on.

Erich turns away from the mirror and takes the sack underneath his arm and puts it in a chest that lies at the end of his bed. This he carefully locks when he is done. But instead of getting up he kneels in front of the chest, takes off his shirt, and pulls out a leather riding crop from underneath his bed. This he takes and soundly hits his back with, raising long dark welts along the surface. You notice there are previous scars. This is not something Erich does on a lark. You think it's a pretty weird hobby to have.

You decide it's about time to leave when Erich gets up. He puts the crop underneath his bed, puts on his shirt, and turns to the door.

"I must warn Phillip," he says to himself earnestly. He goes to the corner where his armor and weapons are, and pulls out his great sword.

Without strapping it on he exits the room. You follow him closely. Out in the hall a guard passes by and casually says, "Evening, Erich."

"Evening," Erich replies. But the tone is strange. What they are saying seems normal, but sounds rehearsed. "See anything strange?" he asks.

"Nope," the guard replies, and moves on.

Erich passes him and waits until the guard reaches the end of the hall before knocking on Phillip's door.

Grover had been in his room all night. He had managed to leave the welcoming party early, feigning fatigue and illness so he wouldn't have to meet anyone he was expected to know. Beogoat had guided him to his room and advised him to stay there. So Grover had gladly settled into his new room, which turned out to be an apartment made up of four rooms. There was his waiting room, right off the main hall, and from there you walked into his sun-room, which had large windows, several couches, and a fireplace in the corner. And off the sun-room was his bedroom, which contained a giant four-poster bed, and had entrances to a large walk-in closet which contained a wardrobe which he sincerely approved of. "This guy definitely has taste," Grover said, caressing the fabric of one of the shirts. And off the bedroom was his bathroom, with a giant tub and many soft towels. But the tub was dry, and he didn't see any water, so he had to content himself with a change of clothes.

He settled into the sun-room, which was well lit with various lamps, and started to read *Dude Knights Die Young*, to get an idea of how he was supposed to act. Beogoat had said it was a manual on how to be a knight, supposedly written by Phillip himself. So Grover tried to read diligently, but all he could get out of it was that every custom had an exception, and after every sentence you were supposed to say "dude." He was just about to start a new chapter when he heard a knocking at his door.

Thinking that it might be Beogoat, he hopped off the couch and ran to the anteroom. Here he skidded on the tiled floor and slid into the door with a thump. "Who is it?" he stopped to ask.

"It's Erich," he heard from the other side of the door.

"Oh no," Grover said. He grabbed at the ponytail he had made of his hair so that he would resemble Phillip. He wondered if he should claim sickness or just tell him to bug off. But instead he said, "What is it?"

"I must speak with you," he said insistently.

Grover looked at the door in fear and realized he had no choice but to open it. Phillip wouldn't refuse entrance to his best friend for any reason. He heaved a sigh of resignation and opened the door. "Come in," he said.

Erich came through the door quickly. His face was flushed with excitement. Outside there was a cry of alarm from a guard.

"What's that?" Grover asked.

"He's here, Phillip," Erich said. "I saw him."

"Who's here?" Grover asked. He couldn't imagine who could be here, but it was probably someone he didn't want to see. "Hans," he blurted out.

"No," Erich said. "It's . . . I'm sorry I have to be the one to tell you. I know we thought we killed him the last time, but he's back."

"Oh no," Grover said, playing along.

"I know, my friend. The Black Avenger is back."

"The Black Avenger," Grover said in surprise. He didn't like the sound of the name at all. The chance that he was one of Phillip's old drinking buddies was slim.

"Yes," Erich replied. "He's back. And you know he has sworn to kill you."

Grover wasn't sure what to say to that so he said nothing. Everything was happening too fast. One moment he was worrying that he might say something that would show Erich that he wasn't Phillip, and the next he had to worry about someone called the Black Avenger who had sworn to kill him.

"Kill me," Grover finally said.

"The guards have already been alarmed," Erich said.

"They're alarmed. I'm alarmed," Grover said. He feared the adventure might be up already and he would have to do something about it. "You don't think he's here to take Winona."

"He might be," Erich said. "You never know with that scoundrel. But he was sworn to bring you down and all who support you."

"He has," Grover exclaimed, and then quickly added, "Yes, right. We must stop him."

"And so we will," Erich said. "I will personally lead the search. I swear to you that I will bring him down, or I will die trying."

"Good, you do that," Grover said, glad that he didn't have to lead the search.

"I'll be off, then," Erich said, and turned to go out the door.

"Get him, ah, dude," Grover said in parting, and then closed the door.

He could hear the cry of alarm going up all around the castle now. He heard shouts of many men, and the sound of heavy-booted feet running outside his door. He stood there for a moment with his back to the door, staring blankly into his sun-room. Finally he heaved himself away from the door.

"The Black Avenger," he said. "Beogoat never said anything about a Black Avenger."

The Sign of
the Black Avenger

Grover waited until the commotion in the halls died down before he went out. In his haste to leave he forgot to put on his shoes and went out barefoot. But he had not forgotten to bring his great sword, *Biff*, which was his only protection against the myriad persons who seemingly wanted to do Phillip in, just because he had wanted to unite the empire and bring peace to all peoples. Some people just couldn't appreciate a good thing.

He wasn't sure in which direction he should go, since Beogoat had never told him which tower he lived in, so he had to stop and ask a servant who was rushing by with a lantern for the search going on in the courtyard.

"I'm confused," Grover told the servant. "Did Beogoat change his quarters? I thought his tower was down the hall."

"So it is, Lord Phillip," the servant said. "We moved his quarters as far as possible from you like you ordered. A pox on all wizards."

"Ah, right," Grover said. "Thanks."

"My pleasure, Lord Phillip," the servant responded.

Grover pushed past the servant and made his way quickly to the tower steps. It was becoming more and more evident that Beogoat wasn't dealing with them squarely or any sort of rectangle, for that matter. It hadn't been so bad before when he had simply forgotten that Winona had to be rescued and that she would rather die than marry Phillip, but now he had learned that someone wanted to kill him *and* that Phillip didn't even like Beogoat. Which raised the puzzling question: Why did Beogoat want to help save the empire? It couldn't have been because he liked Phillip. It had to be something else.

Grover climbed the steps two at a time, cursing the fact that wizards—like the ever-so-annoying damsels in distress—always seemed to reside at high altitudes.

"I don't care if this is aerobic," Grover muttered to himself. "I wish they lived on the ground floor like normal people."

Grover stopped at what he thought was the final landing and

knocked on the door. A strange muttering ceased and there was
the sound of soft slippers. The door opened a crack and Beoweasel's pinched face peered out. "Oh, it's you," he said. "What do
you want? I'm busy."

"Nice to see you too," Grover said. "The least you could do is
treat me nice. Isn't that how you would treat Lord Phillip?"

"But you aren't him," Beoweasel said. "So why should I?"

Grover frowned. "Because it might look suspicious if you
don't."

"So what do you want?" Beoweasel insisted. It was obvious
that he didn't want to be disturbed. And because he only opened
the door a crack, it was obvious he didn't want to show what was
within his room.

Instantly Grover grew curious. "What are you doing in there?"
He looked over Beoweasel's shoulder and caught a glimpse of
candles and a whiff of very mild incense.

"Nothing, nothing," Beoweasel said hastily. "You've already
disturbed me long enough. Tell me what you want and leave."

"I thought this was Beogoat's room," Grover explained. "What
are you doing with all the candles and incense?"

"None of your business," Beoweasel said. "Beogoat lives at the
top of the tower. Right up those stairs."

"Oh," Grover said. "I thought those went up to the roof." He
then looked back to the room, and since Beoweasel was being
rude, Grover decided to be obnoxious. "So aren't you even going
to invite me in?" he asked, pushing on the door.

"No, no," Beoweasel protested, pushing back. But Grover was
the stronger of the two by far and the door was pushed wide open,
revealing a small chamber adorned with fat candles, lit in rows of
ten on each side of the room. To either wall was a small cot and
a writing table. In the very middle of the room was a plain white
rug, and on it was a text of some sort, open to a marked page.

"What's this?" Grover asked, looking around the room.
"Doesn't look like the room of an apprentice wizard to me."

Beoweasel shut the door quickly. "You didn't have to open the
door wide."

"What's wrong?" Grover asked.

Beoweasel looked at him with annoyance and then walked
away from the door. "If you have to know, I'm studying to be a
priest."

Grover's mouth fell open. "A what?"

"Not a 'what,' " Beoweasel said. "A priest. I was in the middle
of purifying myself of the taint of magic when you so rudely

interrupted me. Magic is evil, unholy, wicked, and causes cancer in rats. Your very presence offends me."

"Well, you offend me," Grover shot back.

"Go, just go," Beoweasel said. "It's bad enough you had to interrupt me in my cleansing ritual, but now you have to defile my room."

"Defile," Grover said. "I'm just standing here."

"Just leave," Beoweasel said. "Beogoat's room is upstairs."

"Is he in?" Grover asked.

"How should I know?"

"I thought you were his apprentice. Shouldn't you know about that sort of stuff?"

"No," Beoweasel said. "He has his room, I have mine. Now, please go."

Grover started to move toward the door. "Does Beogoat know how you feel about magic?"

"He should," Beoweasel said. "I tell him every day."

"And yet you still work for him?" Grover asked.

"Yes," Beoweasel said.

Grover shook his head. "That's the stupidest thing I ever heard."

"It is our way," Beoweasel said.

"It's a stupid way," Grover said.

"Just go," Beoweasel said again.

Grover could think of nothing else to say, and so allowed himself to be pushed out of the room. He watched the door close in his face and heard Beoweasel mutter, "Unclean, spawn of the devil. I wash my hands of you."

"Well, well," Grover said, and paused for a moment. When no other snappy reply came to his mind, he proceeded up the stairs to find Beogoat's door open and a stiff cool breeze coming in from an open tower window.

Grover sensed something was wrong and stopped before entering the room. It was too quiet. And why would Beogoat leave the window and his door wide open? But then again, Beogoat was a wizard, and this could be normal.

Grover gripped the sheathed sword in front of him and called out, "Beogoat?" There was no response. "Beogoat, I need to talk to you," he called out again. There was still no response. Could the wizard just be hiding from him again? It was possible. So he took a step into the room and gave a once-over at the clutter of the room, the overflowing shelves, the thick rugs, the unmade bed, and the messy desk. "Are you here?" he asked.

Grover saw no evidence of him, though the room still smelled vaguely of pipe smoke. "I guess you're not here," he concluded.

He searched around for a pen and paper to write a note on and came across the courtier pen standing above the open text. On it were written four lines of dialogue.

"Argh, get him."

"Stop, I say stop."

"Grab him."

"Quickly, before the guard comes back."

Grover placed a finger above these last words. "Hmm," he mused. "Must be writing an action-adventure novel." He then flipped back a few pages and read the description of a meeting with a rude demon, and then flipped back to the former page. "Weird stuff," he commented. And turned to look for paper.

"Phillip!" croaked a shrill voice.

Grover jumped in fright and turned around quickly, his sheathed sword held out in front of him with one hand. In the doorway, he saw a bent-over old man, his blond hair thinning so that his skull showed pink beneath, and his pale face wrinkled and sagged around the jowls. He wore a heavy fur coat that covered him from shoulders to feet. In one hand he supported himself with a heavy oaken staff. The head was carved like the face of a satanic koala bear.

"Who are you?" Grover asked without thinking.

"Has it come to this, Phillip?" the old man rasped. "That you do not even recognize your own father?"

Grover drew back, lowering the sword. "Ah, hi, Dad."

The man grabbed at his heart and seemed to sink to his knees. "Oh, how you wound me. It's 'hi, Dad.' Why do you mock me so?"

Grover eyed the man strangely and fingered the scrolled sheath of his great sword. "I . . ."

The man held out a hand to Grover and then rose to his feet on his own. "No," he cried out. "I don't want your help."

"I . . ." Grover started again.

The old man looked around the room. "And have you come to kick out Beogoat? My only friend in my old age. Have you come to take over completely?"

"Ah," Grover said in response.

"Why don't you kill me now?" the old man shrieked. He pulled open his fur coat and tore open his shirt to bare his chest. "Why don't you kill me now? You think I'm too old to fight? Well, I still have honor." He looked hard at Grover and cried out, "Coward."

"Coward," Grover said, and shifted his position.

The old man stiffened.

Grover, unsure of what to do, did nothing. And the moment of indecision would surely have gone on had not Erich burst into the room.

"Your room was empty," Erich explained. "I was told you had come here. What is it with you and wizards?"

"He wishes to destroy Beogoat," the old man explained.

"I do not," Grover said.

The old man reached out and touched Erich. "If only you were my true son, instead of my sister's son."

"You don't mean that," Erich said, gently taking the hand off him.

"Yes, I do," the old man insisted.

"No, you don't," Erich repeated softly.

"Yes, I do," the old man said once again.

"No, you don't," Erich repeated once more.

"Okay," the old man said. "I was just exaggerating. I'm an old man and my son never became the goat herder I wanted him to be. Why couldn't he have been a goat herder, Erich? Why?"

"Because he hates goats," Erich explained.

"He just says that," the old man said.

"Please," Erich pleaded.

"All right," the old man said. "I'll be quiet."

Erich turned to face Grover. "I have bad news. The Black Avenger has escaped."

"Shit," Grover gasped.

"Yes," Erich said fiercely. He pulled something out from a pouch. It was a long red scarf. "And he left his sign on a dead guard."

Grover stared at the red scarf with idle curiosity, wondering how he was supposed to act. Was he supposed to scoff or was he supposed to show fear? He wasn't sure.

"The red scarf," the old man repeated. And his hand went to his chest for the second time.

Erich looked expectantly at Grover and then waved the scarf. "You see."

"Yes," Grover said, and looked to the old man, who was grabbing for a chair to sit down in, and then back to Erich, who dangled the scarf.

"It's the red scarf," Erich emphasized.

Grover shrugged. "So? So he left his scarf? So what?"

Erich looked amazed. His mouth dropped open and then clamped back shut. "He has been befuddled by wizards."

The old man slumped in the chair. "Oh, to have lived to see the day."

Grover was confused. "What?" he cried. "What?"

Erich threw the red scarf on the floor. "Fool, not to take warning. I warned you it would come to this." He turned on his heels and exited the room.

Grover turned to the old man and demanded, "What?"

"Leave me," the old man said, waving one weary hand. "Leave me."

Grover shrugged, bent to pick up the scarf, and left the room.

You are left alone in Beogoat's tower with the old man. From the tower you began your journey tonight and in the tower your journey has come to an end. In that time you have seen betrayal, death, abductions, rudeness, and confusion. All in all it has been a pretty good evening. But you are tired now. So you go back to the tower window and descend into the courtyard. The rain has stopped, and you can even see a bit of the moon through the departing clouds. As you cross the courtyard, you pause to look back at the castle. You wonder what will happen to Grover and Cilla and all the rest. It seems premature to leave right now when the action seems to be getting good. But then you realize that you can always come back tomorrow and find out what happens. It's just as easy as turning the page.

PART IV
Where Matters Are Further Complicated

An Unexpected Excursion

Beogoat was still unavailable. Grover asked the messenger again, "Did you see him?"

"No, I did not see him," the messenger replied.

"Then how do you know he is not there?"

"Lord Phillip, he did not answer the door."

"Did you knock?"

"I knocked."

"How many times?"

"One time."

"I told you to knock three times."

"Lord, you know that I cannot count."

"And when you knocked, what happened?"

"Nothing."

"Did you hear anyone inside?"

"You did not ask me to listen at the door."

"But did you hear anything?"

"I heard nothing," the messenger said.

"Did you talk to Beoweasel?"

"No, I did not."

"Did you put the message under the door as I asked?"

"Yes."

"What did the message say?"

"It said . . ."

"When did I tell you to read the message?"

The messenger turned red. "Forgive me, but my curiosity got the better of me."

Grover shook his head. It had been two days since Beogoat had disappeared. Knocks at his door went unanswered, as did the messages placed under it.

"If I may ask a question, your lordship?"

"Yes," Grover said.

"What would you want with a filthy, dirty, conniving wizard?"

"The usual," Grover said, and closed the door in the messenger's startled face.

A moment later there was a knock.

Grover opened the door to see the messenger there, his hand extended palm upward.

"What about my tip?"

"Don't walk in dark alleys," Grover said, and once again closed the door in the messenger's face.

"Still no luck," Cilla commented when he returned to the sun-room in Phillip's apartment.

"No luck," Grover said. "Where could he be?"

"Maybe it slipped his mind where he was," Cilla commented.

"Maybe," Grover said. "But I'm worried. Why aren't you worried?"

"Because I'm the leader," Cilla explained.

"Oh," Grover said, and threw himself down on one of the couches.

Cilla looked up from where she was reading *Dude Knights Die Young*. "I've been meaning to tell you something."

"Is it about the tattoo?" Grover ventured.

"How do you know about the tattoo?" Cilla asked suspiciously.

"I didn't. But now that we're on the subject . . ."

"We're not on the subject," Cilla said.

"We aren't?"

"No. I have to tell you, Grover, that I'm involved in a plot to kill Phillip."

"You're what?" Grover cried.

"I didn't want to alarm you," Cilla explained.

"Alarm me, you're out to kill me."

"No, I'm involved in a plot to kill Phillip and that's a whole different thing."

"You're just confusing the issue with details."

"No, I'm explaining the issue with details. Voss is in on a plot with the Black Avenger to kill Phillip and to disrupt the wedding."

"I'll kill Voss," Grover said, his hands reaching out to choke an imaginary neck.

"I'm Voss," Cilla said.

"You dirty betrayer," Grover cried. "And after all these years of service."

"What years of service?" Cilla asked.

"Well, that's what Phillip would have said," Grover explained. "I can't believe this, my own partner betraying me. What are you, bored? Don't have enough to do here that you have to join in on plots to kill me?"

"It just sort of happened," Cilla said. "How was I to know?"

"You should have known," Grover said. "You've probably known all along. You and Beogoat have been planning this for a long time. I'm the fall guy, aren't I?"

"Yes," Cilla said. "You're right. I've been planning to betray you since the first day I met you in Parda. It all started then."

"I knew it," Grover said.

Suddenly there was a knocking at the door.

"Go away," Grover said. "I'm sick and not seeing anyone."

There was more knocking at the door.

"They can't hear you," Cilla explained.

"Tell them to go away," Grover told her.

"You can't order me around," Cilla said.

"Yes, I can."

"Well, I'm not going."

"Fine," Grover said. "We'll just listen to the knocking on the door, then."

The pounding continued. Finally they heard a muffled voice. "I know you're in there, Phillip. Come out or I'm coming in."

Grover looked at Cilla. "They're coming in."

"Not my problem," Cilla said, pretending to find sudden interest in the book she was holding.

Grover threw himself before Cilla's feet. "Will you please answer the door?"

"Well . . . you promise me half of your profits?"

"Half?" Grover cried.

"Done," Cilla cried, and sprang to her feet.

"Wait a second," Grover cried, but Cilla was already on her way to the door. "I didn't mean 'half,' I meant 'half?' It was a question, not an answer."

Grover heard the outside door open. "Phillip isn't seeing anyone. He is ill. So bug off."

"Out of my way, toad," Grover heard Erich say.

And then Erich was standing at the entrance of the sun-room. "You're not sick." He pointed straight at Grover.

"I'm not?" Grover asked in surprise.

"We're going hunting," Erich declared. "And you can't refuse."

Cilla reentered the room. "Lord Phillip is ill, he can't leave."

Erich turned to look at Cilla and he winked at her. "Yes, he can." And nodded to her knowingly.

Cilla was confused. "No, he can't," she said firmly.

"Really, I can't," Grover added. "I don't feel well. I couldn't kill a thing today."

"I won't hear of it," Erich said, rushing off into Phillip's bedroom closet and pulling out riding leathers, boots, and other hunting apparel. "Fresh air and sunshine are just what you need to feel healthy."

"But it's partly cloudy," Grover protested.

Erich returned to the sun-room with his arms full of clothes. "No, it's not. It's partly sunny."

"Really," Grover said, "I command you."

"You can't command me," Erich said.

"I can't," Grover said.

"Not in the matter of your health," Erich said. "I know you're just moping around, and the only way to get out of it is by direct action."

"It is," Grover said.

Erich nodded. "Let's go."

Grover looked at Cilla for help but she just shrugged her shoulders.

"Change," Erich said.

Reluctantly, under Erich's watchful eye, Grover changed into Phillip's hunting clothes. And before he knew it he was being herded out of the room.

"But can't Voss come with us?" Grover asked.

"No, just the two of us," Erich said.

"I was afraid of that," Grover replied.

"Have a good time," Cilla cried after them.

"Wait a second," Grover said before he went into the hall. "I forgot my scarf." A moment later he returned with the red scarf of the Black Avenger.

"The scarf," Erich said.

It took a moment for Cilla to realize. Erich was the Black Avenger.

Cilla pointed at Erich behind his back to indicate to Grover what she had discovered.

"What, Voss?" Grover asked.

Erich turned around. "What are you doing back there?"

"Nothing," Cilla said, shoving her hands in her pockets.

Erich shrugged and walked out into the hall, saying, "You really shouldn't wear that scarf, you know . . ."

Cilla got up on her toes and whispered into Grover's ear as he walked out, "Erich is the Black Avenger. Be careful."

"What?" Grover cried.

But Erich was already pulling him down the hall. "I got the best horses . . ."

How to Persuade
Your Wizard

Hans was troubled—had been, in fact, since the day when the man he had personally killed had suddenly and mysteriously returned to life. Now, that was troubling. How a man could survive decapitation threw his mind into paroxysms of . . . well, the whole thing discombobulated him, and left him wondering if the entire incident hadn't just been some sort of pipe dream. But he didn't smoke pipes and the event had a clarity that was almost too real. But then so did dreams when you were having them, and it was only when you woke up that you realized it hadn't been real at all. So maybe it had been a dream.

Except he hadn't woken up. He, in fact, had never been asleep. There was no sudden bright light of consciousness, no muscle spasm jerking him forward to what was real. The whole thing had been real. Phillip had returned. And so had Voss.

The nightmare of the three omens that would portend his destruction had come true. He had laughed at the predictions when they were made, scrawled as they were in crayon on the back of construction paper. But now it seemed that he had laughed in haste.

The omens had stated that his original curse was correct and that he was doomed to rule all of Hoven and then would be killed by his closest friend. But they also said there were three things that would prevent him from ruling all of Hoven. First, it said the beheaded man would walk again. He had stopped reading right then and there and had laughed so hard that tears came to his eyes. So he would rule Hoven. He was pleased. The other two omens were that the earth would move against him and that he would be defeated by a common servant in battle, which were equally ridiculous terms. So he had paid them no mind.

That had been years ago. Years. And he had deemed it as foolishness until now. Until Phillip had come back from decapitation to once again walk the earth and to lead his united forces against him, thus forcing him not only to lose Winona but to retreat across *The Stream That Rushes Too Fast in the Wrong*

Places, so he could reach the safety of his own shore. It had been very humiliating and hadn't done much for his ego either, or the gloom which persistently plagued him.

He had called out for information from his spies but they had not been able to come up with anything useful. Some people even doubted that he had killed Phillip. But those who did possess such feelings kept them quiet to his face, and only said them in hushed whispers as he walked through the gardens, or shouted them across crowded, noisy rooms, so that they wouldn't have to suffer his displeasure. It was a law in his land that no one could refute the leader openly. It was only legal to do so in underground groups, but only if the group was licensed and its agenda set by the state. Few underground groups ever applied for a license, and so when they were caught—because they were always caught—they were charged with operating a treasonous, underground political group without a license, and thus suffered the penalty of hanging. And no one could say that Hans had done any wrong because, after all, it was the law.

So days went on while he had to suffer these humiliations until two things happened. One, a new piece of information had surfaced that Phillip and Voss had been seen departing the reflecting pool in the company of Beogoat and Beoweasel; and two, he had been approached by Wizard Collectors who had Beogoat in their clutches and wondered if he, Hans, wanted to buy him. So with these two events he determined that whatever had happened to Phillip and Voss, Beogoat had something to do with it, or knew something about it, and thus was the only one, save Phillip and Voss themselves, who could provide him with the proper answers. But he also knew that Beogoat, being the cagey wizard he was rumored to be, probably wouldn't tell him. He had to be persuaded. And wasn't it auspicious that Hans had experience in that sort of area?

Beogoat wasn't happy. He sat across from Hans, in the grand dining hall, dressed in the same brown bathrobe he had been wearing when he was abducted, trying to convince himself that this cold chicken leg was worth eating. He didn't know how long it had been since he was abducted. He felt disoriented and sick to his stomach, and the seasoning on this chicken leg wasn't too good either. He rubbed his temple and murmured an incantation to warm up the food. It didn't work. He wasn't surprised. None of his magic worked since his abduction. The chemistry in his body had been altered by some drug that would prevent him from doing magic for some time. And not only that, it didn't make him feel good. This wasn't the first time he had been given the drug, but that didn't make him feel any better.

"Not hungry, I see," Hans said.

Beogoat shook his head and dropped the chicken leg.

Hans did not join him in his feast, being rather frugal in his habits and proper in his appearance. He sat with his hands on his lap and observed the wizard.

They weren't alone. Besides the two of them, there was a contingent of guards at the far doors, and a priest who sat at the next table, with a hand clutching his holy book just in case Beogoat decided to do something unholy and vile.

When Beogoat finally gave up trying to eat, Hans leaned forward and asked, "Finished now?"

"For now," Beogoat said. "Maybe I'll feel hungry later."

Hans nodded. "Still feeling weak?"

Beogoat shrugged. "I've felt better."

Hans relaxed. He knew that as long as Beogoat felt weak he couldn't practice any magic. But you could never be sure, so he still had to be careful. That's why he didn't have wizards in his court. You couldn't control them and they wanted at least three-fourths of the credit for any good thing that happened in the principality, and zero blame for anything that went wrong.

"So did you pay a high price for me?" Beogoat asked.

"My money is not your concern," Hans said. "But from what I heard, you're lucky that they were willing to sell you to me when they did."

"Lucky for you," Beogoat said. "Not for me. Luck is a strange thing, don't you think? You take gamblers, for instance. One guy gets lucky and he wins the whole pot. But what about the rest of the players? There's four or five guys who lost, who were unlucky. Not really fair, if you ask me. Strange thing luck, don't you think? It's just a thought that popped into my head."

"I see," Hans said. "That's very interesting, but I didn't buy you so that I could discuss the nature of luck. I . . ."

There was a burst of voices at the door, and a guard brought over a sandy-haired, youthful fellow who carried a black sack that jangled. "Hi." He waved to Beogoat.

"Hi," Beogoat answered.

Hans nodded to the man. "You can take a seat. We won't be needing you for a while."

"Who is he, your advisor?" Beogoat asked.

"No, my torturer," Hans replied.

"Pretty jovial fellow," Beogoat observed.

"I don't like unhappy people," Hans said. "They bring me down."

"Oh," Beogoat said.

"I'm doomed," Hans went on, explaining. "And I don't want to be reminded of the fact."

"Trust me," Beogoat said quickly. "I won't bring it up."

"Incidentally," Hans said, "you wouldn't happen to know any good jokes."

Beogoat shook his head. "Sorry."

"Pity," Hans said, and he snapped his fingers. A lute player emerged from behind a curtain and started to play a haunting tune in descending minor chords. The kind of song that rattles in your chest and makes your blood chill.

"Nice tune," Beogoat said as goose bumps appeared on his arm.

"He tells jokes too," Hans replied.

Beogoat nodded and started to pick at his teeth slowly.

Hans drummed his fingers on the table. "As you know, or may not know, it is illegal for any citizen of Reichton to practice wizardry."

"But I'm not a citizen of Reichton."

"Ah, but you are. Because any person who practices wizardry in Reichton, for the purposes of the law, is considered a citizen."

"That's absurd," Beogoat said.

"That's the law," Hans replied. "And in Reichton we obey the law or suffer the penalty of the law."

"Because that's the law," Beogoat offered.

"Exactly," Hans said. "I'm glad you understand."

"I don't," Beogoat said. "But I had a feeling if I said something absurd it would turn out to be correct."

Hans shrugged. "Now that I have made you aware that you are practicing wizardry illegally in Reichton, it is my duty to inform you that the penalty is . . ."

"Death," Beogoat answered.

"No," Hans said. "Killing a wizard in Reichton is illegal. It's also bad luck. But don't worry, the punishment is equally unpleasant and I'm sure you would want to avoid it."

"So," Beogoat said, "did you purchase me from the Wizard Collectors to invite me to be a citizen of Reichton, just so I could be punished? Or did you like me so much you just had to have me for your own?"

"No, not at all," Hans said, shaking his head. "Though you're welcome to apply for citizenship once you renounce all wizardry. But that's not why you were brought here. I asked you here because you are the only person who might be able to answer my questions."

"Ah," Beogoat said, finally understanding. "You have heard of my reputation as a man of wisdom. After all, I was frat brothers with Gandalf and Merlyn."

"Yes, yes," Hans said. "That's all very well and good on your résumé, but I didn't call you here to ask you questions important to all mankind. I came to ask you questions of a more personal nature."

"I didn't know we were going to get personal," Beogoat said.

Hans looked closely at Beogoat. "I know you left the reflecting pool in the company of Phillip and Voss."

"Is that a crime?" Beogoat asked.

"Here it is," Hans said seriously.

Beogoat knew he had to be careful now. He wasn't sure what Hans had wanted at first, though it might have just been some old grudge they had between them, but now he knew it all had to do with Phillip and Voss. Of course it did. It all became clear now. Why had he thought that Hans would overlook the fact that Phillip and Voss were alive again? But then, he had hoped Cilla and Grover would have killed him, so Hans would never have enough time to put the pieces together.

But since Hans was alive, and was here asking the questions, he had to be very careful with what he said, because if he told Hans what really occurred it could not only threaten the Westerhoven alliance, it could possibly affect his own life, especially when Cilla and Grover found out he had betrayed them and came after him to exact revenge. He wasn't on the best of footings with them now, and exposing them as impostors wouldn't help his position with them at all. So he had to be very, very careful.

"So you do not deny that you were with Phillip and Voss?" Hans asked.

"Maybe your information is incorrect," Beogoat replied.

"Maybe it is," Hans said. "That has been known to happen, but I don't think that applies in this case."

"So what are you saying?" Beogoat asked. "Are you accusing me of something?"

"Not yet," Hans said. "I'm just asking you things. But first I will tell you something. On," and he named a day, "I met Phillip and Voss at the reflecting pool. And there I beheaded Phillip and had Voss executed for betrayal. I don't deny this. In fact, I boasted of it the very same day."

"But Phillip and Voss are alive," Beogoat said. "Everyone knows that."

"And I know I killed them," Hans said. "After all, I was there."

"Maybe you dreamed it," Beogoat suggested.

"I thought so at first," Hans admitted. "But the memory is too vivid, and I have witnesses. I did kill him. He just didn't stay dead."

"Maybe you didn't really kill him," Beogoat said. "Maybe he was only wounded and recovered from it."

"From a decapitation," Hans scoffed. "I don't think so. So what I want to know is how you are involved in this. We know that you and Phillip didn't get along. It's common knowledge. So why were you seen leaving the reflecting pool with him?"

"Because we were walking out at the same time," Beogoat answered. "I don't see the point of this discussion."

"You will," Hans said. "In time. Everyone begins to understand in time."

"I cannot tell you anything," Beogoat said. "I am loyal to the Westerhoven cause. Giving information to you, even as innocuous as who I walk out of reflecting pools with, is betraying those who trust me. I cannot tell you anything."

Hans frowned. "That's too bad. I was hoping we could wrap this whole thing up by dinner. Are you sure you don't want to answer my questions?"

"Yes," Beogoat said.

"Okay," Hans said, nodding his head. "If that's the way you feel, then that's the way you feel." He looked to the youthful fellow who had come in. "I guess that means I'll have to have you tortured."

"Tortured," Beogoat cried out.

"Yes, tortured," Hans repeated. "You are familiar with the term?"

"Yes," Beogoat said. "It's the inflicting of severe pain to force information or confession."

"Well," Hans said, clapping his hands. "I'm glad you're familiar with the topic. I'm sure you can discuss it in detail with Frederick." He gestured to the youthful torturer. "He happens to be a scholar on the subject. But as for me, the whole thing makes me squeamish. I prefer straight death myself, rather than lingering pain and mutilation, but we all have our preferences. Of course, if you answer my questions you don't have to choose torture."

Beogoat gulped and looked at the grinning Frederick. Frederick looked like the type of good-natured boy who would be sitting around having fun with his friends, telling jokes to pretty girls, or daydreaming on a hill looking up at the beautiful sky; not the kind of face you imagined bending over you with a pair of red-hot pokers.

"I cannot betray Westerhoven," Beogoat said.

"Betrayal," Hans said, "only depends on which side wins."

Beogoat was silent. The musician started another haunting tune.

The Hunter and the Hunted

Erich raised his hands to his lips and drank the cool spring water. Behind him Grover stood with his back to the trees, a spear in one hand, and the bridles of the horses held in the other. Within the *Very Dark Forest*, the very thickness of the trees and the preponderance of foliage cut out the light until it seemed as if it were almost twilight. A coolness hung in the air that stuck in your throat.

Erich let out a sigh of contentment as he slaked his thirst. He then dipped his hands back into the stream to wash his face. The coolness of the water brought a clarity to his thoughts.

Erich had come out here to speak with him man-to-man, old friend to old friend, to save Phillip from himself. Didn't he realize that no one wanted Phillip to be King of Hoven? Not the Sousterhoven people, not even the Westerhoven people. Why didn't he pay attention to such signs as the Black Avenger? Weren't troublemakers like that sign enough he was doing things wrong? Apparently not for Phillip, who boldly wore the red scarf the Black Avenger had left as a sign that Phillip was marked for death.

Erich got up from the bank and turned to Phillip. "Remember the last time we came here?"

Phillip looked up and said, "What?"

"Remember the last time we came here?" Erich asked again.

Grover trembled a bit. It had only been a matter of time before Erich would ask him a question about something he didn't know. Now that the time was here, he didn't know what he was going to do. Finally he decided to be honest.

"No, I don't remember," Grover said, and then added, "dude." The handbook had said to say "dude" after everything. But it hadn't become a common practice yet.

Erich shrugged. "Really? Well, the last time we were here you told me of your vision of a united Westerhoven."

"I did," Grover said.

"Yes, you did," Erich replied. "And it was here I pledged to

97

help you. Because I believed in your vision. I thought it was about time we became united under one ruler again."

"I'm glad you thought so—dude," Grover said.

Erich looked up at the tops of the trees for a moment. "But what I didn't know was that you planned to unite *all* of Hoven."

"You mean I didn't mention that?" Grover asked. "I thought I told you that. I swear I told you that."

"Don't mock me," Erich said coldly. "You said no such thing."

Grover felt a chill at his words. And it finally occurred to him that he was alone in an isolated area with a psychopath. In his hero guidebook, it said if you ever got into that situation, the one thing you should never do is piss off the psychopath. That was seen as very bad. But how could Grover take Erich's gravity seriously? So what if Phillip forgot to mention he wanted to rule all of the empire? Erich had forgotten to mention that he was the Black Avenger. Beoweasel had forgotten to mention he hated magic. And Beogoat had forgotten to mention everything. Forgetting to mention something seemed like the normal course of events in Hoven. It was only remembering to mention something that seemed out of place. So why should Erich be getting upset? But then again, Erich was a psychopath.

"Sorry—dude," Grover said. "But what does it matter? You'll always be my right-hand man."

"I know," Erich said. "And I will always be there to support you."

You mean, Grover thought, when you're not putting on a black cloak and a mask and running around betraying me.

"But that is not what I'm talking about," Erich said. "There was a time when we shared a vision, but now that vision has gone astray. Uniting Westerhoven was a good thing. But marrying Winona isn't in your best interest."

"It isn't?" Grover asked in surprise. Was this some further irony he was involved in due to Beogoat's seemingly endless spotty memory? Was it really not in Phillip's best interest to marry Winona? If so, why had he been brought here? What was his real purpose? "Why not?" Grover asked.

"Astertov will not recognize you," Erich said. "You will agitate the Sousterhoven nations to further aggression. It is better just to have peace within our own borders. Including Souster-hoven in your plans will only ruin what we already have."

Grover was silent. "So what do you think I should do—dude?"

"Call off the marriage," Erich said. "And stop calling me dude."

"Sorry, du . . . Erich," Grover said.

"And consolidate Westerhoven before it's too late. Before you do something that you'll regret."

"Like what?" Grover asked.

"You know what I'm talking about," Erich said. "You don't fool me."

Grover gulped. Erich had seen through him. Next would come the denouncement and after that he would be killed as an impostor. He was sure that once he was dead, they would all see he was Grover and not Phillip.

"What else could your quest be, then: except to find the *Sacred Stone*? Why else would you be consorting with Beogoat after all the bad things you have said about him? It's because you think you are meant to be the next king. Admit it, you desire the *Sacred Stone*."

"The what?" Grover cried.

"Don't play the fool with me," Erich said. "I know you've discovered the location."

Grover felt he was on treacherous ground. There was a strange magic glow in Erich's eyes. If he denied knowing where the *Stone* was he would have to explain his presence at the reflecting pool, which he could not do. And if he admitted knowing about the *Stone* it seemed he would only enrage Erich's wrath. There seemed no safe choice. "Maybe I have," Grover said. "But that is my concern."

"Your concern," Erich said. He seemed about to go on but stopped and brooded for a moment. "We were brothers once."

Grover was quiet. The space between them seemed very tense.

Erich stood still, almost completely still, his face stretched taut. He held the pose for what seemed a long time and then slowly relaxed. "I must relieve myself," he said, and wandered slowly off into the trees.

Grover let out a gush of air. That had been close. Whatever the feud between Erich and Phillip was, it obviously ran deep. He promised himself that as soon as he returned to Castle Wunderkinde he would seal himself off in Phillip's room and wouldn't see anyone, no matter what, until the wedding. And this time he would barricade the door.

It was quite a time later, after he had sorted through these thoughts, that he looked around his surroundings to see that Erich had not returned. He looked past the horses, and into the brush, but saw nothing. Just trees and more trees. But by the bank of the stream was Erich's spear. He hadn't even noticed him laying it down. Now where was he?

And then he heard it. The sound behind him.

He whipped around and saw a man dressed in a black cloak wearing a black mask.

"Erich," Grover let escape from his lips.

The man pulled an ornate scabbard out in front of him, and from this he pulled forth a gleaming sword.

"No," the figure said. "The Black Avenger."

No Sympathy for Her Sex

Winona was dressed as usual, in a yellow dingy dress that looked more like a smock. Her hair was uncombed and she was biting on one of her nails. She sat on a stool near the window, gazing out into the courtyard, with a contemplative look on her face.

Erika sat patiently near the fireplace, looking pretty as usual. Her hair was combed and her cheeks were rosy. Her clothes looked fresh and clean. And she was smiling as she worked on her knitting.

Winona turned away from the window when Cilla entered, and Cilla looked clearly into those amazing green eyes. Like emeralds.

"Ah, brother," she said. Her voice was neutral.

"Ah, sister," Cilla replied carefully. "I was told you wished to see me. Have you missed me?"

Winona gazed at her thoughtfully. "Yes, I have."

"You have," Cilla said with some surprise.

"I have thought long and hard," Winona went on. "And I think I have made a mistake. I want to ask your forgiveness. I was wrong to turn on a family member."

"I know," Cilla said. "But I didn't want to say anything."

"I'm serious," Winona said.

Cilla looked at her skeptically. "But what about all that stuff you said when we came to rescue you—about renouncing me, how I was no longer an Astertov? Or your brother."

"I was upset," Winona said.

"You nearly jumped out a window," Cilla pointed out.

"I was very upset," Winona explained. "But you have to understand how I felt at that moment."

"I do," Cilla said.

Winona gestured to a chair that was next to her. "Come. Sit. We must talk. Don't stand so far away."

Cilla walked cautiously over to the chair. "I can't stay for long."

"Pity," Winona said. "I'm so lonesome in the tower."

"But you have Erika," Cilla pointed out.

"Lonesome for real company," Winona explained.

Erika looked up momentarily and then returned to her knitting.

"What about Romeo and Bill?" Cilla said.

"Get serious," Winona said. "Those two should be executed. I know Phillip sent them here just to irritate me."

Cilla sat down in the chair. "Don't say that. You know Phillip worships you. He wants to marry you after all."

"You know very well why he wants to marry me," Winona said. "And it's not because he appreciates me."

"But that's not why people get married," Cilla said. "Marriage is just a business contract. I'm sure he appreciates your assets."

"Oh, you don't know anything about women," Winona said. "You're just a typical male."

"I am not," Cilla said firmly, sitting up sharply.

Winona shook her head and reached out with her hand to touch Cilla's arm. "Oh, don't be that way. You know what I mean. You just can't understand what it's like to be a woman. You'll never understand unless you are a woman."

"I think I know a few things," Cilla said. She had sincerely believed what she said about marriage.

Winona smiled. "Dear brother of mine, let's not fight. I didn't ask you here to relive old arguments."

Cilla relaxed in her chair, and Winona removed her hand.

"What did you ask me here for?"

"For your understanding," Winona said.

"What do you want me to understand?" Cilla asked.

"I cannot marry Phillip," Winona told her.

"But you must," Cilla insisted.

"I know I am pregnant with his child but I do not love him," Winona said.

"What does love have to do with it?" Cilla asked.

"That is where you do not understand," Winona said. She turned to Erika. "Erika, is not love the most important thing?"

Erika paused in her knitting and looked up with a glow in her face. "Truly love is the most beautiful thing. How can a woman marry a man she does not love? It will not work and both will be made unhappy by it."

"Even so . . ." Cilla started.

"But," Erika interjected, "I don't see how you could not love Phillip. He is handsome, strong, a leader of men. He is all a woman could want."

"But I do not want him," Winona said. "I want another."

"Who?" Cilla asked.

"I cannot say," Winona said, blushing.

Cilla ran her fingers up and down the arm of her chair. "So what you want me to understand is that you cannot marry Phillip because you are in love with another man."

"And another man loves me," Winona said.

"The same man?" Cilla asked.

"Of course it's the same man," Winona said.

"Just asking," Cilla said, and turned to Erika. "You have anything to say to this?"

"Isn't it romantic?" Erika asked.

Cilla sighed. "So what do you want me to do?"

Winona answered, "There is one thing you can do."

"Yes?" Cilla said wearily.

"You promise to help me?" Winona asked.

"Well . . ." Cilla hesitated.

"You're my brother," Winona said. "You must help me."

"To help reunite you with your love?" Cilla suggested.

"Yes," Winona said. "You understand how important this is. I could not live and marry Phillip. You know that. I'd rather die than marry him."

"There's worse things," Cilla said. "Having a red-hot poker shoved up your butt, for one."

"But not for me," Winona said.

"So what do you want me to do?" Cilla asked with an air of detachment.

"I want you to help me kill Phillip," Winona blurted out.

"Kill Phillip," Cilla said. "But he's my lord."

"He's the enemy," Winona said.

"I couldn't do that," Cilla replied. "In fact, I promised not to."

"If you don't," Winona said, "I'll find someone else who will and I'll make sure they know you were involved. That's what I'll do."

"You wouldn't," Cilla cried.

"She would," Erika chimed in from across the room. "She's done it before."

"You have?" Cilla said in shock.

Winona smiled innocently. "Some suitors just don't get the hint to leave me alone."

"Oh my," Cilla said.

"You men," Winona went on. "Always shocked by how women conduct themselves when you yourselves go about killing and warring with one another. We just poison a few people."

"Poison a few," Cilla replied.

"Yes," Winona said. "So will you help me?"

Cilla realized that if she didn't participate in the plot against Phillip and help Winona, then Grover would be in even more danger because she wouldn't be able to stop it. She had to participate against him or she wouldn't be working for him, and would thus be threatening the success of the adventure. But it seemed highly strange that no matter where she turned she kept getting in plots against Phillip, and thus Grover. It was as if she were becoming her own worst enemy.

So in a voice that didn't seem like her own, she found herself asking, "So what do you want me to do?"

All in a Hero's Day

Grover answered the door to his room. "Oh, it's you," Grover said when he saw it was only Cilla standing out in the corridor.

"Who'd you expect?" Cilla asked.

"I ordered out for some food," Grover said. "The servant's been gone for over two hours."

Cilla walked into the sun-room and slumped down on one of the couches. "This isn't like the big city, we have to wait for things. Seriously a quest could take years in a place like this."

Grover made affirmative noises.

"So how was your day?" Cilla asked. "With Erich."

"Fine," Grover said. "Fine."

"And the hunting," Cilla asked. "Was it a true test of your manliness?"

"I really don't want to talk about it," Grover said, turning away from her.

"What happened?" Cilla demanded.

"Do we have to talk about this?" Grover asked, obviously irritated. He fidgeted with some pieces of his armor which were laid out to be cleaned. He picked up a codpiece and then set it back down.

"What happened?" Cilla asked again. "Did he change into . . ."

"Yes," Grover said. "And it was awful."

"Tell me about it," Cilla said, tugging her legs in under her buttocks.

"We were in the forest. We stopped for a drink of water. We had some words. He said I was doing the wrong thing. That I should not marry Winona. That I shouldn't try to consolidate the whole empire. And something about a sacred rock."

"Don't you mean a sacred stone?" Cilla asked.

"Stone, rock, pebble, what's the difference?"

"He asked me about a sacred stone when I first met him."

"What is it?" Grover asked.

Cilla shrugged. "I don't know. I don't think Beogoat ever mentioned it."

"Well, apparently Erich is upset about it and he thinks I, or Phillip rather, knows where it is."

"So what happened?" Cilla asked.

"Well, he told me everything I just told you and to forget about the stone and all that. And when I denied knowledge of the stone he didn't believe me. He seemed to get upset. But then he relaxed and said he had to go take a leak. And the next thing I know he's back, wearing a black cloak and waving a sword and apparently really pissed off about how Phillip is running things, and calling for retribution, justice, and lots of other self-righteous stuff."

"So he made a speech, did he?" Cilla nodded. "And you let him."

"What did you want me to do?" Grover demanded. "Attack him? It's not like I'm any good with a spear, and the guy was probably wearing armor anyway."

"I told you to kill anyone who makes a speech."

"Well," Grover said. "Then how could I, as Phillip, explain killing Erich?"

"Just say he was the Black Avenger," Cilla suggested.

"It isn't that simple and you know that," Grover said. "Nothing is what it seems to be here."

"So what happened next?"

"I ran away," Grover said. "Christ, I thought he was going to kill me. I didn't come here to be killed. I just came here to be a stand-in for Phillip's marriage. I didn't know everything was going to get complicated. Honestly, these people are really psycho here."

"Almost makes you like villains, huh?" Cilla asked.

"Yeah," Grover said. "At least you know what motivates them—greed, basic meanness, and thirst for fame. But when you get motivations like justice, revenge, retribution, it starts to get really dangerous."

"I know what you mean," Cilla said, plucking at the fabric of the couch. "I miss villains too. But the wedding is in three days."

"Thank God," Grover said. "Which reminds me. I almost forgot. The Black Avenger challenged me . . ."

Cilla lifted her head up sharply. "Wait, I thought you ran away . . ."

"This is before I ran," Grover explained.

"Okay," Cilla said. "I just wanted to picture this correctly in my mind. Go on."

"He challenged me to ah, ah, I forget what it's called. Some sort of combat where honor is involved. He was fed up that I refused to acknowledge the red scarf and so he had to personally challenge me. Then he took the scarf. And I liked that scarf too."

"And then you ran away?" Cilla asked.

Grover shook his head.

"Then you accepted," Cilla cried. "What the hell were you thinking? You don't have the training for this sort of thing. And what if you get killed before the wedding?"

"I was just doing what Phillip would have done," Grover said defensively.

"You're not Phillip," Cilla said.

"I know, I know," Grover said. "But I have to be like him. To get in his head and find out what he's all about. His character interests me."

"Hey," Cilla snapped, pointing a finger. "Wake up. You are not a method actor. This isn't a play. You don't have to get into character."

"What's it matter anyway? It's just a duel, right?"

Cilla shook her head. "I don't think so. Maybe you should have looked closely at Chapter Six on battles of honor."

"Besides," Grover said, "he wants to fight me in five days. That's two days after the wedding. So it really doesn't matter anyway."

"Oh," Cilla said, and looked chagrined. "Well, you still shouldn't have done it."

Grover wrung his hands and walked to the window, pushing aside the heavy curtains. "I wish Beogoat would return from wherever he went off to."

"Me too," Cilla said.

Grover looked out at the ground where they were making some preparations for the wedding. Tents were being erected, carts of foodstuffs were being hauled in, and decorations were being displayed. All very colorful, in bright greens, yellows, and blues.

"So how was *your* day?" Grover asked, putting his back to the window.

"Oh," Cilla shrugged. "It was the usual. I walked around the castle. Talked to your cringing sycophants."

"How are they?" Grover asked.

"Cringing," Cilla said.

"They bug me," Grover said.

"They bug everybody," Cilla said. "And afterward I saw Winona."

"Saw Winona?" Grover exclaimed, starting forward.

"Saw Winona," Cilla repeated. "Had a nice chat with her,

agreed to help her poison Phillip. Afterward I felt a little tired and took a nap."

"What was that?" Grover asked. "Did I just hear you say you agreed to help her poison Phillip?"

"Apparently so," Cilla said.

"What?" Grover cried. "You're going to poison me? Isn't it enough that you're in with the Black Avenger in betraying me? Do you have to poison me too?"

"Not you," Cilla said. "Phillip. Why can't you make those distinctions? Are you having some sort of personality break-down?"

"But for all intents and purposes I *am* Phillip," Grover said. "What do you have against me anyway?"

"Nothing, nothing really," Cilla said evenly. "Except for that time you called me psycho in Jolinstive, and that time you made me carry the luggage out of Parda."

"I had good reasons to do so," Grover said. "Besides, you never told me why Parda is so confusing."

"Mirrors," Cilla said.

"What?" Grover asked.

"Parda is so confusing because of smoke and mirrors. The whole town is an illusion. It really isn't that big."

"That's stupid," Grover said.

"Well," Cilla said, "that's why no one would tell you."

"Anyway, that's beside the point. It still doesn't change the fact that you're going to poison me."

"I'm not," Cilla said. "I just agreed with Winona to help her poison Phillip. It's not the same thing."

"So you're not going to poison me?" Grover asked.

"Depends on your behavior," Cilla said.

"What?" Grover cried.

"Apparently there's good reason for it too," Cilla said. "I mean for poisoning Phillip. She's in love with another man . . ."

"Who?" Grover asked.

"She wouldn't say," Cilla said. "And after all, Phillip did take advantage of her while she was drunk."

"He did?" Grover said.

"That's what she said," Cilla said.

"What a scumbag," Grover said.

"Yeah, makes me almost want to poison him myself," Cilla said.

"But you won't," Grover said.

"I might have to," Cilla said. "Just to keep my cover as Voss. After all, I am honorbound to help my family."

"But . . ." Grover said.

"Well, you wanted to be the hero in this adventure," Cilla said.

"Yes," Grover said. "But I never knew you would get so upset that you would poison me over it. If I had known that, I would never have insisted."

"See," Cilla said. "It's always in times of crisis that we regret the bad things we've done to others."

"So what?" Grover said. "You're threatening to help poison me." One hand went to clutch at his throat, which suddenly felt tight. "Death makes me very tense. *My* death does, I mean. Do you really have to go through with it?"

"I don't believe this!" Cilla said, hitting the couch arm for emphasis. "You act as if I already poisoned you. Be a hero for a moment."

Grover caught his breath. "I never meant all those bad things," he said. "Really."

Cilla smiled. "That's nice to hear. But I never really was going to poison you."

Grover relaxed.

"I just have to appear to poison you so I can play Voss's part and not arouse suspicion."

"So what's the plan?" Grover asked.

"She wants to do it at the wedding."

"Great," Grover said. "This is going to be some wedding."

Beoweasel's Secret

Finally Beogoat was out of his life. It had been over three days now and Beogoat hadn't returned, and that was a sure sign he was never coming back. That's what the Wizard Collectors had told him anyway.

It was he, Beoweasel, who had tipped off the Wizard Collectors that Beogoat had missed some payments on some scrolls. Otherwise, Beogoat would still be in his tower, threatening the status of Beoweasel's soul. He knew that working with a wizard was leaving an evil taint on him that he had to get rid of.

He would have left Beogoat had he not been honorbound to serve him. It was his father who had given him as an indentured servant. So if he left he would be dishonoring his father as well. If Beogoat released him from service then he would lose no honor at all, but Beogoat wouldn't release him. He said that good help was hard to find. Beoweasel had been happy with the compliment until Beogoat added, "But I'll have to do with what I can get."

That's when Beoweasel had begun to plot. Or maybe it had begun when Beogoat named him Beoweasel. His real name was Benjamin, but Beogoat said all wizards needed to have a name starting with the prefix *Beo,* then the name of the animal he resembled. Thus, he had been named Beoweasel. That was the first real humiliation. And after that he had plotted to get rid of Beogoat. Murder was out of the question, since it would hurt his chances at salvation, but politics weren't.

He had gotten cozy with Phillip and managed to convince him that all wizards were bad. Under this campaign Beogoat fell into disfavor, and Beoweasel hoped Beogoat would get the message that he wasn't wanted and would give up shop, releasing him in the process. But Beogoat was tenacious, and endured whatever had happened. Beoweasel had almost given up hope of escape when he had learned of the Wizard Collectors. Beogoat had said, if you ever see these guys, tell them I moved away. So Beoweasel had immediately contacted them, informing them of the name and location of the owner of certain scrolls that were unpaid for. They said they would take care of the rest.

The next day they discovered Phillip had died. Beoweasel forgot about what he had done in the chaos of helping Beogoat make impostors of Phillip and Voss. And then a week later, he had let the Wizard Collectors in out of the rain and had sent them up to the tower room where they abducted Beogoat.

He was finally free. He was already packing to go back to Meistertonne to pursue the priesthood when he remembered Grover and Cilla. They were his obligation now. If they were discovered as impostors it would be him that was executed, since Beogoat wasn't around anymore. But the wedding was only in a few days. Once the wedding was over, the two heroes would leave. So he decided he could wait a week more. He would pretend to help them, and then leave. How the two returned home wasn't any of his business. Just as long as they didn't get him in trouble.

And if they asked where Beogoat was, he would just tell them that he had gone on vacation and would be back in time for the wedding.

Erich Makes a Discovery

Erich kneeled in the center of his room, dark but for a single candle, and once more applied the riding crop to his back. "Damn it," he said softly, as he felt the sharpness along the ridges of his back. "Why do I keep doing this to myself?" he asked. "Why? Am I some sort of masochist?" And he lay down the riding crop for a moment and shook his head. "What's wrong with me? What am I doing here?" And then his focus shifted and once again he was hitting himself on the back. And then he stopped. "This is weird. I better get some help." And then he reached over to his storage chest and noticed the lock. "Hey, who put the lock on here?" he asked. "Has someone been going through my stuff?" But strangely enough he had the key. He must have put it on. But he had forgotten. There were so many things he had forgotten.

He unlocked the chest and looked inside. There, right in front of his eyes was a black cloak and a mask. "Hey," he said, "someone's been putting stuff in my chest." And then he looked further and found papers and notes all signed the Black Avenger. One of the papers was a detailed plan to infiltrate the wedding and seize Winona, complete with maps, diagrams, and code names for everyone involved. There was also a letter explaining the Black Avenger's love for this woman and why he couldn't allow Phillip to marry her.

"I must warn Phillip," he declared. "The Black Avenger has been using my storage chest to hold his things. Oh, he is the foulest of the foul." And he clutched the papers tightly. "I must tell Phillip right away. He is in danger. And look. Even his own father, Old Lord Phillip, plots against him. I can't believe it. This is horrendous, horrible." He stood up immediately, ready to go out and warn Phillip. To explain that by the sheerest luck he had stumbled upon the Black Avenger's plot when he discovered that the Black Avenger had been secretly using his very own storage chest.

And then he noticed the riding crop on the floor. "Wait a moment," he said. "This doesn't make sense. Why would the

Black Avenger be using my storage chest? That doesn't make sense. Unless he wanted to be caught. Unless . . . " He thought about his blackouts, the things he had forgotten. A terrible image formed in his mind. The Black Avenger hadn't been using his chest without permission after all. It was all very clear. "Then I . . . I am the Black Avenger," he said. He looked over to the mirror and laughed. "All right!" he cried.

In that one moment of realization he became radiant. The dilemma he had been facing had been solved. No longer would he have to play lackey to Phillip's whims. He already had his own force ready to seize power. Now he could do all that he had dreamed of. He could marry Winona and consolidate the Westerhoven principalities under himself, and then use them to crush the Sousterhoven principalities that he hated. All along he had served Phillip faithfully when he felt it was wrong. But now it was all clear.

And he had the plans right in his hands. Details of the security of the wedding, lists of secret passages, and the members of the plot, including even Phillip's servant Voss. "It's no wonder I feel tired all the time," he declared. "I've been up all night plotting against Phillip."

Bringing the candle closer to the chest he began to read the papers carefully and for the first time consciously realize what he needed to do. The time for blackouts was over. He knew who he was and accepted that fact. Now he needed to study the most ambitious and daring plan he had ever read: How he and his black cloakers would infiltrate the wedding and take the Lady Winona right away from Phillip.

It was enough to make him laugh. And in doing so he spied the riding crop once more and regarded it ruefully. Picking it up he threw it out the window. "I won't be needing that anymore because I'm the Black Avenger."

PART V

The Wedding
of Winona and Phillip

How to Calm
a Nervous Groom

"Okay, okay," Grover said, looking at Beoweasel. "But I still don't understand why I have to wear armor. It feels like I'm going to battle." Grover looked at his arms, covered with chain mail, and shook his head.

"But you are, in a sense," Beoweasel said.

"I was just hoping it was some weird form of birth control," Grover commented, hitting his codpiece with the back of his hand to make a ringing sound.

"So do you understand what you have to do?" Beoweasel asked. "I won't be able to advise you once you're down on the floor."

"Maybe we should go over it again," Grover said. "I'm still having trouble remembering the names of the Lords. Young Dianna, Prince Thorn." They had gone over the name of each ruler of Westerhoven just in case he had to talk to them. But he could only remember the rulers he had met at the city of Hoven.

"Okay," Beoweasel said. "But we don't have much time. The wedding is to begin shortly. Where's Voss?"

"Voss?" Grover repeated, and then remembered he was talking about Cilla. "He went off to talk to Winona."

"Voss is supposed to act as your swordbearer in this endeavor," Beoweasel reminded him.

"I know," Grover said. "Apparently, Winona wanted to see her brother about something." But Grover had an idea about what that something was. Winona had probably discovered their counter-plot.

Beoweasel shrugged.

There was a sound at the door, and Grover turned hopefully to greet Cilla's arrival, but instead saw Romeo and Bill come walking through, dressed gaily for the affair, in bright pantaloons and blouses with lots of frills. Romeo carried a lute in his hand, and Bill had his requisite sheaf of papers.

"Are we late?" Romeo asked, his gaze going all over the balcony.

"Yes, sorry we didn't arrive earlier, but we had some last-minute composing to do," Bill clarified.

Grover looked at Beoweasel. "What are they doing here?"

"I thought I told you, they were part of your entourage for the wedding," Beoweasel said.

"Yeah, dude," Romeo said. "You didn't think your cringing sycophants would miss you getting married."

"No," Grover said. "But I was hoping you'd do it from further away."

"Oh," Romeo said. And he went over to the balcony and leaned over. "Hey, look," he said, pointing. "You can see down their dresses."

"You can?" Grover asked, looking toward the balcony railing. "Can you see Young Dianna?"

"Nah," Romeo said. "But you should see the . . ."

"Lord Phillip," Beoweasel interjected. "We were going over the procedure for the wedding."

"Yes, right," Grover said, taking one last reluctant look at the balcony. "The procedure for the wedding."

There was another noise at the door, and Grover once again turned hopefully to look for Cilla, but only saw Old Lord Phillip come walking in through the door with his staff. He looked around and then spotted Grover.

"Ah, my son," he said. Grover looked at him skeptically. "How do you like the arrangements? I did the wedding just as you told me."

"You did," Grover said, and then added, "dude."

"Do you find fault with anything I have done?" he asked.

Grover shrugged. "It's fine, fine." Grover had hardly noticed the arrangements.

The Old Lord smiled and then backed out of the small room. "I have to be there for the start of the ceremonies. I hope you are pleasantly surprised today."

"You do?" Grover repeated.

The Old Lord nodded. "You deserve this."

Romeo turned to the Old Lord. "Come over here, you can see down their dresses."

The Old Lord laughed. "Maybe later."

"Cool, dude," Romeo said.

"Always a pleasure," Bill chimed in, who was just standing around looking at his notes.

The Old Lord nodded and then exited the room.

"You were saying," Grover prodded Beoweasel.

"Ah, yes, the procedure," Beoweasel said. "It's very simple."

Romeo turned away from the balcony. "Anyone for a song?"

"No, thank you," Grover said.

"Would you like to hear 'Dude Knight,' 'Catch a Troll,' or 'Hang a Villain'?"

Grover shook his head. "Whatever pleases you." And then turned to Beoweasel. "Now what am I supposed to do?"

Romeo sang softly with Bill harmonizing. ". . . catch a troll and you're sitting on top of his stash, catch a troll, catch a troll . . ."

"According to custom," Beoweasel began, stopping only to glare at Romeo and Bill, "in the marriage of two nobles, you are supposed to, in fact, win her."

"Win her?" Grover repeated. "I already rescued her. Am I suppose to play dice for her too?"

"It's tradition," Beoweasel explained.

"A stupid tradition," Grover said. "Why couldn't we have eloped? That would have been much easier."

"Then the Lords wouldn't have acknowledged the wedding. It's very important that they acknowledge the wedding."

"Oh," Grover said.

". . . that's because Dude Knights die young, when you get real old you have no fun, so you might as well be a Dude Knight and die young, oooh yeah, play that lute, Romeo . . ."

"So how do I win her?" Grover asked.

"Okay," Beoweasel said. "This is how it goes. You enter the church from the far door. Right over there. You walk in and challenge anyone to refute your claim to Winona as your bride. This is traditional. If anyone disputes your claim, you will have to fight him to win her."

"I'll have to fight," Grover said. "No one said anything about fighting." He glanced at Bill and Romeo, who were grooving in their song and weren't paying attention to any of the exchange between himself and Beoweasel.

"Well, Phillip is a renowned warrior. Anyone challenging his claim is unlikely."

"Good," Grover said. "So then it should be a piece of cake."

". . . there was a Dude Knight, and he was all right, all right with me . . . he had a long sword, so we called him Lord, until the mutiny . . ."

"Maybe," Beoweasel said. "And after that, you will approach Winona and woo her with a love song."

"Woo her? With a love song? I don't even like her, let alone her liking me," Grover said. "You sure we can't dispense with that part?"

Beoweasel shook his head. "This part you have to do."

"That's where we come in," Romeo said, stopping in mid-song, as if on cue. "I'll be accompanying you. Get it, I'll be accompanying you."

"No," Grover said, shaking his head, not noticing the lute that Romeo was shaking in front of him.

"Oh," Romeo replied, disappointed.

"Yes," Bill started. "We wrote the love song for you. It should be pretty good. Here." And he handed Grover a piece of paper.

"What's this?" Grover asked, scanning the writing.

"The lyrics of the Woo Song," Bill explained. "Though, of course, you don't have to give me credit for them, being that I am your cringing sycophant."

"Thanks," Grover said, stuffing the lyric sheet into his belt.

"It was my pleasure," Bill said.

Beoweasel shrugged. "See, you have nothing to worry about, my lord, it has all been taken care of."

"Is someone going to sing for me too?" Grover asked.

"Sorry," Beoweasel replied.

"Let me guess," Grover said. "It's traditional."

"Yes," Beoweasel said. "But after that it should get easier. Once you have wooed her, you approach the altar with her, the priest takes the wedding goblet, consecrates the wine, addresses the assembly, and then you drink the wine and are married."

"Sounds simple," Grover said flatly. A thought just returned to him that he had forgotten.

"Are you all right?" Beoweasel asked, noticing the change in Grover's face.

"Is Voss back yet?" Grover asked.

Beoweasel looked around the balcony. "Apparently not, and we're starting soon."

And then there was the sound of a gong, deeply reverberating throughout the church.

"Correction," Beoweasel said. "We're going to be starting almost immediately. That's the gong signaling to get to our places."

"But what about Voss?" Grover asked.

"You may have to go in without him," Beoweasel said.

"But at least you got us," Romeo said, pulling Bill close in a hug, and beaming a smile at Grover.

"Now I feel better," Grover replied dryly.

"See," Romeo said to Bill. "I told you he appreciated us. He was just going through one of his moods again." Bill nodded.

The door to the corridor was opened and Beoweasel was motioning him to come out. Grover gave one last look around the balcony. It was all starting and he could do nothing to stop it.

Winona Has Made
Other Plans

"You can't come in," said the stern face behind the door. "Tradition states that the bride cannot be tarnished by the sight of a male before she is presented for marriage. It would violate her chastity."

"What chastity?" Cilla responded. "She's already pregnant."

"You have a foul mouth," she said, and began closing the door.

Cilla interposed her booted foot, which was successful in stopping the door from closing, but not very good in stopping the pain it caused. Cilla grunted, and regretted the fact she had to wear dress boots for this wedding affair. But at least it was almost over. That is, as long as Winona was still fooled by the substitute poison she had given her. She and Grover had decided it would be better to give her something instead of nothing, so she wouldn't suspect. As long as Winona thought Voss was cooperating it wasn't likely she would get any other outside help. And so Cilla had given the harmless substitute to Winona and hoped she wouldn't discover it was a fraud. How could she, unless she tried it on someone else? So they would be safe. Safe until now. Winona had asked to see Voss all of a sudden, and it probably wasn't just because she wanted Voss to hold her hand.

"Let me in," Cilla demanded.

The woman pressed harder on the door.

"Ack," Cilla cried out in pain, and then reflexively looked about to see is anyone had noticed. "The Lady Winona has specifically requested my presence. I am her brother, Voss."

The door swung open suddenly as Cilla pushed again and she was spilled to the floor, her face in the hem of some woman's dress. Cilla got to her feet instantly and said, "Nobody saw that."

"Why didn't you say who you were in the first place?" the woman asked.

Cilla answered with a question. "Where is the Lady Winona?"

The woman nodded her head in a direction that indicated she must go further into the room. "She's in the back room."

"Thank you," Cilla said. "You've been a great hindrance."

The woman's face looked vexed but she said nothing.

Cilla moved to the back room, where she presumed Winona was being made ready for the wedding. Cilla had first gone to Winona's tower only to find her gone. It turned out that Winona was being prepared in a room right off the church. So now Cilla had wasted precious time in finding her. The wedding was supposed to go on at any moment and she had as yet to complete her task.

Cilla passed by ladies-in-waiting, dressed in pink gowns, and flower maidens, who had baskets full of unblemished petals, and stern older matrons who were overseeing the whole process. Finally she reached the back room and let herself in. Only Winona and Erika occupied this room. Erika was straightening out the gown as Cilla entered.

"Voss," Winona cried out. "Fair brother. I thought you would never arrive. I was going to have to send another person to fetch you."

"I thought you were still in the tower," Cilla said. "I didn't know you had moved."

"Sorry," Winona replied gaily. "I should have told the messenger to bring you here."

"You should have also told the messenger what this was all about. The wedding is about to start and I'm supposed to accompany Phillip in."

"I just had to see you," Winona said. "I had to see your face when I told you what I am about to tell you."

"And that is?" Cilla asked.

Suddenly there was the deep sonorous sound of a gong reverberating throughout the room.

"It's time," Erika announced.

Cilla heard a courtier shout out to the ladies in the next room that it was time to get ready.

"What is it?" Cilla asked. "I have to be going." She sounded impatient, but she really knew that she couldn't leave until she found out what Winona wanted.

"And so do I," Winona said. And she laughed. "My, Voss, you look so serious. Are you having second thoughts about poisoning Phillip?"

"No," Cilla said firmly. "I said I would do it. And I'm doing it."

"That's not what I think," Winona said.

"It really doesn't matter now," Cilla said. "I've already given you the poison. It should be in the chalice already."

"That's what I wanted to talk to you about," Winona said.

Cilla stared straight into Winona's green eyes, and didn't evince any emotion. "Yes?" Cilla asked.

"I suppose you thought you were clever," she said. "But I'm no fool. You didn't think I would use the poison without testing it?"

"You tested it?" Cilla cried out in surprise. She wasn't sure how she should react. Should she admit to her deed or just play dumb? She finally decided to say nothing at all.

"Yes, I tested it," Winona said. "I gave some to Erika here one night."

"You did?" Cilla exclaimed.

"You did?" Erika cried. "Is that why you were being so nice to me?"

"Un-huh," Winona answered.

"You poisoned me?" Erika clarified.

"Yes," Winona said. "And as you can see, you didn't die."

"You used her as a test subject," Cilla said. "What kind of woman are you?"

"Well," Winona said, "I guess I would have been an awful and evil one had I not been such a distrusting one. Somehow I didn't think you would come through and deliver the poison. But you never know. People could change. But it didn't happen this time."

Cilla wasn't sure of what to say. She had been caught. "So is this what you wanted to tell me?"

"It was part of what I wanted to tell you," Winona said. "I wanted to see your reaction when you were caught lying to me. I never knew you would be so loyal to Phillip. Over the family, no less."

"I guess you don't know me very well," Cilla said.

"I know you're a man," Winona said. "And you can predict that when it comes down to the wire, men will stick together against women. So I wasn't that surprised. I was only disappointed. I thought maybe you had understood my problem."

There was a knocking at the door.

"What is it?" Winona asked.

"It's time to go," the courtier cried from the other side of the door.

"I'll be out presently," Winona said. And she looked back at Cilla. "So I guess you're proud of yourself, that you've saved your master?"

"Have I?" Cilla asked carefully.

"This time no," Winona said.

"How's that?" Cilla asked. "I suppose you've found someone else to help you."

"Very good," Winona said. "That I have."

"Who?" Cilla asked.

"It doesn't matter," Winona said. "But when Phillip goes to drink from the cup, he will find a surprise. I can just see it now. It'll go like so many other fine poisonings. He'll lift the consecrated goblet, full of his gloating self, for tricking me into marriage. And then he'll drink. He'll have a smile on his face. But then a few seconds later that will change, as his throat constricts and his heart begins to beat faster. He'll choke for breath and die in a twisting, convulsive agony. Poetic justice, don't you think?"

"Where's the poetry come in?" Cilla asked.

"I don't know," Winona said. "But I'm sure somebody will write a poem about it. But by then I'll be free. And so will you, my dear brother. You don't have to thank me now."

"But how will you get away with it?" Cilla asked. "You don't think you can poison Phillip and just walk away?"

"Sure I do," Winona said. "No one will suspect me. They'll probably think the Black Avenger did it."

"So you have this all figured out," Cilla said with a calm she did not feel. She was really disappointed because she had been fooled. All along, while she had been counterplotting against Winona, Winona had been counterplotting against Voss. And now she was in almost the same position she would have been in had she not helped Winona. Except for the fact that she knew the wine goblet would definitely be poisoned. She had to warn Grover.

"But what if you drink the wine first?" Cilla asked.

"I already have taken the antidote," Winona explained, and smiled.

Cilla's face fell.

"Now," Winona said, "that was the expression I was waiting for."

There was another knocking at the door. The courtier's voice calling again.

"Well," Winona said, "I have to go and get married." And she walked toward the door with Erika in tow. But she stopped by Cilla. "You will wish me a happy marriage, won't you?"

Cilla blinked her eyes. "What?"

Winona smiled. "I'll see you after the wedding."

"But what makes you think I won't warn Phillip?" Cilla asked.

"To marry me, Phillip has to drink through the chalice," Winona said.

"Not if he knows it is poisoned," Cilla replied.

"Then *I'll* drink from the chalice," Winona said. "To show it is not poisoned."

"But we can stop that too," Cilla said.

"Can you?" Winona asked. "Do you really think you can stop the whole wedding?"

"I can try," Cilla said.

"Well, try, then," Winona said. "But I think you'll be disappointed." And she brushed by Cilla to exit the room.

"No," Cilla said in parting. "I think it is you who will be disappointed."

And then Winona was gone. The ladies-in-waiting, the flower maidens, the elder matrons were all exiting the room. The wedding was moving inexorably on and Cilla was still standing in Winona's room.

How to Win
Your Bride (Part I)

Grover, Romeo, and Beoweasel stood outside the church doors waiting for the cue to enter. Bill had already gone in and taken his place, since he wouldn't be involved in the wedding.

"Where's your sword?" Beoweasel asked.

"Voss was supposed to bring it," Grover explained. And Grover looked down the hallway to see if Cilla was returning. "What could be keeping her?" he asked.

"Her?" Romeo asked.

"Voss," Grover said quickly, and started to sweat beneath his armor. How long could he last without making another slipup? He had been doing pretty well so far. But as yet he hadn't been consulted on crucial matters. It was only a matter of time before he made a crucial mistake.

"Well, you should have your sword," Beoweasel said.

"Why?" Grover asked. "You said yourself that I won't be needing it. No one is going to challenge me."

"Did I say that?" Beoweasel asked.

"Yeah," Grover said. "What's the problem? You don't think anyone's going to challenge me, do you? You said no one would challenge me." These last words were said in almost a panic. Grover didn't know how to use a great sword very well. He had avoided using it at all times. From watching others do so he had determined that he would probably die if he had to actually enter combat using one. He was just happy that everyone thought Phillip was such a great warrior that no one would dare attack him.

Beoweasel hesitated. "Well, I don't think anyone would actually challenge you . . ."

"Then what are you saying?" Grover asked. "I thought this was going to be a piece of cake."

"It should be," Beoweasel replied. "It should be but . . ."

"Then what are you saying?" Grover asked again.

"Chill out," Romeo interrupted. "You sound tense."

"Bug off," Grover shouted at Romeo.

"Okay, okay," Romeo said, walking away. "God, you're uptight."

"Why do I need my sword?" Grover demanded of Beoweasel.

"Well," Beoweasel explained, "I didn't want to get you worried, because you seemed so nervous before, but . . ."

"But what?" Grover interjected. "But what?"

"Well, it would be unseemly for you to just take Winona without any effort. Almost an insult to your manhood."

"I wouldn't be insulted," Grover said. "Trust me, I wouldn't be insulted."

"That's not what Erich thought," Beoweasel went on.

"Erich," Grover gasped, and turned pale.

"You turned pale," Beoweasel said. "Are you eating properly?"

"I'm just fine," Grover said quickly, a hand passing quickly over his face.

"You sure?" Beoweasel said.

"Yeah," Grover said. "Now, what's this about Erich?"

"Well, Erich thought it would be unseemly for you to take Winona without any effort, and it would make the wedding much too short. He thought he would come out to challenge you, to make the wedding a little more interesting."

"A little more interesting," Grover said. "Couldn't we just have had some dancing girls?"

"Hey, that would have been keen," Romeo said.

Beoweasel shook his head. "It's traditional. It's not really a battle anyway. It's just a mock demonstration. A play. You aren't really fighting."

"But we'll be using swords?" Grover clarified.

"He'll let you win," Beoweasel said. "You don't think he would interfere with the wedding?"

"Oh no," Grover said dryly. "Not at all."

"This is just entertainment," Beoweasel informed him. "You have nothing to worry about. I don't see why you're getting so upset."

"Well . . . it's all so sudden," Grover explained to Beoweasel. What he was really worried about was that Erich might be challenging him as the Black Avenger. Since he had learned of Erich's secret identity, Cilla and he had done nothing, because that wasn't part of their adventure. They were just supposed to go through with the wedding, that's all. So they had not attempted to kill Erich, even though that might have been in their best interest. They didn't even know if they could get close enough to kill him, and even if they did kill him, there was always the off chance they could be caught and their identities revealed, so they had done nothing. At the time it had seemed the right choice. But now it looked like they had made a mistake.

But had that been a mistake? Was Erich going to interfere with the wedding? Or was this really just a mock battle?

"God, where's Voss?" Grover asked in an exasperated voice.

Romeo shrugged. "Don't look at me."

"You'll need a sword," Beoweasel said.

"But if I don't have a sword, then I won't have to go through with the fight, right?" Grover asked hopefully.

Beoweasel shook his head.

"Why don't you ask that knight for a sword?" Romeo interjected, pointing behind them.

"What?" Grover asked.

Beoweasel saw a knight who was standing guard at the entrance to the building. "Good idea," he said, and went over to ask the knight for his blade.

Grover watched as Beoweasel argued for the blade, his hands gesticulating to explain the situation, first pointing at himself, then at the knight, and then at Grover. At first the knight seemed reluctant but then he was handing the blade over to Beoweasel, who bowed to him, apparently thanking him. Then Beoweasel was coming over to Grover, blade in hand.

"He said it would be a great honor," Beoweasel told him.

"Great," Grover said, taking the blade in both hands.

"And he wants it back once the wedding is done," Beoweasel added.

"Okay," Grover said.

"And if you could make sure it was sharpened he would be really pleased."

"All right already," Grover said. And looked around again. "What could be keeping Voss?"

"I don't know," Beoweasel said, and then there was a trumpet blast. "But you're supposed to be going in now."

"Now," Grover repeated with dread.

"And don't forget to make the challenge," Beoweasel said.

"But . . ." Grover said hopelessly.

The doors to the church were opened. Grover saw that the benches had been pushed to the side to give a wide space between himself and the altar, presumably for the challenge. Lords and Ladies stood up and turned their gaze to him. He could see a few faces he recognized but the names slipped his mind for the moment. At the end of the church was the Lady Winona, waiting to be won. She was dressed in a pink gown and looked dumpy even in that. Beside her was her handmaiden, Erika.

There was silence now, except for a few coughs and the rustling of fabrics.

"Go," Beoweasel said, and disappeared.

Now it was up to him.

Romeo came up and stood by his side. He didn't say anything.

Grover took the first step in. He was looking for Erich. But no one obstructed him from reaching the dais and marrying Winona. Something jabbed at his ribs, and he saw the Woo Song lyrics tucked into his belt. He wondered if he would ever get to sing his Woo Song. But maybe he was just being overdramatic. Of course, Erich would let him have the bride. Erich was Phillip's best friend. It was only the Black Avenger who might stop him.

More confident now, Grover walked into the church about one-third of the way, and then remembered he had to issue a challenge.

"I have come to claim the Lady Winona as my bride. Is there anyone who would lay doubt to this claim? Then let him step forth."

Grover was surprised at how easily he was able to speak the challenge. He glanced around the assembled Lords and Ladies, but didn't see anyone jumping out to stop him. Maybe Erich had changed his mind. Maybe he had decided to let Phillip win her without a challenge. Maybe he had had a cerebral hemorrhage and dropped dead. Maybe he had been swallowed by a vortex. There were an infinite number of possibilities.

Grover glanced at Romeo, and Romeo just shrugged. He didn't know what was going on either.

Grover shrugged too and moved on more confidently. If he reached the stage without a challenge, he presumed he could just sing the Woo Song and that would be it. So Grover increased his pace across the church floor, his boots making an ominous clicking noise.

And then there was a stirring in the crowd.

"Wait," someone cried out.

Grover stopped and looked back. There was someone dressed all in armor, stepping out of the crowd at the back of the church. Grover couldn't tell who he was, since he wore a helmet that obscured his face. Was this Erich?

"Wait, I claim this bride," the man said.

Romeo looked to Grover. "Go ahead, kick his ass."

Grover licked his lips and pulled the sheath off his great sword.

"Sorry, I didn't catch your name," Grover stated boldly.

Behind Walls
and Secret Doors

It was in this moment when some sort of action was needed most that Cilla couldn't decide what to do. If there had been a call for direct action, involving violence and lots of bloodshed, Cilla would have been able to handle it. But Cilla wasn't in her normal environment. Stripped from her natural surroundings, cast into the role of a man, and not only any man but a servant to boot, without her customary weapons or authority, in a land that ran by different rules, she was confused about how she should proceed. If this had been any city in Vardan—Rigersdown, Jolinstive, Parda—she would have used her knife first and had a glass of wine later. Questions were for sissies anyway. Maybe she would have asked more questions had not the answers been so damn long. When it came down to it, Cilla was an impatient person. She felt she had a calling in life—a place and position she had to be by a certain time and she was already late in getting there. Every obstacle, every long-winded speech, locked door, wrong turn, mistaken assumption, was a setback and only made her angrier. And ever since she had come here, there had been many setbacks: the bride who had to be rescued, the Black Avenger who wanted to kill Phillip, and the absence of Beogoat. One after another, a never-ceasing parade of setbacks. And having them didn't mean she got used to them. So the pressure inside her had begun to build.

The pressure had actually begun long ago, and was always there, just below the surface. And when too many things had gone wrong, she exploded. Death and anarchy soon followed. It always seemed that people and things moved beyond her realm of control. And it made her angry. Very angry. Not "scream at the top of your lungs" angry, with exhaustive temper tantrums, but rather "rush and push everyone who got in your way out of the way" angry.

This all went through Cilla's mind in a microsecond. These thoughts did not come in complete sentences, or even words, but rather in reverberating urges and violent flashes of emotion. All she knew was that she had to do something. She had to make sure

the adventure went right or . . . or she didn't know what . . .
She could think about that after. Not now. She just didn't know if
she could handle any more setbacks.

With these thoughts reeling through the back of her mind she
took a deep breath and stepped forward. That's all she needed to
get moving. Winona had made a mistake in warning her. The
bride-to-be had been too cocky. She thought that Voss would do
nothing to warn Phillip. But she hadn't known that Voss was Cilla
and Phillip was Grover, and that Winona was going to get married
whether she liked it or not. Cilla would personally see to that. But
first she had to warn Grover about the wine being poisoned. She
still had time. It hadn't been long since the gong had rung. The
wedding probably hadn't even begun yet. These affairs never
began on time anyway.

Before she finished these thoughts she was out the door.

The hallway was empty. She was one floor above the church
ceremonies. No problem, she could make it. And then she
remembered she had to get Grover's sword. She had thought there
would be time to get it after speaking to Winona, but she didn't
know that getting to Winona would take so much time. So she
stopped and looked toward the passage that led back into the
castle. She didn't have time to get the sword. Grover would just
have to go without it. Grover was in danger of being poisoned,
not skewered. God, how this mission was getting fouled up.
Beogoat had been such a liar. All you have to do is marry her,
that's all. Yeah, right.

She swiveled to go back the other way toward the ground floor
of the church, and just as she was rounding a corner she saw
something out of place. A figure slipping into the wall. Into the
wall! Now, how could a man slip into a wall, unless that wasn't a
wall there at all?

And not only that. The man was wearing a black cloak. Then
Cilla recalled that night out under the bridge when she had first
met the Black Avenger. He had said the plan for the wedding was
still on. She hadn't given it much thought then or since then,
because she no longer had any contact with the Black Avenger,
and the Black Avenger had already challenged Phillip to a battle
of honor anyway, so why would he bother with the wedding? She
had put away any concerns she had about the Black Avenger,
because Grover would have married Winona and they would have
been out of here by the time they needed to deal with him again.
But now a man in a black cloak was slipping into the wall. She
couldn't just ignore that.

The thought of getting to Grover was pushed back. She still probably had some time before Grover went in. It would only take a moment to look into this. And this might be more important after all. Or so went Cilla's mind, which flipped from action to action, like a stone skipping from wave to wave. She ran forward, her hand reaching at her side for her short sword and *Argh* knife.

"Damn," she muttered when she found them missing. And that was just one more irritant she had to suffer.

She pulled up her hands and clenched her fists.

The black-cloaked figure was out of sight. She reached the portion of the wall she had seen him disappear into. There was a hairline crack. Not so obvious if she hadn't known to look for it.

"Secret doors," she muttered. "This whole place is filled with secret doors and secret plots."

She pushed on the door and the crack widened. She pulled the tapestry out of the way and pushed harder against the false stone surface. The door slid inward easily as she leaned forward, and now she was disappearing into the wall.

Looking in, she saw that the man had already disappeared. She hesitated as light from the hallway filled in the darkened passage. Should she go on and investigate? Or should she warn Grover? The former idea seemed more important. And she could always warn Grover any moment preceding the drinking of the wine. This *was* more important. The Black Avenger was here. Which could only mean he had his own plan to kill Phillip. She couldn't let that happen.

Decision made, she went in, leaving the secret door wide open behind her. What need did she have for secrecy?

The passage was narrow. But why would it be wide? It was secret after all, and they certainly weren't smuggling elephants through it. And it was dirty. Secret passages were always the worst places to travel, concluded Cilla. They're dark, dirty, and you never know what's waiting for you at the other end. Sort of like one-night stands.

The light from the entrance was enough to lead her to a T-shaped bend. She could either go left or right. Right or left. Last time she was in one of these she had stepped on a decaying body. She could almost remember the feeling of her foot sinking into the rotting stomach cavity of some dead guy. She could still imagine the feel of aging fat squishing through her toes, and that thought made her squirm.

"Pah," she spat out the memory. That adventure hadn't been successful.

She fancied she saw some light at the end of the left passage and started that way. At least it looked like light, as if coming under the crack of some door. A thin crack. One you would have to turn sideways to squeak through.

She patted her side again for weapons and only came upon the belt she was wearing. She loosened this and held it in her hands like a garrote. She reflected that it also could be used as a whip if she had to. She went forward and stopped at the door. Taking a second to gather her energies, she kicked on the door, knocking it open, and squeezed through.

How to Win
Your Bride (Part II)

Grover couldn't tell who the person was beneath the mask. Was it Erich, the Black Avenger, or was it just someone else who had decided to crash the party?

The unknown knight did not at first respond to Grover's question requesting his identity, but instead removed his own blade from its sheath. A hush fell across the assembly. Everyone was waiting to see what would happen. Someone had actually challenged Phillip.

Grover gulped, but stood his ground. After all, he realized, he had nowhere else to go. But if everything was going according to plan, he should be just fine. All he had to do was fake a fight with the guy. How hard could that be?

"My name is not important," the knight finally said, his voice distorted by the mask, so Grover couldn't tell who he was.

"Then who will sing your song?" Grover asked.

"I will," Romeo whispered.

Grover glared at Romeo. "Whose side are you on anyway?"

"Well, you haven't paid me recently," Romeo said. "That is a factor in my loyalty."

Grover shook his head. Servants were the same everywhere.

"They will know whose name to sing after the battle is done," the knight explained.

Grover's eyes widened. That's it, the knight was the Black Avenger. Beneath all that armor he was wearing a black cloak. Any moment now he would be ripping off his mask and ranting about retribution and justice for the common man. Grover looked at the doors of the church. Where the hell was Cilla when he needed her? Why wasn't she here? He needed her to fight with him back-to-back against the Black Avenger.

There was a murmuring in the crowd now. Voices wondering who the knight was, and what principality he was from, and why he wanted to marry Winona. Many thought the challenge was for real, while others waited to see what the true story was.

Grover thought it was real too. But he couldn't back down. He had to play the part of Phillip to the very end, and he had to marry Winona. If not for himself, then for Cilla, who really wanted the adventure to succeed. As far as Grover was concerned the adventure could fail. He didn't have any reputation to live up to.

"You're right," Grover finally said, his voice steady as if he had carefully deliberated what he was going to say. "Names are not important."

"I'm glad you see my point," the knight replied.

"By what right do you claim this bride?" Grover asked.

"By right of love and of superior force," the knight responded, waving his sword.

"Well," Grover said, "I cannot test the strength of your love, for no one can ever know the measure of one's love, but I can dispute your claim of strength by superior force."

"You will find that my claims are not the kind that can be disputed by rhetoric," the knight said boldly.

"Hey, dude, I was aware of that," Grover said, simultaneously thinking, Oh my God, what am I getting myself into?

"There is only one way that a claim of superior force can be disputed," the knight said. "And that's if you are able to overcome me in a battle of force."

"I was wondering when you'd get around to mentioning that," Grover said.

There was some laughter in the crowd at this remark. Grover started to feel more confident. Maybe he could pull this off. It was probably just Erich under the mask anyway. He would have declared himself the Black Avenger long before if he actually meant to do him in. At least, that's what Grover hoped. You could never really tell with psychopaths, though. They were an unpredictable lot, which was why they were so annoying.

"And," Grover asked, "how will we determine who has the greater strength in arms?"

"We will fight until the other concedes defeat," the knight answered.

"So this is also a test of endurance?" Grover asked.

"Endurance and skill," the knight said.

"Are you sure what we're actually fighting about here?" Grover asked.

There was more laughter from the Lords and Ladies. They were eating up Phillip's, and thus Grover's, performance. Grover started to smile openly. He was sure he could handle this now. Erich would just put up a fake fight and he would win. There was no danger at all. He was actually beginning to enjoy this. It didn't seem so bad that Cilla wasn't here now. In fact, she probably would have spoiled the moment if she had been here.

"I'm sure what I'm fighting about," the knight responded. "Are you sure you want to defend your claim?"

Grover looked over his shoulder at Winona. Did he really want to defend his claim? She surely didn't seem like any prize. And he knew that she didn't want to marry him. Maybe he shouldn't be knocking himself out over this woman. But then Cilla would be pissed. He'd rather fight than face Cilla pissed. "I'm fairly sure," Grover said.

"Then you agree to my terms?" the knight asked.

"But what if no one acknowledges the other one's skill in arms?" Grover asked.

"Then that person will die," the knight said.

Grover's smile faded. The lighthearted expressions on the Lords and Ladies disappeared. The last statement had sounded serious.

"And how do we begin?" Grover asked.

The knight raised his blade and walked forward. "We begin like this."

Cilla Uncovers a Plot

The room was empty except for a lantern on the floor that was burning low. Cilla whipped around thinking that maybe she had gone the wrong way when she spotted another door. Behind it she could see stairs. Stairs curving upward.

Cilla opened the door as wide as it would go and clearly saw the narrow steps that curved upward. But they were so steep that it was almost like climbing a ladder. At first Cilla tried to use them like normal steps, one foot after the other, with her hands to the walls to steady herself, but it soon became clear that if she was going to get anywhere fast, she would have to crawl up.

"The things I do," Cilla muttered as she stuck the belt between her teeth to hold it.

The stairs weren't very long but since they were so difficult to negotiate and Cilla was in such a hurry to get up them, she kept slipping and falling, and precious minutes slipped by until she came abruptly to the top, her head hitting some solid surface. Cilla backed down a bit and with one hand reached up to feel a wooden board above her head. She braced herself on the stairs so she could give the board a push when she suddenly felt the board lift without her help.

Light streamed in and she saw a black-cloaked, demon-masked figure above her, lifting the board aside. It was him, the guy she had been following. He must have mistaken her for one of them and was going to help her up.

Cilla scrambled up before the black-cloaked figure could turn around and ripped the belt out of her mouth.

When the black-cloaked figure finally turned around he saw her rising from a crouch with a belt in her hand.

"What the hell?" he cried.

"So what are you doing here?" Cilla asked. Her eyes scanned the room and saw it was just as small as the chamber she had left. Only enough room for a few people to sit around in. Behind the black-cloaked figure there was a corridor. She also saw one behind her. It was easy to see because there were small slits in the wall where light from within the church was coming in. She was above the ceremonies. She could hear the clang of swords but wasn't sure where the sound was coming from. It seemed the Black Avenger had made his move after all.

"I'm supposed to be here," the man said. "What are you doing here? You're supposed to be on the floor."

The guy believed she was Voss. He recognized her. He must have been one of the fellows out at the bridge that night.

"What do you mean, down on the floor?" Cilla demanded. "I thought I was supposed to be up here with the others."

"That's not what I was told," the man said. "What the hell are you doing up here without the costume?"

"There wasn't time," Cilla said.

"You shouldn't be here," he said. "You could ruin the whole thing. Do you even know how to use a bow?"

"A bow," Cilla said, and that's when she noticed that there was a strung bow at the side of the wall, with a sheaf of arrows. Obviously the guy wasn't using a bow just because it was the most handy weapon to have in a small enclosed passage, which it wasn't. He had to have the bow for some other reason, and it probably wasn't just to shoot at any hay bales. Cilla then noticed the slit windows again, which suddenly seemed perfect for firing on people in the church below. Just like target practice. How convenient. But was this the only guy here? Was he just a lone assassin who would kill Grover at a crucial moment, or was he one of many? "Of course I know how to use a bow," Cilla said.

And that was when the fellow seemed to get a better idea about what was going on. "What are you doing with that belt?"

"This?" Cilla said, holding up the belt. "Well, you see, I didn't have any weapon to kill you with when I came up here. So I thought the belt would do."

"Kill me," he said. And then he lifted his mask and cried out, "Louis, Gerald."

"Now, why did you have to do that?" Cilla frowned. "Why did you have to cry for help?"

"Louis, Gerald," he cried again.

"Stop it," Cilla said. "You're really pissing me off."

The man seemed about to yell again so Cilla made her move. She lashed out with the belt, the buckled end striking the fellow in the face. The man grabbed out at the belt and yanked it away from Cilla's grasp.

Cilla stared at her empty hands and said, "You weren't supposed to do that. Now you're really pissing me off. You don't understand how this works, do you?"

"You're crazy, Voss," the man said. "You'll die for this." And he dropped the belt to the floor.

Cilla didn't know how long it would be until this man's friends arrived. She had to act quickly. "All I want to know is what the plan is."

The man seemed to be reaching for something at his side. That's all it took to set Cilla off. She took the opportunity to leap at him, pushing his body to the ground, her knee driving fast and furiously into his groin.

The man cried out in pain, and Cilla ripped the man's mask off to see who lay beneath. Behind the mask was a startled but unfamiliar face. "I don't know you," Cilla said.

"What . . ." the man cried. And then Cilla punched him in the face.

Cilla struggled to keep the man down, but he was stronger and heavier. Cilla had no recourse but to slip off and let the man regain his feet. But before he could cry out again, or grab a weapon, Cilla had regained the belt and was using it to encircle the man's throat. She pulled the belt tight and felt the man gasp. One of his booted feet kicked into Cilla's stomach, and she collapsed backward, pulling the guy with her.

They both fell to the floor, the man on top of Cilla. Cilla momentarily lost the grip of her belt, but then she pulled tight. The man struggled, twisting in her grasp.

"What's the plan?" Cilla cried. "You think I'm just playing around here. Tell me the plan and I'll stop."

But the man twisted and pulled, and Cilla felt her body pressed into the floor. Then two things happened. First Cilla pulled tightly on the strap, and second the man fell to his side and into the open trapdoor feetfirst. Suddenly the man was falling and flailing out with his hands, and Cilla was pulling back on the belt trying not to be dragged down with him. She heard the snap, like it was an explosion in her head. And then she was letting go of the belt as the man started to slide down the stairs.

Cilla looked at her hands and then beyond where the dead man was disappearing from sight with a slithery sound. "I just wanted," she gasped, "to know the plan. You were the one who took it so seriously."

Cilla then collapsed to the floor and gazed up at the ceiling.

"Oh well," she said to herself, breathing heavily, "there's more where they came from."

And that's just about when Gerald and Louis decided to show up.

How to Win
Your Bride (Part III)

Grover hadn't actually believed, until the moment when the knight had come forward with his blade, that he would really have to fight. Somehow he had hoped that all through this talk they would have been able to settle their differences peaceably. This was a fantasy he indulged in often, when he and Cilla were fighting villains. He always believed that because they were supposed to be better, and that they were the good guys anyway, the villains should just give up. But they didn't, and that was always exasperating to Grover, who found battle to be an anxiety-producing event, not to mention it tended to ruin a lot of his good outfits. So when he was bantering with the knight, he thought that since he was supposed to be Phillip, and Phillip was the greatest warrior, somehow the knight would just say, "Well, okay, you can have Winona." But that didn't happen.

So there Grover was, standing two-thirds of the way to the dais where Winona was, with a crowd of Lords and Ladies on either side of him, and this knight who might or might not be the Black Avenger rushing toward him. It was in this moment that Grover came to the conclusion that action was indeed called for. Action on his part, because Romeo, who had been his faithful and cringing sycophant up to that moment, was now cringing away from him, and he was all alone.

The only thing that troubled him—or rather, it should be said, one of the things that troubled him—was that he was unfamiliar with how to conduct such a battle. All his life he had spent practicing the art of the rapier. This was the only weapon with which he had any familiarity. The vagaries of the great sword eluded him. How was one supposed to artfully dodge, and to parry, and to riposte, and put on a good show? All he knew about this weapon was that it was very useful in the area of wholesale killing and dismemberment. His first experience with the blade had been watching Phillip's Dude Knights throwing themselves boldly into the Sousterhoven forces, swinging their swords as if they were light as sticks and using them to cut their opponents into pieces. This sort of battle didn't seem like it could be faked. If one practiced battle in that manner, either he or the knight would end up dead, and it would probably be he since he wasn't wearing a helmet.

But even though he had all this against him, he did have his superior size and superior strength to help him out. Unfortunately this is about all he had going for him. That and the fact that he was *supposed* to win this fight.

So with little mental preparation on his part, Grover entered the contest between himself and this unknown, unnamed knight, and tried to do his best. And to be fair, Grover did do his best. But that wasn't really what mattered in this contest. What mattered was that you did better than the other.

He matched the knight's blade, blow for blow. Grover found that the sword could be used to parry, except stopping the other's sword often resulted in a numbing feeling up one's arms. Not the best of feelings. And for the most part that was all that Grover did. He would see the knight's sword whistling down, and in a frenzy would lift up his own blade to counter. There would be that ringing sound, followed by a numbing reverberation, and then both of them would be stepping back to appraise the situation. In that moment Grover would think, God, how long is this going to last? Then the knight would attack again.

All along there would be cheers of encouragement from the various Lords and Ladies, telling him how to take on the knight. But Grover didn't use any of this advice, or even hear much of it, because he was caught up in his own world. Wondering, wondering, how long this would last.

At the moment when it seemed that it would never end, when the knight seemed like he wouldn't stop coming, and when Grover thought about giving up, the fight did come to an end and the knight did stop coming. Just as Grover was wondering why the knight was taking so long to resume the fight, he suddenly pulled off his helmet, and everyone could see that it was Erich who had played the part of the challenging knight.

The next moment, Erich was shaking his hand, there was a healthy bit of clapping going on, and Romeo was pulling him toward the dais to get the rest of the wedding over with.

"Not bad," Romeo was saying.

Grover felt weak all over, but happy. He had actually managed to stand his ground. He thought that maybe this great sword fighting was for sissies after all. "It wasn't so hard," Grover responded.

"Are you ready to sing the Woo Song now?" Romeo asked.

"Woo Song," Grover said.

"Yeah," Romeo said, and plucked the lyric sheet out of Grover's belt. "It's your turn for the solo, dude."

Grover stared at Romeo. "I've got to sing?"

"Yeah, time to show your sensitive side," Romeo said.

Grover gulped. This was worse than the fight.

Option Number Four

At this point, Cilla might have wished her only problem was singing a love song to Winona, or, knowing Cilla, she might have found that problem to be worse. But since she didn't have the option to choose from a convenient menu of problems, where anxiety over self-worth was always the special of the day, she had to deal with the only problem she had. And since the problem she had was one of her own making, she might have regretted her former actions—namely, running into a secret tunnel after a member of an underground organization that was prone to stabbing its own members to keep their faces secret—but she didn't. She only regretted that she didn't have her *Argh* knife by her side, because then she might have been able to handle the situation better.

As she lay there on the floor, not really thinking about much of anything, Louis and Gerald entered the room in a state of confusion and flux, and saw only Cilla there, and not one sign of their friend, who had managed to slither even further down the stairs.

At this point in time, several things could have occurred. One, Louis and Gerald could have invited Cilla on a picnic in the countryside. Two, Louis and Gerald could have pulled out knives and killed Cilla without thinking much about it. Three, they could have turned around and left the room because their friend obviously wasn't there. Or four, they could have investigated the matter further. Of these choices, which Louis and Gerald weren't aware they had, they managed to pick number four, though if they had realized they had the option of number one, going out on a picnic, they would have done that, because they were sort of nervous about all this behind-the-scenes, backstabbing stuff. Even the best of rebels sometimes had qualms about what they were doing, and Louis and Gerald happened not to be the best, with many qualms. They weren't the type to stab first and then stab second and then maybe consider who they were stabbing and why they were doing it. So at that moment when something had to be

144

done, because otherwise there is nothing to write about, and the scene ends, Louis and Gerald exercised option number four.

"Where's Thearin?" Louis asked. He was the one in the black cloak and mask.

"Yes, where's Thearin?" asked Gerald. He was the other guy in the black cloak and mask.

"Thearin?" Cilla uttered, rising to a sitting position.

"We heard him cry out," Louis said.

"Yes," Gerald agreed.

"I haven't seen him," Cilla said.

"This isn't good," Louis said to Gerald.

"Not good at all," Gerald replied to Louis.

"Thearin should be here," Louis said. "What are *you* doing here?"

One may venture to ask at this point, and with valid substantive reason, why two followers of the Black Avenger would simply ask Cilla what had happened to their friend, when they would most likely see any intruder as a violator, and one not just to be idly questioned. And the answer is that things took a darker turn at this point.

"Hey," Gerald cried out. "There he is. He killed him."

Cilla stood up. "I'm sorry you had to see that."

It was at this point that Gerald and Louis called out for help.

It must be said for Cilla that she made a desperate attempt to kill these two gentlemen, and thus single-handedly subvert the whole plot of the Black Avenger, saving Grover and whoever else from death, but her attempt failed, and several members of the Black Avenger following came into the small chamber and were able to subdue Cilla, whereupon Cilla was to remark, "Oh shit," and would have said a great many other unprintable things, had not one of the black-cloaked figures decided to have her gagged as well as bound, and so Cilla was never, ever able to adequately voice her frustration, but instead had to sit in that chamber and endure the humiliation of being captured.

You may ask again at this point why they just didn't kill her. But then my only answer was that they promised to.

"We'll let the Black Avenger deal with him later," remarked one black-cloaked figure.

Which didn't really boost Cilla's spirits a whole lot. Because not only had she failed to stop the plot, she had failed to warn Grover about drinking the wine, and now she was going to die by the hand of the first guy she had been attracted to in a long time.

All in all, Cilla wasn't a very happy person at this moment. But we will leave her in her predicament, as we go back to Grover, who happened to think that everything was going according to plan, and that the adventure was going to be a success after all. Which shows how little Grover knew.

Do You Take This Woman?

Winona waited and watched patiently as Phillip made his challenge to the room. When the unknown knight accepted the challenge she became excited because she thought it might be the real thing. She hoped that Phillip would be defeated. But that didn't happen, and the knight turned out to be Erich. Apparently it had all been set up between them. And she thought she had Erich under her thumb.

After that incident she started to get fidgety. Now that she was close to poisoning Phillip she could hardly wait. She kept glancing over at the altar where the wine chalice sat filled with the tainted wine. Soon it would be all over. Phillip would be choking and gasping for life, and she would be free. She was so eager to get the wedding over with that she said she accepted Phillip in only the first verse of his Woo Song.

"What?" Grover asked.

"I accept," Winona was saying. She was standing up and declaring she wanted to marry him.

"I told you the song was good," Romeo said, nudging Grover. Grover glanced down at the lyrics that he had sung.

> I love you, and I'll give you the reasons why.
> First of all you're a woman and I'm a guy.
> If that shouldn't convince you we should be together
> Just listen up and I'll tell you better.
> Second of all, you're already with my child.
> Face it, babe, you're already defiled.
> If that isn't enough I'll tell you more:
> I'm the only one who doesn't think you're a whore.

Grover shook his head. "Something's wrong here. This song's awful."

"It's not the song," Romeo said. "It's how you sing it."

"I sung it awful," Grover said.

"Well, there's no accounting for taste," Romeo said.

147

Winona was speaking again. "I accept you for marriage."
Grover shrugged and looked up at Winona. "Well, okay."

Up above the wedding, Cilla was tied up and trying to work her
way out of her bonds. One of the black cloakers was in the room
to watch that she didn't escape. He stood with his back to her and
stared out the slitted window. In his hand he held a bow, and had
an arrow loosely hanging from the string.

They had taken her belt and tied it tightly around her wrists, and
they had taken another belt and used it to tie her feet together.
While they had applied the restraints Cilla had flexed her muscles,
so that when they were done tying, she could relax and have a
little room with which to work. Even though she had been
captured and had been left to sit, she wasn't ready to give up. So
very quietly she worked at the bonds, loosening them, grabbing at
the knots with her fingers. The knots weren't very difficult to
loosen. You couldn't tie really complicated knots with belts. So it
would only be a matter of time until she was free.

Grover ascended the dais to meet Winona. In front of him was the
altar where the wine stood in the goblet. Nearby was the high
priest who was presiding over the wedding. And hovering not far
behind him stood Old Lord Phillip, who was overseeing the whole
affair.

To his left were Winona, Erika, and the ladies-in-waiting.

To his right were Romeo and a few of the Dude Knights who
had been assigned as an escort.

Once the wedding was over, Grover and Winona would file out,
the flower bearers preceding them to make a path of petals to walk
on. Behind them would follow the ladies-in-waiting and the Dude
Knights as they made their way to the ballroom for the feast.

But for now, Grover stood facing Winona, taking her small
plump hands in his own. He stared into her extravagant green eyes
and for a moment lost himself.

"What?" Grover asked when he came out of the spell.

"I didn't say anything," Winona said.

"How come you seem so happy?" Grover asked.

"No reason," Winona replied.

Grover shook his head.

Behind them in the church, the benches had been moved closer
and the most prominent Lords and Ladies in the land sat near the
dais. Grover saw the faces of Thorn, Richard, and Young Dianna.
He couldn't recall the other people's names.

Grover whispered to Romeo. "Where's Voss?"

Romeo shrugged. "You can worry about Voss after the wedding."

The priest had completed his private prayer in front of the altar and was now turning to address the assembly. He smiled at Grover and then at Winona.

"I am here to oversee that the wedding of Phillip and Winona is right in the eyes of God. When they drink from the chalice and taste the wine, which symbolizes the commitment and ties that bind them together, they will be drinking the wine of life that God has to offer. If for some reason these two should not be joined together the wine will change into vinegar and their union will be dissolved."

"Yeah, yeah," Winona whispered. "Let's get to it."

Grover gulped. This was it.

The priest raised the chalice into the air. "This wine is the wine of life. Bless this wine and see your will be done." He then lowered the chalice and brought it to where Grover and Winona stood hand in hand.

"When you both drink from this wine your marriage will be consummated in the eyes of God."

Grover nodded.

The priest held out the golden chalice.

Winona gazed up into Grover's eyes. "Take the chalice, dear."

Grover hesitated. "You first."

"The man should drink first, isn't that right, Father?" Winona asked.

The priest nodded. And he placed the chalice near Grover's hands. "Take it," he said.

Grover took the chalice from the priest. He looked down and saw the red fluid against the gold interior of the cup. He hesitated to drink.

"Everyone's watching," Winona said.

Grover sighed and lifted the cup to his lips.

Cilla Saves the Day

The stained-glass window behind the altar shattered into thousands of pieces as the Black Avenger broke through the glass. He walked through the window and onto the dais calmly as the church broke out into pandemonium. The Lords and Ladies got up to either flee or pull out their weapons, while those on the dais backed away from the Black Avenger's advance. Behind him came others dressed in black cloaks and masks and the only way one could distinguish who was actually the Black Avenger was by the red scarf he wore around his neck.

"Oh no," Grover said, lowering the chalice from his lips. "I knew this was going to happen." The Black Avenger was here to kill him after all. And after he had been so close to getting married and succeeding with the adventure.

The contingent of Dude Knights went to pull out their swords, but arrows promptly came from above and landed in their backs, their arms, and their skulls and they fell to the ground. The ladies-in-waiting screamed and ran from the stage.

On the church floor, the rest of the guests were finding that the exit was also blocked by members of the Black Avenger.

Grover, seeing he had nowhere to go, stood his ground.

The Black Avenger walked past the altar and approached Grover and Winona. Grover looked around for his sword but didn't see it anywhere. He had handed it off to one of the Dude Knights to hold until the ceremony was over.

"Where's your invitation?" Grover asked.

"All I want is the Lady Winona," the Black Avenger said.

"You can't have her," Grover said. "She's mine."

"No, I'm not," Winona said, and took a step away from Grover. "It's about time you got here," she said to the Black Avenger.

"Hey," Grover protested.

The Black Avenger took Winona's hand and then pushed her slightly behind him.

"Hey," Winona cried out. "I don't have to go with you."

The Black Avenger stood still and the rest of the church grew quiet and looked to see what he had to say.

"As you have already seen, I have this room under control. You will do what I say. If you resist, specially placed archers will ensure you don't resist for long. I have not come here to bribe or extort you, but to take what is mine. All I want is the Lady Winona."

Cilla's forehead was covered with perspiration when she finally broke free of the bonds that tied her wrists. Carefully she lowered the belt to the floor so as not to make a sound. With her free hands she removed the gag from her mouth. She wanted to spit out the taste but knew that would only attract attention.

She looked at the black cloaker closely to see if he was paying attention. Just then she heard a tremendous crashing sound. It was glass. Lots of glass breaking. The black cloaker stiffened and pulled back the arrow in his bow.

That was the sign. The Black Avenger had made his move. They were going to kill Grover. Cilla grabbed out at the walls with her hands to pull herself up. She didn't have time to untie the belt around her feet. She had to stop the archer.

She heard the twanging sound of other bows sending arrows in flight. In her mind she imagined them all going for Grover. But even though she couldn't stop the others she could stop this one. And she leaped across the room.

But instead of preventing the arrow from being launched, she knocked the man's arm so that the arrow, which had been aimed at Grover, was knocked off course and went flying off at a different angle.

The arrow flew straight and true and ended up in the right eye socket of Winona, who was killed instantly. She fell to the ground in sight of everyone but the Black Avenger, who had to turn around to see what the commotion was. After that, the room could no longer be contained. The guests scattered in all directions and the Black Avenger fled back out the broken stained-glass window.

Grover was left standing on the dais as knights ran past him to chase the Black Avenger, and the representatives from Winona's principality of Astertov came up to see about Winona. With a sigh, Grover looked at the chalice of wine in his hand and raised it once again to his lips.

Only to hear, "Don't drink the wine, Grover, it's poisoned," shouted from up above.

Grover dropped the chalice and the wine spilled to the floor.

Up above, Cilla sagged to the floor of the small chamber, her task completed. She had saved Grover from being poisoned, and the plot of the Black Avenger had been foiled.

"Not bad," she said, patting herself on the back. "Not bad at all."

PART VI

Scenes from the Aftermath

Call Me Floyd

It was the middle of the afternoon, and a servant carried a tray with two glasses along a white gravel path. The path took him by a section of azalea bushes, over a gaily painted wooden bridge, and to the entrance of a pagoda where Beogoat and Frederick sat in reclining chairs. In the background there was framed the beautiful Castle Reichton, almost glowing in the reflection of the sunlight of its high spires, which did not take away at all from the beauty of the great gardens stretched out all around them.

The servant bowed to Frederick. "Thank you," Frederick said, and accepted the tray, setting it down on the small table between him and Beogoat.

Beogoat reached out and sipped his drink casually, making a face. "Not enough alcohol," he finally said.

Frederick pushed back his hair to regard Beogoat, but it was a futile effort since it fell directly back into his face again. "You understand that this is going to be a question-and-answer session."

"No torture?" Beogoat asked.

"We've been over that," Frederick said. "It depends. The application of pain as a stimulus to mental performance has been debated for some time, and the conclusions I think are rather doubtful. I've written a treatise on the subject."

"How civilized," Beogoat replied dryly.

"We think so," Frederick said, and reached out to take a sip from his drink. "I'm not really in favor of the pain methods of my counterparts in the profession. You have to clean up all the blood . . . and the screaming, begging, and pleading really get on your nerves after a while."

"I can imagine," Beogoat said, who could imagine no such thing. "Must be horrible," he added in what sounded like a sympathetic voice.

"It was," Frederick said ruefully. And then he looked straight at Beogoat. "But if I have to," and here he lifted up his infamous black sack that jangled, "I can deliver unbearable amounts of pain, without causing any undue damage to your general appearance. I'm rather proud of that."

"As you should be," Beogoat said. And he noticed that his hand trembled as he set down the glass.

"Thank you," Frederick said.

"So what are we doing today?" Beogoat asked. He had been here for almost two weeks and as yet nothing had happened. He thought he had been forgotten about until he had been brought out of his cell today to this pagoda in the Reichton gardens to meet with Frederick. He had thought about escape the past few days, but that's as close as he got to it. He still couldn't do any magic.

Frederick didn't answer his question immediately, but instead pulled out a sheaf of papers and a lead pencil. These he made room for on the small table, placing the glasses on the floor. "I'm going to ask some questions and you're going to give some answers."

"No pain?" Beogoat clarified. "Just questions?"

"Yes," Frederick said. "And answers."

"That's all?" Beogoat made sure.

Frederick nodded. "Yes, and you can call me Floyd."

"Why?" Beogoat asked. "Is this all part of your hidden agenda?"

"I don't have a hidden agenda," Frederick said, horrified. "I'm surprised you made such an assumption."

Beogoat, baffled by the reaction to his offhand remark, mumbled, "Whatever."

Frederick scribbled on the paper without looking at Beogoat and explained. "The idea behind this interview is to understand what motivates you and why you answer or won't answer as you do. I do this because the philosophy behind torture is to ultimately arrive at the truth. The truth, as you know, can be painful. But I'm a believer in truth. A passionate believer in truth. Us torturers despise lies. It only gets in the way of truth and clouds the issue. We want everything to be made clear and precise. Lies make us angry. That is why we have to resort to pain." He looked up at Beogoat now. "You understand what I'm saying?"

"Lies make you unhappy, and you hurt people for it," Beogoat said.

"Something like that," Frederick replied. "I just want you to understand what I'm trying to do before I begin. Do you have any questions?"

"What happens after I'm done answering your questions?"

"You mean when I am satisfied that we have arrived at the truth?"

"Yes," Beogoat answered.

"I don't know," Frederick said. "That is up to Hans and the law of the land."

"Oh," Beogoat said. "The law again."

"Yes, the law again," Frederick said. "So now that we are clear on what we are doing, here is the first question. The last time you spoke to Hans you would not answer his questions. The only thing you would admit to doing is exiting the reflecting pool in the company of Phillip and Voss. Is this correct?"

"That is correct," Beogoat said.

"Now," Frederick stated, "Hans says that he killed Phillip and Voss two days prior to the time you were seen exiting the reflecting pool with them. Hans has witnesses to verify this event, and I am satisfied that Hans and his witnesses are telling the truth. Phillip and Voss did die that day. Phillip was decapitated and Voss was killed by several missile wounds. Now, you exited the pool with them two days later than their death and they were alive at this point. Is that correct?"

"If they walked out with me," Beogoat said, "then they must have been alive."

"Then they were alive?" Hans clarified.

"Apparently so," Beogoat said.

Frederick scribbled down something on his paper and then looked up. "So what we have here is . . . that between the time Hans last saw Phillip . . . and the time you were last seen with Phillip . . . he came back to life."

"Is that a question?" Beogoat asked.

"No," Frederick said. "It's just a statement. We have a discrepancy here. Phillip died, ergo he should not be alive walking out of a reflecting pool with you."

Beogoat nodded.

"Were you aware of his death?" Frederick suddenly asked.

Beogoat said nothing.

"I asked a question," Frederick informed him.

"I know," Beogoat said. "But it would not be in my best interest to answer."

"So you do not know the answer, or you know the answer and you do not want to say?" Frederick asked.

"It would not be in my best interest to answer that question either," Beogoat explained.

"I see," Frederick said, and wrote something down on his

notepaper. "Can you tell me why it would not be in your best interest?"

"That also might not be in my best interest," Beogoat replied.

"Okay," Frederick said. "Let me ask you this, then: What is your best interest?"

"To not tell you anything," Beogoat answered.

"Why should you not tell me anything?" Frederick inquired.

"Because you are a representative of a government that is hostile to the one I serve."

"I see," Frederick replied. "So you are doing this out of loyalty?"

Beogoat thought for a second. "Yes. Yes, I am."

"And who exactly are you loyal to?"

"I am loyal to Westerhoven over Sousterhoven, and Wunderkinde over Westerhoven," Beogoat explained.

"And this loyalty forbids you to speak?" Frederick asked.

"Yes," Beogoat explained.

"Why are you so loyal?"

Beogoat thought for a moment. "Because it is my job here to be loyal."

"Why is it your job here to be loyal?" Frederick pressed.

"Well," Beogoat replied, "I was sent here a long time ago and my job was to make sure that Hoven was once again united. It was my assignment. And I'm not allowed to leave or move on until it is completed."

"So you are really loyal to those who sent you here?" Frederick asked.

"Well, yes," Beogoat replied. "I suppose so. I haven't really thought about it in a long time."

"But you serve Wunderkinde now?"

"Yes."

"And you support Phillip because you think he is the one who will be able to unite Hoven peacefully?"

"Yes," Beogoat said.

"And this is why you will not answer my questions concerning Phillip?"

"Yes," Beogoat said firmly. "It is not in my best interest to do so."

"Well," Frederick said, "that is very interesting. I wasn't aware of all this before. But this is all important in understanding your motivations, which is necessary if we want to arrive at the truth."

Beogoat nodded solemnly.

"So why do you support Phillip?" Frederick asked.

"Because he is the one who will unite the empire."

"Why do you think this? Is it just some gut feeling . . . or you're tired of working here and are willing to support anyone so your assignment will be over . . . or what?"

"It was prophesied," Beogoat explained.

"Well, Hans was also prophesied to rule the empire," Frederick said. "So why did you support Phillip?"

"Because it was my prophecy that predicted Phillip. He was the one I was waiting for."

"I see," Frederick said. "Did it ever occur to you that your prophecy might be wrong or that you supported the wrong man?"

"No," Beogoat said, shaking his head. A kernel of doubt began to grow.

"Which brings me to a question I always wondered about. How can two people be prophesied to do the same thing?"

"They can't," Beogoat explained. "It's not possible. There's no record of any such instance. One prophecy has to be false."

"And you believe that Hans's prophecy is false?"

"Yes," Beogoat said.

"And why is that?"

"Because it did not fit the one I foretold," Beogoat explained.

"And Phillip fit the one you foretold?"

"Yes," Beogoat said.

"Did it ever occur to you that your prophecy might be the wrong one and not Hans's?" Frederick asked.

"No," Beogoat said instantly, and then looked doubtful. "Well, a couple of times. But you can never be sure until it comes true."

"So what you're saying is that your prophecy might be wrong and thus you supported the wrong man for uniting Hoven?"

"I am?" Beogoat said. "I don't know. I'm not sure anymore."

"What aren't you sure of?"

"I don't know," Beogoat said. "I thought my prophecy was correct. I thought I supported the right man."

"But now you're not so sure?"

"Apparently," Beogoat said.

"So how can you support someone who you are not sure is the correct man?"

Beogoat shrugged.

"Okay," Frederick said, going back to his previous piece of paper. "Let's start with the relationship between you and your father."

The *Sacred Stone*

Erich paused at the entrance to the tomb of the last Hoven king. Years of research, thousands of leagues of traveling, hundreds of conversations, books, overheard rumors, and vain searches had led up to this point. He had finally discovered, where all others had failed before him, the final resting place of the *Sacred Stone*. Erich put a hand to the tomb inscription and recited, "Let the trees be my soldiers, the rocks be my missiles, and the birds be my spears, and I will have no need of an army of men."

The tomb had lain hidden for centuries, buried under vegetation and obscured by the surrounding forest, but he had found it. Behind him, his followers, dressed in the black garb which was both fashion statement and political statement, milled around, waiting for further instructions.

"What did he say?" one man asked who had overheard Erich's mumbling.

"Don't ask," another one advised him. "He's been getting weirder every day."

Erich heard none of this. He was full of the moment of discovery. And he was also impatient. He backed up and shouted, "Open it."

Three of the black cloakers moved to the entrance.

Erich stood back and watched.

It had been several weeks since he had fled Wunderkinde after the disaster of the wedding. He had ridden for his life, realizing that he could never go back now that Winona had died by one of his archers. But it wasn't only Winona who died that day, it was also the part of him that was Erich. He could never go back to his dual life. Now he could only live one life, dedicated to keeping Westerhoven pure from the taint of Sousterhoven. He saw Winona's death as a sign. He had been tempted and now she was dead. And that's what would happen to anything Sousterhoven. They only brought bad luck.

A few days after his departure he had begun to make plans. He had gathered all his followers about him, each faithful to the cause of bringing back the glory days of Westerhoven. But he realized soon that his forces were too small. He only had about two hundred knights at best. He needed to find the *Sacred Stone* so that he could have the power he needed to fulfill his goals.

For years he had known of it, but had been unaware of its location. He had spent all his private time away from the duties of knight or to liege Lord, devoted to searching for the *Stone*'s final resting place. The last written record of its location said it was in the possession of the final King of Hoven, King William X. He should have passed the *Stone* on to his son as all the kings did, but no mention of that transaction was ever recorded. William X's son, Patrick, never ruled a united Hoven. After William's death, the empire had divided into the South and West over a dispute of who should rule. The rulers of both South and West were both brothers to William X. Since neither would allow the other to rule, South and West had remained split and each ruled as king in his own territory. But this didn't last very long, and soon Hoven was divided into many different principalities, each claiming its right to the throne. But none ever succeeded in securing that right.

If Patrick had the *Sacred Stone* within his possession, he hadn't used it, because no mention of it was ever made. And so, Erich reasoned, William must have hidden the *Stone*. But no book or tome, or any sage, could say where he had hidden it. Many said he had broken it and that is why the empire broke, and he had given half to each brother and that's why the empire divided in half. And each half of the stone was further divided and with each division a principality was born. But that was pure myth.

And so for years Erich had searched for some clue, for any reference to the final resting place, until one day he found a small reference, in an old musty book, about an old Lord who had served under William. The book was actually a memoir, and the Lord seemed to think everything he did was important, which actually wasn't, except for the mention of William X's burial. In it he listed all the articles buried with William, and among the items a strange stone was mentioned. It was white as pearl, as big as a fist, and round as a sphere, with a green streak running through it. And even though no one had ever described the *Sacred Stone* except to say it was beautiful and powerful, Erich knew that this was it. The last king had presumably subscribed to the theory that you could take it with you.

So then it all came down to finding William X's tomb. But no mention, anywhere, was made of the location of his tomb, except to say that William desired to be buried in a safe and secret place, and not in the crypts under the palace in the ancient city of Hoven. And so he wasn't, because when Erich had looked for William's name on those deteriorating nameplates, he had not found it.

This was as far as his search went until he put two unrelated facts together. One was the legend that the location of the *Sacred Stone* could be revealed by gazing into the reflecting pool, and the other was that the *Sacred Stone* was buried in William's tomb. These two facts clicked in his mind. To look in the pool all you would see is the sky. But what you were really seeing was William X's tomb. Because the pool had been built at the same time as William's death. Unbeknownst to everyone, he had had a chamber dug beneath the pool with a tunnel extending out into the forest. It was the only way in. So the reflecting pool did reveal the location of the *Stone*, but one had to look beneath the surface, not on the surface.

The three men pulled at the stone slab that covered the entrance of the tunnel. They used sticks and knives and finally were able to open it a crack. They pulled harder and the stone covering fell to the ground with a thud and the dark smell of earth and decay hit their nostrils.

Erich smiled and went up to the three. "Good work, Ulrich, Benson, Alfred." He slapped them on the back.

"I'm not Ulrich," one of them said.

"Who is?" Erich asked, looking at the similarly clad men, their faces covered by demon masks.

"Ulrich didn't even come with us. He stayed at the camp," the second one said.

"Oh," Erich replied.

"And I'm not Alfred," the third one said.

"And I'm not Benson," the second one said.

"Oh," Erich said, tugging at his chin.

"It's the damn uniforms and masks," the first one said. "We can't tell who's who with them on. Can't we take them off once in a while?"

Erich stepped back, horrified. "What? What! No, absolutely not. How else will we strike fear in the hearts of our enemies?"

"You know," the third one said, "I wasn't even here when we voted on the costumes."

"Uniforms," the second one corrected.

"Uniforms," the third one repeated.

"That's because we didn't vote," Erich said. "It's traditional that we all wear the same thing so they don't know how many we are or who are our leaders."

"Oh," the first one said. "So we're just doing this to protect your skin. Doesn't do much for us. Some fool will attack us just to get to you."

"Well, yes," Erich said. "If you wish to extend the theory . . ."

"Now," the third one interjected, "if we at least had some different masks. I don't know—pigs or cows or something. Something to make us different. My brother-in-law is great with that sort of thing and . . ."

"Yeah," the first one said. "If we could just have a little individuality of expression, I'm sure it would boost morale, besides the fact we would know who we were talking to and . . ."

"Shut up," Erich said. "No more discussion of the costume."

"Uniform," the second one corrected.

"Uniform," Erich spat out. "Now get back to your posts and when I'm done I want to know who the hell you are so I can discipline you."

The three men said nothing and walked out silently. When they were out of earshot the first turned to the second and said, "Did you notice he's been acting a little tense lately?"

Erich didn't waste any time getting to the tunnel. He paused for a moment once inside and ignited his lantern. Not much was revealed except for the unusual arched ceiling of the tunnel. The walls and ceiling had been worked with stone and in places the stone had fallen in and there were piles of dirt, but not enough to constitute any impediment to his progress.

When he reached the end of the tunnel he found a wooden door, but it had rotted through and had fallen to the floor. And beyond the door was a simple rectangular chamber, decorated like a sitting room. Chairs and tables were set out as if someone were expecting guests for tea. And in the middle of the room, on a raised platform, was the coffin of William X.

Erich ignored all else and walked directly to the coffin, placing his lantern on one of the tables nearby. With his free hands he reached out to remove the lid. "It has to be inside," he muttered to himself.

The lid was sealed shut so he had to take his knife and break the seal. Once broken it wasn't too hard to lift up the wooden top and push it aside.

Inside, among a deteriorated lining, lay the skeletal remains of William X. His clothing was tattered and frayed to bits. Gold ornaments hung loosely on old bone. And in the pelvis area, where it had probably lain on his stomach cupped between two lifeless hands, had fallen the pearl-white and green-streaked *Sacred Stone*.

He reached in and grasped the *Stone* firmly in his hand. It was cold, but felt like it pulsed with life. He rolled it back from hand to hand, marveling at its touch. And then momentarily lost his hold. It fell on his foot, crushing his toe.

"*Ack,*" Erich cried as he reached down for the stone, bumping his head on the coffin. "*Ack,*" he cried again, and chased the rolling *Stone* across the room to the entrance, where it stopped by one his black cloakers' feet. Erich grasped at the *Stone* and looked up.

"Ah, sorry," the black cloaker explained. "You were gone so long and . . . and there's someone here to meet you. I think it's Prince Thorn."

Erich stood up and smiled beneath his mask. He had the *Stone*, and now he might even have the aid of Prince Thorn. It seemed as if everything had worked out to his advantage after all. And to think his mother had never said he would amount to much.

No Way Out

Grover held the lizardskin book in the flat palm of his hand and used the other to massage his forehead while he concentrated.

"You know," Cilla said from where she sat on the couch, "if you keep rubbing your head like that you're going to start losing hair."

"I'm trying to concentrate," Grover said. "Besides, baldness makes you more attractive."

"Who told you that?" Cilla asked.

"No one," Grover said. "It just seemed to make sense."

"You fool," Cilla laughed. "You've been duped by the third-person-omniscient narrator."

"I have?" Grover asked in surprise. "Wow, I hadn't noticed."

Cilla shook her head. "I see your beard is coming in fine."

"Thanks," Grover said, bringing his hand down to caress the blond whiskers that proliferated over his face. He had grown the beard because Phillip had possessed one, and he didn't know how long the disguise spell was going to last. So it was better to grow one, just in case it didn't last, so he could at least look partially like Phillip. "I think it makes me look more mature."

"You mean ripe," Cilla said. "Like you're ready to be plucked or harvested?"

"No," Grover pouted. "Are you going to let me try the spell or not?"

"Are you sure it's the right spell?" Cilla asked. "I don't want to start any fires in here."

"I guess so," Grover said. "This stuff is harder to read than a VCR programming manual. I don't know what I'm doing."

"That's obvious," Cilla said.

Grover made a face. "Well, here it goes." Grover stared hard at the page and wiggled his left foot as he did so. "Iguana, iguana, iguana, banana." And then Grover looked up. "Are we home?"

Cilla craned her neck and peered around the sun-room of Phillip's chambers. "Nope, still here. Are you sure that's it?"

"That's what it says," Grover said.

"Let me see," Cilla said, and took the book from Grover's hand. She stared at it for a moment. "Hey, this is a recipe, not a spell."

"They look the same," Grover said defensively.

Cilla turned the book over and read the cover aloud. "*Great Recipes for Wizards.*"

"Well, it sounded like a sorcery book," Grover said. "How was I supposed to know?"

Cilla made a face and put the book down. "Let me try now," she said, and lifted a book to her lap that was already open. "Are you ready?" she asked Grover.

"I was ready a long time ago," Grover said.

"Okay," Cilla said, and read from the written page. "O sacred kumquat, O foul zucchini, O ichor orange and thong bikini. Take out the trash, and send out for beer, deliver me from this place, get me the hell out of here." And then Cilla sneezed.

Grover and Cilla waited in tense silence. The air seemed to waver before them. But nothing else happened.

Finally Grover asked, "Were you supposed to sneeze?"

"No," Cilla said.

"Well, jeez, Cilla," Grover exclaimed. "Then what did you do it for?"

"The book was dusty," Cilla shouted back. "At least the air seemed to waver on my spell."

"Well, a lot of good that did," Grover said. "We're still here."

"You want me to try again?" Cilla asked.

Grover opened his mouth to say yes, but just then his enthusiasm and verve were deflated. "No, forget it." He sat down on a couch and threw up his legs. "You know, somehow I get the feeling that we're going to be stuck here for a while."

Cilla took a huge bite out of an apple and between bites said, "I think you're right. Want an apple?"

.

Dude Knights

"So there I was, right?" said the first knight. "Just me and Lord Dubois. And he tells me I can't tilt for shit. Well, I tell you that I can unseat any dude from any horse, with my eyes closed. It's all in the wrist. Like this." He pulled his arm back and twisted his wrist, and then lifted up his arm. "And like whoa, the dude is on the ground, totally gone. And he tells me I can't tilt. So I call him an asshole.

"The guy gets offended," the knight went on. "I've got the right to call names when a man criticizes me. It's part of the honor code, right? Or am I from a totally different planet? So he pulls this major shit fit and wants to have it out right there. Well, I say, anytime, anyplace, dude. Because he's really beginning to piss me off.

"So he decides he wants to joust, just to up me, I guess. And I'm still banged up from that fight we had with the Smoles. But I don't say nothin', 'cause I'm cool, and he'll think I'm trying to lame out. So he gets on his high horse. And I get on mine. We get our tilting spears. And then we're riding, right? To see who's the better man. The first time he rides by he lifts his spear just to show he's in no hurry to finish me off. I lift mine, because I can wait too. And then this totally gnarly thing happens. We wheel around for a second pass. He's bearing down on me and I'm bearing down on him. I extend my spear, give it a little twist, like so, I get right up under his shield and boom!" The knight clapped his hands together. "The guy's flipping through the air doing all sorts of gymnastic moves he could probably never do if he tried. Lands right on his left arm, breaks it, and then won't even admit he was wrong. Do you believe that?"

The other knight, who had been picking gristle from his teeth all along, looked up and absently said, "Bogus."

"Right, that's exactly what I'm saying," the first knight said.

There was some commotion, and other knights in the yard started to stand up and look toward the castle entrance. "Phillip must be here," the first knight said. And then they both got up as

166

Phillip came out to the courtyard where practice was held every afternoon.

"Okay, okay," Grover said, stopping in front of the knights who were milling around. "I want you guys to get quiet."

The knights coughed, stamped their feet, and finally became quiet.

"Okay, good," Grover said, and looked at the knights. "I know that lately there's been some changes and that some of you've been complaining. Well, I want that to stop. Complaining annoys me."

The knights shuffled about but said nothing.

"I know in the past we've done things differently, but in the past I was a different man," Grover said. "I'm not the same man today that I was when we went to kick Hans's butt at the ancient city of Hoven. You can almost say that I'm a completely new and different man, and that wouldn't be very far from the truth."

The first knight leaned over to the second knight. "What is he talking about?"

"Beats me," the second knight responded.

"There have been new developments, and experience has hardened me. The woman I loved was killed right before my very eyes and it was instigated by my best friend, who I thought I could trust."

The first knight raised his hand.

"Yes?" Grover inquired.

"You really didn't love Winona, did you? I thought you just got her knocked up so you could forge a political alliance. You always said to make the most of your opportunities."

"Ah," Grover said. "I might have said that before, but I'm not saying it now. I'm a new man now, and yes, I did like Winona, even though we didn't always get along."

"Who is he fooling?" the second knight whispered to the first. The first knight shrugged.

"As you know," Grover said, "it's very likely we'll go to war."

"All right," a cheer went up from the knights. "War, war, war, no longer will life be a bore."

Grover grimaced. "I know you're all excited, and war is an exciting thing. But it's also a bad thing. My former friend says we should keep Westerhoven separate. And to him I say: What do you know?"

"Right, what does he know?" several knights shouted.

"And Hans thinks that he should rule all of Hoven. But I don't think he knows what he's talking about either."

"Yeah," a chorus of knights added.

"But both these guys have made it their mission to kick our butts. And are we going to let them do it?"

"No way," all the knights shouted.

"Good," Grover said when the uproar died down. "I'm glad to hear it. I just want you guys to know that I need your support. There's tough times ahead of us and it isn't always going to be easy." Grover's gaze went to the face of each knight, up and down the line, sensing their feelings. When he was done he asked, "Any questions?"

The first knight raised his hand again.

"Yes?" Grover asked.

"What's your point?"

Grover seemed confused by the question. "Actually I don't know if I have one. Just hang tough, and remember who you're throwing your lives out on the line for. Me. And if you ever get the feeling that maybe I shouldn't be dying for this guy, dismiss it from your mind. You're absolutely wrong. When Hoven is finally united, you guys will all rise with me. Each and every one of you."

"All right," the knights shouted, and came forward to lift Grover up and carry him around the courtyard.

Grover just smiled. He was getting the hang of this Phillip thing after all.

The *Ice Caves*

"Cold, very cold," Hans said, rubbing his arms. His breath shot out and became a small cloud.

"That's why they call them the *Ice Caves*," Floyd said cheerfully.

"Oh," Hans said absently. "I just thought it was one of those picturesque names. You take a pitch-black cave and they call it Dark Cave. And a cave where someone was once scared they call it Scary Cave. Or someone will call it Dave's Cave just because Dave is king and it's a cheap present to give. I never thought there was really going to be ice in the caves. And it's summer. Shouldn't this stuff be melting?"

"This ice," Floyd began, "is the residue of an ice dragon's barf, or the remnants of an ancient ice glacier. Scientists still disagree whether there was really an ice age or if ice was just created, by, you know, God."

"Did I ask for an explanation?"

"Sorry," Floyd said. "I just thought you wanted to know."

"I wanted to know if the ice should be melting," Hans said. "That's all. If I wanted to know anything else I would ask that question."

"Sorry," Floyd said. "But to answer one question raises other questions and if you don't answer them all, all you are left with is a partial truth, and that is a lie."

"Thank you," Hans said, "for deliberately trying my patience further. All I want to know is about the melting."

"Oh," Floyd said. "Well, yes, it does melt. Actually the cave used to be called Smoking Cave because the condensation from the melting ice would form a cloud of vapor in the air. Which brings us to the legend of . . ."

"Floyd," Hans warned, "you're babbling again. Try not to do that."

"Sorry," Floyd said.

"Don't be sorry," Hans said. "Just tell me a few jokes."

"Okay," Floyd replied. "What did the one prisoner say to the torturer when he rammed a red-hot poker up his butt?"

"What did he say?" Hans asked.

"Ouch, that hurts," Floyd answered.

Hans stopped and regarded Floyd, who still had a smile on his face. "That wasn't very funny."

"It's a torturer's joke," Floyd explained. "They're the only ones I know."

"Didn't I tell you to go around and gather more material?"

Floyd shook his head. "No."

"Well, I should have."

"I will do so when we return to Reichton," Floyd replied.

Hans nodded and cupped his hands over his mouth to blow hot air on them. "So Beogoat said that he and Beoweasel took the dead bodies of Phillip and Voss and put them in here?"

Floyd nodded. "Yes, he put them here to avoid the decay of their bodies. He said he was going to thaw them out once the two impostors were done with the job."

"I didn't ask that," Hans said.

Floyd shrugged. "Force of habit."

"So where are they?" Hans asked.

Floyd checked his notes. "He said he put them around the first corner, in a niche, and built a little snow wall to hide them. There's a stick denoting the place."

Hans nodded and they advanced further into the cave.

"You never told me," Hans started, "but did Beogoat ever say anything bad about me?"

"You mean during the interrogation?" Floyd asked.

"Yes," Hans replied.

Floyd shook his head. "No, he didn't. But as I recall, when you banished him, he called you a dirty so-and-so who should rot in . . ."

"Floyd," Hans cried. "I didn't ask that."

Floyd smiled sheepishly.

"Did you get the impression that he didn't like me?"

"Oh no," Floyd said.

"You like me, don't you, Floyd?"

"Yes," Floyd said evenly. "You're all right."

"Good," Hans said, apparently satisfied.

They rounded the first corner and saw a stick standing out of the wall.

"There it is," Floyd said.

Together they moved to the snow wall and pulled it apart. When the snow was all about their ankles and their bare hands were numb from digging, they had revealed the hidden bodies of Phillip and Voss. They lay faceup on the icy surface of the cave. Both bodies were covered with a thin layer of ice. But otherwise, they looked the same as the day they died. Except for the fact that Phillip's head was now lying on his chest, bearing that look of confusion right before it was disconnected from his shoulders. And Voss had a few dark stains on his clothing where the crossbow bolts had punctured his skin.

"And there they are," Hans said, and pulled Phillip's head free from the ice by yanking on the long hair. "I wonder what Phillip would say if he knew that he had died and two hired heroes were taking the place of him and his servant."

"Probably 'No way, dude,' " Floyd suggested. "Or something along those lines."

"Maybe," Hans said. "It's just too bad he's not here so I can say his prophecy was wrong." Hans looked closely at the frozen face. "You were wrong, Phillip, and I was right. How do you like that?"

Phillip's face said nothing.

Floyd waited until Hans was done gloating and asked, "Do you still want the bodies preserved and prepared for viewing?"

"Yes," Hans said. "You said you knew how to do that?"

"Yes, all torturers are versed in the art of taxidermy."

"Very good," Hans replied, and dropped the head back down on Phillip's chest. "But do you know someone else who can do it? I'll be needing you for some other tasks."

"There's Byron, my assistant," Floyd suggested.

"He'll do," Hans said. And he turned away from the corpses. "Come, I must show you something. We'll have the others remove the bodies."

Floyd nodded and they walked out onto the parapet that overlooked the valley below in Westerhoven. They were now in enemy territory, located between the provinces of Hoenecker and Vagner. They had come here secretly just to remove the bodies of Phillip and Voss.

Below them, the valley stretched out into patches of full-blooming forest. Down the center flowed a glittering stream, and some cattle and horses grazed along its banks. But right in front of this beautiful view was a drop of three hundred feet onto jagged rock.

"You know," Floyd said, "those heroes taking the place of Phillip and Voss is what the first omen was talking about."

Hans was startled and a strange look came over his face. "Don't talk of that now."

Floyd nodded.

"Do you see the valley before you?" Hans asked.

"Is this what you wanted to show me?"

"Yes."

"Then I see it," Floyd said. "It's very nice."

"But that's not all," Hans said. "This valley I will one day conquer, as is my doom. I will rule all of Westerhoven and Sousterhoven."

"Unless the other prophecy comes true," Floyd pointed out. "Don't forget that. You might fail in that endeavor."

"Yes, yes," Hans said. "I am aware of it every moment. I feel the weight of the curse on me like a yoke that can't be cast off. Yes, I am aware. And thank you for once again making me conscious of the pain that throbs within me every day."

"Sorry," Floyd said. "But aren't you just being a little over-dramatic about this doom thing?"

"No," Hans said. "But when a man is cursed he needs his friends. I can trust you."

"Thank you," Floyd said. "I like you too."

Hans reached out and put his arm around Floyd's shoulders. "And as you know, once I am King of Hoven I will be betrayed by my best friend."

"But I wouldn't ever . . ." Floyd began, becoming aware of Hans's tone. "And I wouldn't say we were best friends." Floyd tried to disengage himself from Hans's arm.

"But how can I ever be safe?" Hans asked, and pushed Floyd off the cliff.

"Hey . . . I . . ." Floyd cried out, falling face-forward, taking a long nosedive into the stones below.

Hans waited until he heard the thump and then shivered. "It was the curse that made me do it," he said quietly in explanation. "The damn curse." And he looked at his hands, which were still twitching. "Sorry, Floyd, but the parting of friends is always painful."

How to Plan a War

There were eight Lords in Westerhoven, and of the eight, one was dead, one had betrayed the cause, and one suspected something wrong about Phillip. All the others were faithful to the cause in various degrees and fashions, according to the relationship they made with Phillip and how they were brought into the alliance.

The seven Lords, minus the one who had betrayed the cause, had kept in contact throughout the summer to plan how they would meet the Sousterhoven nations in war. For war had come suddenly once the Lady Winona was killed. Soon after, Astertov had aligned with Reichton, and the rest of the Sousterhoven nations had joined in for various reasons that had nothing whatsoever to do with peer pressure. This combined front left Westerhoven in a weak position. Especially Wunderkinde, which was the official target of the Sousterhoven front. It was not only a war of retribution but a war of destiny, or so Hans billed it.

The Westerhoven nations banded together in defense, since they were already allied to Phillip, and this was the big battle everyone had expected. Everyone except Grover and Cilla, that is, who had no choice but to go through with it, until Beogoat returned.

But Westerhoven was split. Erich and his black cloakers had formed a coalition with the Hoeneckers under Prince Thorn. Prince Thorn supported Erich's claim to leadership of Westerhoven, and was rumored to be promised the rule of Sousterhoven himself after they were defeated. Their claims to leadership were denied formally and informally with a lot of name-calling and lunch dates to see each other in hell, which Erich and Prince Thorn didn't take too well. They were now preparing for war with the rest of Westerhoven as well as Sousterhoven. All in all, it was a mess.

At this crucial juncture, more crucial than Beogoat ever imagined, Westerhoven needed a great leader. Someone with vision, with a dream, who could sway masses of men to throw their lives away needlessly for someone else's ambition, who could heal the division within the Westerhoven alliance while being able to defeat the Sousterhoven alliance. Instead they had Grover. Grover and Cilla. Together they alternately dreamed up schemes to help Westerhoven and to get the hell out of Hoven period.

The leaders they had to support them were of varying types, but each held true to the theory of self-preservation that helped destroy the empire three hundred years ago. Among these were Phillip's staunch supporters, Ivan of Dresdel, Sajin of Ubbergammu, and Vince of Kurtonburg, represented by his younger son, Kirk. Each of these nations had pledged a great amount of troops and supplies in support.

Ivan was a rotund man, giving to boasting and drinking, and his support was expected as long as they were winning. In times of strength he was Phillip's most ardent supporter, and in hard times he was always heard to say that Phillip didn't know what he was doing.

Sajin's support was more firm. As long as he believed in a cause, he would fight on until either he or everyone else was dead. He was not a man who sought prizes, and secretly loathed Phillip's desire for the rule of Hoven. But he respected him for being able to fight and gather nations about him.

And last was Vince of Kurtonburg, whose own nations bordered Sousterhoven, and who owed Phillip *and* Wunderkinde favors for coming to support him in the past when he was in need. His principality was under a threat of a fight over leadership once he died, and Phillip had promised to support his son Kirk. So the Kurtonburgs served out of a debt of obligation, and could be counted on as long as Phillip did his part of the bargain.

And then there were the ones less devoted to Phillip. These were represented by Bertrand of Vagner and Richard of Meistertonne. Bertrand was a weathered businessman whose principality was far removed from the battles with Sousterhoven. He believed in peace through prosperity, and didn't feel a need to contribute to the battle as long as he wasn't threatened. But once threatened he would be the first one asking for aid and saying something should be done.

Richard on the other hand was a fierce, religious man who only had loyalty to Phillip out of an ancient treaty, which he respected against his better judgment. Because ever since that fateful day outside of the city of Hoven, he had doubts about the intentions and motivations of Phillip. Especially where the wizard Beogoat was involved. He knew now that Phillip's hatred of all wizards had been a ruse to gain his confidence, and that Phillip really believed in wizardry. He was confirmed in this belief by Beogoat's elevated status during the latter half of the Save Winona campaign. And Phillip's behavior had been markedly different afterward. Thus he was willing to send troops, but not to help Phillip, only to protect himself.

Last but not least was Young Dianna of Helmutov. Of all the principalities of Hoven, only hers was ruled by women, and she wasn't even a ruler. She was representing her grandmother, who was too ill to leave the confines of Castle Helmutov. Her devotion was not to Phillip, but rather to the cause itself. She believed strongly in meeting Sousterhoven in battle and making sure there was one ruler to this land. Of them all, she had the fatal flaw of idealism. Consequently no one listened to her ideas.

It was these people that Grover and Cilla had to lead. It was them they had to convince that the war could be won, even though it looked hopeless. And amazingly they did follow, and they did listen to what their supposed leaders had to say. When Grover and Cilla presented the idea of making their stand on the island of Hoven, because no cavalry could be used by either side, and essentially they would be on equal terms, it was agreed.

But what they didn't know was that there was a spy in their midst. One man who didn't want to see Phillip succeed. One man that Phillip had pushed aside in his ambition to rule. And this was Old Lord Phillip. It was he who had helped Winona get the poison at the wedding. And it was he who had made security lax so Erich and his black cloakers could interrupt the wedding. Yes, Old Lord Phillip felt just a little bit slighted when he had been forced to step aside and showed his anger by being just a little bit vindictive. So while all the Lords planned to meet Sousterhoven face-to-face, Old Lord Phillip was sending information to Erich and Prince Thorn so they could make their own plans. Because Erich had promised to put Old Lord Phillip back in power once Phillip was dead.

While all the Lords congratulated Grover and themselves on a brilliant plan, they didn't know that their plan would never be used. And that when they arrived on the island of Hoven, one drizzly day in the fall, they would find that it wasn't only the Sousterhovens they had to worry about, but Erich and Prince Thorn as well.

PART VII

Suddenly into the Abyss

Revelations in the Rain

Hans waited by the reflecting pool with his new advisor, Byron, beside him, as he watched the other Lords of Sousterhoven arrive. He felt good, better than he had felt in years. The doom that had seemed to press upon him was now lifting at the further prospect of death and destruction. His prophecy would be realized, he would be King of Hoven, and he would die as a martyr betrayed by his best friend, like all great kings were supposed to. He could almost see the epitaph on his tombstone: *He Loved Too Much*.

The first Lord to arrive was Luke of Astertov, the driving force in this whole campaign. Hans considered it sheer luck that Winona had died to make this man's total support possible. Luke was a man driven by feelings of honor and revenge and didn't attack people on a lark, like Hans did. But he was also an unpredictable and often dangerous man, who was one to be watched carefully. He had his own goals and agenda that he kept hidden, and thus it was hard to determine what he was going to do until he had already done it.

Behind him came David of Gustavus, who was probably Hans's staunchest ally. David shared his bloodlust, but unfortunately also shared his ambition for the throne. After he had faithfully supported Hans he would suffer a sudden stabbing pain to the heart caused by an assassin's knife. If Hans was in a good mood the knife might not be poisoned. But for now David was willing to throw all his support to attack Westerhoven, and especially Prince Thorn, who had been a mortal enemy for some time.

After David came Bertold of Teuton, who looked rather nervous. His family suffered from a history of mental illness and thus was easy to manipulate with stories of conspiracies. Hans knew just how to handle him. But Bertold was suspicious of everyone, even his Sousterhoven neighbors. Fortunately for those close to him his suspicion didn't breed in sudden attacks, but only in more rigorous defense. He was persuaded to join the effort only after he was assured that he would be able to leave to protect his own principality if it was in any danger.

Last came Calvin of Auschwitz. His nation bordered Kurtonburg but they didn't have fierce border wars. Calvin was a bit of
a loner and believed in settling things in his own manner and on
his own terms. But like everyone else, Calvin had his first
obligation to the Sousterhoven effort, a loyalty that went back
three hundred years. He could never allow Westerhoven to
humiliate Sousterhoven. There was also the matter of some
territory that Auschwitz had lost to Kurtonburg many years back
that helped as a motivating factor. He thought any battle might
bring concessions that could help him. Hans trusted this man least
of all and planned to have his forces at the forefront of the battle.

All in all, a group united by forces of dubious loyalty and
tradition that had started long ago and could not be changed now.
And Hans thanked God for that.

"I have asked you to come here," Hans said, "because I want
to tell you a story."

"Does this story have a point?" Luke asked. "Or do you just
want to talk again?"

"It has a point," Hans said. "Don't worry. You will all find this
story interesting. But first, does anyone have any jokes to tell?"

The Lords shifted about but said nothing. A few of them noticed
a tarp lying over some supplies behind Hans, but did not ask what
they were, or if it was the special project they had been hearing
rumors about all along. There had been a pall of secrecy in Castle
Reichton lately, about things going on in certain rooms, that no
one would speak about. And no one lived to tell about either,
because there was a rash of executions. Which was termed
"cleaning house" in Reichton. But all this had been superseded by
preparations for war, so no one had asked and Hans had offered no
memos on the subject.

"Last spring," Hans began, "I came to the island of Hoven to
recapture Winona, who had escaped from the evil Phillip."

"And if you had done a better job we wouldn't have to be here
tonight in the rain," Luke said.

"Actually," Hans said, "I did a better job than any of you ever
suspected."

David of Gustavus looked up in interest. Calvin also listened
intently.

"It was here at this pool in the last days of spring while the
forces of Phillip surrounded my own troops in the ancient city of
Hoven that I was able to trick Voss into bringing Phillip here."

"Is this about your claim that you killed Phillip?" Luke asked.

"Yes," Hans said. "And I don't blame you for doubting me.

How could you when Phillip had forced me to retreat across *The Stream That Rushes Too Fast in the Wrong Places*? And after he had recaptured Winona."

"Yes," Luke said. "How could we?"

"So you're saying he *is* dead?" David asked. Had he followed a mad leader into battle?

"I'm not saying that yet," Hans said. "Because you all know he is alive, right?"

"Of course he is," Luke said.

"You mean, of course he is *dead*?" Bertold asked in confusion. "Calvin, tell me what's going on."

"I guess I have to say he is alive also," Calvin said. "Unless you prove to me otherwise."

"I tell you that I did kill Phillip that day and I also had Voss executed for crimes against the state."

"Wait a moment," Luke interjected. "You have no jurisdiction over my subjects." Voss was a citizen of Luke's principality.

"He consented freely to becoming a citizen of Reichton and I have witnesses," Hans replied. "Lots of them. But that's off the subject. Phillip and Voss did die, and for two days I waited for the Westerhoven forces to fall in disarray, but on the third day Phillip and Voss reappeared."

"I don't get it," Bertold said, even more confused than before. "If you killed them how can they be alive?"

"A riddle that has kept me up many a night," Hans said. "And I would have never known the answer had I not escaped that day with my life, and had not the wizard Beogoat been repossessed by Wizard Collectors and offered up to me. It was from Beogoat that I learned what really happened. Beogoat found Phillip and Voss dead the day I killed them and instead of making their death public knowledge, he hid their death, went to another land to hire impostors, and replaced Phillip and Voss without anyone knowing."

"That's stupid," Luke said. "Do you expect us to believe you?"

"Hans's mad," Bertold hissed. "I should know. I come from a family of madness. And he's mad."

"We're all mad," David said. But he was really wondering if he should get out now while he had the chance. Madness was contagious after all.

"Where's your proof?" Calvin asked casually.

Hans turned to Byron. "Byron, remove the tarp."

And with those cryptic words Byron went over to the tarp and lifted it to reveal the preserved bodies of Phillip and Voss, a masterwork of taxidermy. Rain fell on their waxen features.

The Lords moved closer. "My God," Luke exclaimed. "You really messed them up."

"Sure looks like them," David said, picking up Phillip's head. Maybe Hans wasn't mad after all. But could he trust him?

Bertold shivered. "They look dead, all right."

Calvin asked: "Is it really them?"

"It's them," Hans said.

"So you killed them," Luke said. "What good does that do us?"

"Because," Hans said, "besides us and the impostors, only Beogoat and his assistant, Beoweasel, know what really happened."

"So what do you plan to do?" Calvin asked.

"Simple," Hans said. "I reveal to the Lords of Westerhoven who their leader really is. Once they discover he is an impostor they will no longer follow him. Wunderkinde will be forced to withdraw. The alliance will fall apart."

"How can you be so sure?" David asked. This was too simple of a solution.

"Because this is the way it was meant to happen before but never did, because Beogoat intervened with fate. Now fate is back on track. The key to Westerhoven has always been Phillip. Once they know he is dead their alliances will be invalid. Sure a few might stick together, but for the most part they'll withdraw to their separate principalities and we can defeat them there. Or attack them here."

Yep, David thought. All that talk about fate was a sure sign of madness.

"Why do you think they will believe you?" Bertold asked.

"Because I will show them," Hans said. "They will see with their own eyes that Phillip is dead."

"And how will you do that?" Calvin asked.

"You'll see," Hans said. "I told you to trust me, and you should trust me. Tomorrow we shall see the disruption of the Westerhoven alliance."

"And what then?" Bertold asked.

"Then we slaughter them," Hans said.

That Old Magic Feeling

The tall, lanky figure moved familiarly through the ranks of Wunderkinde knights. He passed the outer guard and exchanged greetings, giving him the secret handshake. He moved on, pausing to speak to another knight. A match was ignited, pipes were lit, and there was a bit of talk and some laughter. He passed on. No one challenged him as he walked past the guards and fortifications of the Wunderkinde camp. And everywhere he went, men looked up and whispered his name and nudged their friends so they wouldn't miss out on the event. Some pointed, a few gawked, but many settled back, reassured that he had returned in their time of need.

Looking at the worn-out shoes, one could tell he had traveled a long distance. His clothing, though not the same he had previously worn, also showed signs of wear and tear. And when he paused in conversation with a knight there seemed to be a faraway look in his eyes, as if he had seen too much and didn't understand the half of it. He seemed as if he had died and been born again.

Without challenge he walked past the guard to Phillip's tent and entered as if he were expected there.

Inside, Grover lay sleeping on a cot, furs heavy about him. He had finally drifted off into an uneasy sleep. But Cilla, whose cot was next to his, was not asleep, and she saw the lanky figure enter the tent without being challenged and grabbed a knife from the floor.

The lanky man responded by puffing on his pipe.

Cilla was up in an instant and was heading for the man, crying for Grover to be awake. By the time Grover had managed to rub the grit from out of his eyes, Cilla already had her knife pressed against the chest of a very familiar figure.

"So," Beogoat asked, "did you miss me?"

And that's when Cilla tried to stab him.

So what could have been a tender reunion, of friends long lost meeting once again, wasn't. Instead it was a scene of two frustrated heroes meeting up with the wizard who had messed up their lives. Not very tender, and not very friendly either, but still quite a scene.

"Don't kill him, don't kill him," Grover said, pulling Cilla away from Beogoat.

"Let go, let go," Cilla cried, trying to shake off Grover's hands.

"Not unless you promise not to kill him," Grover said, holding her arms behind her back.

Cilla smiled prettily. "I promise."

"You're such a liar," Grover said, twisting her arms.

Cilla's face changed to a scowl. "Let me go."

Grover tugged the knife out of her hand and let it drop to the floor. "Okay," he said, and let Cilla go.

Cilla turned and slugged Grover in the stomach. Grover collapsed onto his cot in pain. "Don't ever touch me again," she said. And then she turned to Beogoat. "So was your vacation cut short?"

Beogoat puffed on his pipe for a moment. "I guess I've missed out on something. I was . . ."

"Missed out on something," Cilla ranted. "Since you left, I became involved in two plots to kill Phillip, Winona was killed, the Black Avenger joined with Prince Thorn to force Phillip out of power, and Luke, enraged by Winona's death, joined with Hans and the rest of Sousterhoven to attack Wunderkinde. So no, you didn't miss much. In fact, things have been quite dull since you've been gone. Wouldn't you say, Grover?"

"No," Grover said. "I thought the past few months have been rather hectic and . . ."

"Who asked you?" Cilla snapped.

"Why, you did," Grover answered.

"And since when did you listen to me?" Cilla said.

"I always did," Grover said.

"That's beside the point," Cilla said. "So where have you been?" she asked Beogoat.

"I was . . ." Beogoat started.

"And what's the idea of taking leave right when we reach Wunderkinde?"

"Take leave, I . . ." Beogoat started.

"And how come you didn't tell us that Erich was the Black Avenger?"

"Because I didn't know he was the Black Avenger," Beogoat said, glad to get a whole sentence out. "Nobody knew who he was."

"Well, how come you didn't tell us there was a Black Avenger?"

"I meant to," Beogoat said. "But it just slipped . . ."

"Your mind," Cilla finished for him. "We know. And we're tired of the little games you've been playing, aren't we, Grover?"

Grover had a quizzical expression on his face. "He's been playing games?"

"Forget it, Grover," Cilla said.

"You mean Twister . . . ?" Grover asked, feeling totally lost.

"I haven't been playing games," Beogoat replied.

"Then what do you call taking a vacation before all hell breaks loose?" Cilla asked him.

"Well, I don't know if there's just one word to describe it," Beogoat said, who thought it was a hypothetical question.

"Try," Cilla said.

"Well . . ." Beogoat started.

"No, wait," Cilla said. "Let me help you. How about the word 'charlatan,' or 'betrayer,' or 'deceiver'?"

"They don't fit," Beogoat said. "You sure you don't want me to explain how I was abduc—"

"Well, that would be a first," Cilla said. "Actually explaining to us. Why didn't you do that in the first place?"

"I had my reasons," Beogoat said.

"Which were?" Cilla asked.

"If you allow me to explain . . ." Beogoat started again.

"No, let me tell you," Cilla began.

"Cilla," Grover interjected, "will you just let him explain."

"Why should I?" Cilla asked. "He'll just lie to us again."

"Because I'm tired of listening to you," Grover said, rubbing his stomach. "And I want to hear what Beogoat has to say."

"Oh," Cilla said. "Oh, I see. Oh, I get it."

"Good," Grover said. "Now sit down and shut up."

Cilla's eyes blazed.

"Please," Grover said.

Cilla's anger faded and she said, "Okay, but don't think you won the argument."

"You can rest assured that I feel like a loser," Grover said.

"Good," Cilla said, and sat down next to Grover.

Grover gestured to Beogoat, who was still standing, to have a seat on Cilla's cot.

"Why, thank you," Beogoat said. "I have traveled a long way." And he gratefully sat down on Cilla's cot. He puffed on his pipe for a few moments, not saying anything.

"Well?" Grover asked.

"I see you're preparing for a battle," Beogoat said. "Are you trying to unite all of Hoven?"

"It's more complicated than that," Grover said. "Actually we're in a bind. Erich and Prince Thorn have joined forces and are in the ancient city of Hoven. He wants to kill me. And Hans and Luke just landed on the other shore, and they want to kill me."

"I was afraid of that," Beogoat said. "I was hoping to get back in time to prevent all this. There's been a grave, grave mistake. Phillip's not destined to rule all of Hoven. I made a miscalculation. I brought you here to do the impossible."

"You what?" Cilla cried, jumping up. "Are you telling us you didn't even need us to take Phillip's and Voss's places? That this has all been a waste of time?"

"Well . . . yeah," Beogoat said. "It came as a shock to me too. Wasted all that time and money when I didn't need to."

"I say we kill him," Cilla said, bending down to pick up the knife.

"No, wait," Grover said. "When did you learn this? I thought Phillip was prophesied to bring peace to all of Westerhoven."

"Me too," Beogoat said. "But hey, we all make mistakes. I didn't realize mine until I was talking to Frederick. Excuse me, Floyd."

"Wait, who's Fred . . . Floyd?" Cilla asked. "And what does he have to do with all this?"

"He was a torturer who worked for Hans," Beogoat explained. "He helped me realize that I was so eager to get out of Hoven and finish with my assignment here that I made Phillip fit the prophecy that I had made, rather than waiting for the right person to come along."

"Torturer. Who worked for Hans," Cilla said. "What were you doing talking to a torturer who worked for Hans?"

"If you had let me explain earlier, I would have told you," Beogoat said.

"Well, explain now," Cilla said.

"I wasn't on vacation. Who told you that?"

"Beoweasel," Cilla said.

"And you believed him?" Beogoat asked.

"Well, we believed you," Cilla said in weak defense.

"So there you go," Beogoat said. "For your information I was abducted the night we returned to Wunderkinde, by Wizard Collectors. If you had looked in my memoirs you would have read the whole episode."

"Wizard Collectors," Cilla swore. "I knew those guys would come back to haunt me."

"They can't be the same ones," Grover said.

"You know these guys?" Beogoat asked.

"We've met," Cilla said dryly.

"Hmm," Beogoat said. "Well, they sold me to Hans. And gave me a potion that ripped away my magical ability."

"Such that it is," Cilla said.

Beogoat smiled. "Oh, so you know about that too."

"We know everything," Cilla said.

"Except where you were," Grover added.

"I was with Hans. And I was threatened with torture unless I revealed what happened to the real Phillip and Voss. I knew this would happen. If you only had killed Hans when you recaptured Winona."

"You didn't tell us to kill Hans," Grover said.

"And what's this about revealing what happened to the real Phillip and Voss?" Cilla interjected.

"I had to," Beogoat said. "I was in no position to fight back, and when Floyd made me realize that Phillip really wasn't the one prophesied to lead, I ended up telling everything. He also made me realize that I had a bad self-image caused by a domineering father. But anyway I didn't think it would matter because I thought I would get back to you in time."

"You betrayed us," Cilla said. She looked at the knife in her hand with intensity. "That's it. I'm going to kill him."

Grover put a restraining hand on Cilla's arm. "Not yet. He said he tried to warn us."

"He betrayed us," Cilla said.

"And that's why I came back when I could," Beogoat interjected. "It's all over. You don't have to pretend anymore. I can take you back."

"What?" Cilla cried, looking up.

"All *right*," Grover said, joy evident on his face. "When do we leave?"

"As soon as you want," Beogoat answered.

"What?" Cilla cried.

"I'm just glad I was able to get back before Hans could expose you two," Beogoat said. "I was really worried."

"What?" Cilla asked again.

Grover got up and started to pick up clothes he wanted to take with him. "Come on, Cilla, let's go."

"Go," Cilla said.

"It's over," Grover said. "Over. Don't you understand? Beogoat said he would take us back."

"Back," Cilla said. "We can't leave."

"Yes, you can," Beogoat said. "It's no problem. I know how to do the spell."

"Start packing," Grover said.

"I'm not going to leave after I've come this far," Cilla said, shaking her head. "No way."

Grover stopped in mid-stoop to pick up a shirt. "What was that?"

"We're not leaving," Cilla said.

"Oh yes, we are," Grover said. "Beogoat said it was okay. We did our part."

"Yes," Beogoat agreed. "It makes no sense now. What's the point in having Grover pretend he's Phillip if Phillip isn't really the one destined to rule?"

"Destined or not," Cilla said, "we've put a lot of effort into this adventure of yours. We made Phillip and Voss live and breathe. Those people believe in us. We just can't leave them when they're confronted by two opposing forces."

"Sure we can," Grover said. "Phillip is dead. He was supposed to die. And Winona is dead too. So there can't be any alliance. We even tried to leave before. Now's our chance."

"Well, I don't want to go," Cilla said. "I want to finish the adventure."

"Fine," Grover said. "Stay. But as for me, I'm leaving."

"You can't leave," Cilla said. "I need you to be Phillip."

"Yes, I can," Grover said. "Right, Beogoat?"

"It's fine with me," Beogoat said.

"You can't go," Cilla said.

"What do you mean I can't go?"

"When we started this adventure we agreed that even though you were Phillip, I was in charge. I'm the hero, and I say we stay."

"Damn, damn, damn, damn it," Grover swore. "I did agree to that, didn't I?"

"I don't understand," Beogoat said. "There's no reason for you to stay. You might end up dead. I admire your conviction. But this is unnecessary. Hans knows your true identities. It's foolish to stay."

"That's a risk I'm willing to take," Cilla said.

"I'm not," Grover said.

"But you have no choice," Cilla pointed out.

"So what are we going to do?" Grover asked.

"We're going to stay and defeat Hans and Erich and bring peace to Hoven," Cilla said.

"Just great. And how do you propose to do that?" Grover asked.

"I'll figure out a way," Cilla said absently.

Beogoat shrugged. "It's better if you leave at night."

"You hear that?" Grover said. "It's better if we leave at night."

"I heard," Cilla said. "But we won't be leaving until I say so."

Grover fell to his cot wearily. "Well, this sucks."

"Whenever you're ready to leave," Beogoat offered.

"I'll tell you," Cilla said. "Thanks for everything you've done, or actually, haven't done, but we're going to finish this one for ourselves."

"Very well," Beogoat said. "But if you change your mind in the morning you know where to find me."

"In another country?" Grover asked.

"No, at breakfast," Beogoat said.

Sudden Beginnings

The next morning, the battle began suddenly, unexpected by all sides. Only a few principal members remember how it began. The rest who were involved are now dead.

It all started simply, while Beogoat, Grover, and Cilla stood on a hill looking at the city of Hoven, where the red and white flags of Prince Thorn of Hoenecker and the black ones of Erich flew. The city had been silent, and no one knew how large Erich's forces were, or what he intended.

But danger didn't come from the city, but across the field, on another hill. There the Sousterhoven forces were encamped. Their banners snapped in the stiff breeze that blew that morning. And it was from their camp that they saw two men walk forth.

"Look," Cilla said, pointing to the opposite hill. "Those two men. I think they're walking our way."

"You sure they're not going to the city?" Grover said. "He may be dealing with Erich."

"Not likely," Cilla said.

After a few moments of observation it became clear that the two men were indeed traversing the field toward them. They walked slowly, carrying a flag of truce.

"I wonder what he could want?" Cilla mused.

"Maybe he's given up," Grover said. "What do you think, Beogoat?"

"I don't think that's it," Beogoat replied. "But I don't see what Hans would be doing. He certainly can't believe that Westerhoven will submit to his claim as the one ruler of Hoven."

"And Luke has a vendetta against Wunderkinde anyway," Cilla added.

"I guess we'll find out soon enough," Grover said. "Maybe we should get the other Lords." He turned to go back up the hill.

Beogoat put out a restraining hand. "Don't. Maybe it would be better if we found out for ourselves what he has to say."

"Or *if* he has anything to say," Cilla said. "Do you suspect something?"

"Well," Beogoat said, "Hans does know the truth about you two."

"But who would believe him?" Cilla asked.

"Right," Grover said. "It's his word against ours."

"True," Beogoat said. "Unless . . ."

"Unless what?" Cilla demanded. "This wasn't something that slipped your mind, was it?"

"Well, I wasn't sure," Beogoat said. "But I did tell him where the bodies were hidden."

"You what?" Cilla cried.

"I told him where the bodies were stored," Beogoat repeated.

"You kept the bodies?" Grover asked. "Why?"

"Because I was going to have Phillip die a little later," Beogoat said. "I needed his body for afterward."

"Christ," Cilla said. "If he has the bodies we're screwed. There's no way we can keep on pretending that we're Phillip and Voss."

"Exactly why we should leave," Grover added.

The two men were halfway across the field now.

"They'll be noticed soon," Cilla said. "If someone else hasn't seen them already."

"Then we should leave before anyone talks to them," Grover said. "While we still have the chance."

"But he might not even have found the bodies," Cilla said. "Right, Beogoat?"

"If it pleases you to think so," Beogoat replied. "You never know."

"And besides," Cilla said, "they're probably so decayed by now that no one could tell who they were."

"Maybe," Beogoat said.

"What do you mean, maybe?" Cilla demanded. "It's been several months."

"I hid them in the *Ice Caves*," Beogoat said. "To preserve their bodies."

"You preserved them," Cilla said. "Why'd you have to do that?"

"I already said . . ."

"Well, they can't be in good condition," Cilla said. "Bodies don't keep that long."

"I don't like this," Grover said. "I don't think we should just wait here until we find out if he does or doesn't have the bodies. I think we should leave."

Cilla said nothing, but seemed to be thinking.

"Well, that may not even be why they're coming over," Beogoat offered.

"You hear that?" Cilla told Grover.

"Can you think of any other reason?" Grover asked Beogoat.

"Nope," Beogoat said. "To paraphrase Hans: We're doomed."

"I don't like this," Grover said.

"It's only natural not to like being doomed," Beogoat replied.

The two men were now three-quarters of the way over. Just then a detachment of Meistertonne knights descended the hill to confront the envoy.

"Well, what are we going to do now?" Grover asked.

"I suggest leaving," Beogoat said.

"No," Cilla said firmly. "There must be some other way. I'm not going to be chased off like this. I didn't come this far to have Hans ruin everything."

Beogoat smiled. "That's what I thought one morning a couple of months ago. And you see where it got me."

Cilla looked up. "We're going to prove your prophecy was right, even if it was wrong."

"What are you going to do?" Grover asked Cilla. "Change the world?"

"If I have to," Cilla replied.

The Meistertonne knights had met up with the two Souster-hoven men. They stood in the field and talked and gestured. The two Sousterhoven men were checked for weapons. They then were brought forward under guard.

Other knights and functionaries were beginning to appear at the crest of the hill, now that word of a Sousterhoven envoy had spread. They stood in ever-increasing numbers watching the Meistertonne knights bring the envoy forward.

"So what are we going to do?" Grover asked Cilla again.

The Westerhoven forces might have won the battle that day had not another man intervened. It wasn't this man's intention to hurt Westerhoven, but rather to help it. It must be said to his benefit that in his heart he thought he was doing the right thing. And to that we all reply: So what? At one time he was known as Beoweasel. But now he had joined the Meistertonne church and had become a devoted subject. He was worried about the status of his soul and had confessed to dealings in magic. In his confessions he had admitted to his foul deed with Beogoat, and his superior told him to immediately report this to Lord Richard. So while Lord Richard enjoyed a cold breakfast in his tent and waited for the Sousterhoven envoy to arrive, a young lay brother was announced, bearing a very important message.

"Cilla," Grover said, unaware that he had called her by her real name. "What are . . ."

But Cilla wasn't listening. She wasn't even staying put to listen to Grover's outburst. She was already dashing across the side of the hill to meet up with the Meistertonne escort.

"What's she doing now?" Grover asked. And then added, "I don't care what she thinks, we should go back now."

"I can't take back just one," Beogoat said.

Grover watched as Cilla met up with the leader of the escort and exchanged words with him. Grover kept seeing the knight shake his head. He did this repeatedly. The leader kept pointing up the hill, toward the encampment, and Cilla kept pointing over to him and Beogoat.

"I don't like this," Grover said again.

Cilla kept arguing and finally the knight wasn't shaking his head anymore. Cilla pointed one more time, insistently at Grover and Beogoat, and suddenly the knights were walking their way.

"She got them to come to us," Grover said.

"Yes," Beogoat agreed.

Cilla walked hurriedly toward them, the knights trying to keep up. The face of the leader didn't look too happy. He kept turning his head back to look up at the hill. And would occasionally say something to Cilla, who just shook her head. Finally the whole entourage came to a halt before Grover and Beogoat.

"I brought over the envoy for you, Lord Phillip," Cilla said.

"Ah . . . very good," Grover said, not sure of what to say.

"Lord Phillip," the leader of the knights said, "the envoy has stated that they have a message for all the Lords. Yet your swordbearer insisted that she bring the envoy over to you. Is this your order?"

Grover looked at Cilla, who nodded her head.

"Ah . . . yeah," Grover said. "I wanted to speak to the envoy first."

"This is against protocol," the knight said. "Lord Richard will be . . ."

"Just tell Lord Richard that Lord Phillip ordered it," Beogoat said.

"But I have orders to bring any envoys to . . ."

"We understand that," Beogoat said. "But the authority of Lord Phillip supersedes that of Lord Richard in this matter."

"But Lord Phillip does not have the power to overrule all the Lords," the knight pointed out.

"He is not overruling all the Lords," Beogoat said. "He's just overruling you, if you get the drift."

"But . . ." the leader of the knights protested.

"You may go," Beogoat said. "Your duty is done. We will escort the envoy into camp."

"I cannot let the envoy go in unguarded," the leader said.

"It's all right," Grover said. "You can go. You've done your duty."

"In all fairness, Lord Phillip, I cannot return to Lord Richard failing in my duty."

"But you haven't," Beogoat said. "You have escorted the envoy to us. We'll take over from here."

"But . . ." the leader said, and looked over his shoulder once again. His face twisted with great reluctance and finally he looked to the other knights. "Come on." And he looked at Phillip. "We'll only draw a little way off. Just in case."

"Fine," Grover said.

"But I still . . ."

"Duly noted," Beogoat said.

The leader turned around and drew off some distance, with the knights leaving Grover, Cilla, and Beogoat with the Sousterhoven envoy.

The envoy consisted of two men. One dressed in the black and white colors of Reichton and one in the green and white colors of Astertov. It was the one from Reichton who spoke.

"Our message was intended for all the Lords of Westerhoven," he explained.

"We understand that," Beogoat said. "But what is the nature of your envoy?"

"We can only disclose that to all the Lords of Westerhoven. Lord Hans made that very clear. I don't understand why you have detained us. We bear the flag of truce and have come to parley."

"This is the Lord Phillip," Beogoat said, pointing to Grover. "And he speaks for all the Lords of Westerhoven."

"That's right," Grover said.

A shade of doubt crossed the envoy's face. The Reichton envoy exchanged looks with the Astertov envoy.

"This is very irregular," the Reichton envoy replied.

"Just tell us why you've come," Cilla said.

Bargaining for Time

The Reichton envoy had pulled out a letter from his pouch. "I was supposed to read this to all the Lords of Westerhoven."

"Look at it this way," Cilla said, taking the letter from him. "We're saving you a walk."

"Lord Hans will be displeased with me," the Reichton envoy replied.

"And Lord Luke won't like it much either," added the Astertov envoy.

"We didn't ask you to like it," Cilla said.

The two representatives said nothing.

"You can go now," Cilla told them.

"We're supposed to wait for your reply," the Reichton envoy explained.

"What's the letter say?" Grover asked.

Cilla broke the seal of Lord Hans and read the letter to herself. "This isn't good," she said when she was done.

"What does it say?" Grover asked.

Cilla looked at the two members of the envoy. "Do you know what this message contains?"

The two representatives shook their heads.

"We were sent to deliver the message and to receive your reply. And to guide over anyone who chose to accompany us," the Astertov representative explained.

"Guide over," Grover said. "Why would they guide us over?"

"Look at this," Cilla said, and handed the letter to Grover.

Grover reached for it, but Beogoat interposed himself and took the letter for himself, quickly scanning the contents. "This is worse than I feared."

"What?" Grover demanded. "What is it?"

Cilla looked to Beogoat. "What do you think we should do? We can't give this message to the other Lords."

"Unless you have a death wish," Beogoat said.

"What?" Grover cried.

"Here," Beogoat said, and handed Grover the letter.

Grover took the letter and read it carefully. It read:

To the Lords of Westerhoven, it is my duty to inform that there is an impostor in your midst. Actually two impostors and they go by the names of Grover and Cilla. You think these two are really Phillip and Voss, but the real Phillip and Voss are dead, and their bodies are lying over here by the reflecting pool for you all to see. I know you probably won't believe me, but that's why I'm asking you to come over under the flag of truce and see for yourselves how all of you have been deceived by the machinations of Beogoat and his assistant, Beoweasel. Since you may think that it is a trap that I am asking you to come over here, all you have to do is tell my envoy that you wish to have the bodies brought over to you, and you will see the truth for yourselves. I do not do this out of spite, but out of our desire to see truth have its day. Do you really want an impostor leading your armies?

"My God," Grover said when he finished reading the letter.

"Prayer never helps," Beogoat said.

"Oh no, it's . . ." Cilla exclaimed.

"What now?" Grover asked.

"I think it's Lord Richard," Cilla said, pointing.

They all looked up to the top of the hill and saw that it was indeed Lord Richard, wearing the brown and red colors of Meistertonne, and not looking a bit too happy. He stopped at the top of the hill and looked down. His gaze swept the slope and then stopped on them. He pointed at them, but it was too windy and he was too far away for them to hear what he had to say.

"He doesn't look like he's come to invite us over for breakfast," Cilla said.

"We already had breakfast," Grover said.

"This might complicate matters," Beogoat observed coolly.

"Should we refuse the breakfast invitation then?" Grover asked.

"What?" Cilla cried.

The two envoys looked over their shoulders to see Lord Richard storming down the hill, and then looked back to Grover, Cilla, and Beogoat.

"Well?" Grover asked. He still held the letter in his hands and he waved this to Cilla. "Should we include him in our deliberations?"

Cilla saw the letter and ripped it away from Grover and stuffed it deeply into her pants. She turned to the envoys. "You can both go now."

"But we were told to wait for a reply," the Reichton envoy explained.

"Tell him . . ." Cilla started. "Tell Hans that no one is coming over."

"Then he'll send *it* over," Grover said. Meaning the bodies.

"Tell him . . ." Cilla said, and then she looked to Beogoat. "Do you have any ideas?"

Beogoat shook his head. "I was never very good under pressure."

"Shit," Cilla said, and then she looked to Grover. "Lord Phillip, I advise you to send the envoy back with a message that the Lords of Westerhoven will follow."

"You do?" Grover said.

Cilla nodded vigorously.

Grover glanced up the hill and saw that Lord Richard had stopped to speak to the leader of the knights who had acted as escort. They were only about forty or so yards away. Not very far at all.

"Then I will take your advice," Grover said. "Give Hans the reply that all the Lords will come over shortly under the flag of truce to parley."

"But . . ." the Astertov envoy began to protest.

"I speak for all the Lords," Grover said as commandingly as possible. "You may depart now."

"But we are supposed to guide you over," the Reichton envoy explained.

"We know the way to the other side," Cilla said.

"Yes, go," Grover said. And he saw that Lord Richard was breaking away from his knights now.

"Go," Grover said again.

And then the two representatives were turning around and were walking down the hill. Lord Richard saw them and shouted at them. The two representatives halted and looked toward Lord Richard. Grover waved to them to go on. But they just stood there. Lord Richard asked them to come forward once more and the representatives started to do so.

"Go back." Grover waved once more. "Go back."

"Over here," Lord Richard said, pointing in front of his feet.

The representatives came walking back.

"Traitors," Grover swore. "Now what do we do?"

No one said anything, but almost on cue they moved closer to hear what Lord Richard had to say.

"Come here," Richard said once more, and the representatives stopped in front of him.

"Why did you leave?"

"Because Lord Phillip ordered us," the envoy explained.

"I was told you had a message for all the Lords of Westerhoven," Richard said.

"That is true," the envoy said.

"And what is that message?" Richard asked.

"We have the message," Cilla said, coming up.

"You," Richard said, and scowled at Cilla. "Since when do you speak for all the Lords of Westerhoven?" Richard asked.

"About a few moments ago," Grover said, "as I recall."

Richard's face went a deeper shade of red. "I have never liked you or your methods . . ."

"Well, I haven't liked you much either," Grover said. "And I don't like you recalling an envoy that I have sent away."

Richard looked stunned. "How dare you insult me . . ."

"How dare you insult *me*?" Grover asked back. He turned to the envoy. "Go back."

"Stay," Richard said.

The two members of the envoy shook their heads in confusion and didn't move.

"I said go," Grover said. "Go back. Now. Shoo."

"Wouldn't it be better if we waited for all the Lords?" the Reichton envoy asked.

"Yes," Richard said.

"No," Grover said. "And I didn't ask for your opinion."

The Reichton envoy was silent.

"What are you hiding?" Richard asked.

"Nothing," Grover said quickly.

Richard glanced past Grover and looked at Cilla and Beogoat. "All three of you are hiding something. I can tell." He turned to the envoy. "What was the nature of the message?"

"We do not know," the Astertov envoy replied. "We gave the letter to Lord Phillip."

Richard turned back to Grover. "Where's the letter?"

"I have no letter," Grover said.

"That's because his swordbearer tucked it in his pants," the Reichton envoy said.

Cilla glared at the Reichton envoy. "Your days are numbered."

"Let me see the letter, Voss," Richard said.

"No," Cilla said, and shook her head.

"If you don't give it to me I'll have my knights forcibly take it away from you," Richard said.

Beogoat turned to Cilla. "Give it to him."

"But . . ." Cilla protested.

"Beogoat," Grover said.

"He's turning on us too," Cilla said.

"Trust me," Beogoat said.

"Thank you," Richard said to Beogoat.

"Don't mention it," Beogoat said.

Cilla reluctantly pulled the letter out of her pants. She stared at the contents and then looked at Beogoat. "Are you sure?"

Beogoat nodded.

"Give it here," Richard said.

"You could at least ask nicely," Cilla said.

"Give it here," Richard said.

"No wonder everyone thinks you're an asshole," Cilla said, and handed him the letter.

But just as Richard reached for it, the paper burst into flames.

"What the . . ." Richard exclaimed, and looked up at Beogoat, who was smiling.

"I love that trick," Beogoat said. "It's good for lighting pipes too."

Grover laughed.

Richard glared at Beogoat. "You'll regret that." He turned to Grover. "What was in that message?"

"Lord Hans wanted to say you were an asshole," Grover said.

Richard's eyes blazed. His mouth opened but nothing came out. He pointed at Grover, then Cilla, and then Beogoat, but he could only make grunting noises. Then he turned and stormed off.

"Great going," Cilla said as she watched Richard storm off.

"What was I supposed to say?" Grover asked. "I couldn't . . ." And then he noticed the two representatives were still waiting. "You two can go now."

"Has the message changed?" the Reichton envoy asked.

"Has it?" Grover asked Cilla and Beogoat.

"Yeah," Cilla said. "Tell him Lord Richard won't be able to come."

"Very well," the Reichton envoy said. They then both bowed and started to walk off.

"What did you expect me to do?" Grover asked when the envoy was gone. "I couldn't tell him what was in that message."

"Still," Cilla said, "you could have made something up."

"I think he's the least of our problems," Grover said. "We still have to deal with Hans. If we don't do something fast then we're really going to be in trouble."

"Well, what do you want from me?" Cilla asked.

"A plan," Grover said. "You were the one who wanted to stay."

"Well, that's when I thought we still had a chance," Cilla said.

"So do you want to leave now?" Grover asked.

"Anytime," Beogoat said.

"No," Cilla said. "No, I don't."

"You're crazy," Grover said. "You're crazy if you want to stay. "Isn't she crazy, Beogoat?"

"Probably," Beogoat said.

"Shut up," Cilla said. "I didn't ask you. And where are you with all your bright ideas?"

"My idea was for you two to leave," Beogoat said.

"Hans is going to send over those bodies when the Lords don't show up," Grover said. "Unless we do something."

"Then we'll do something," Cilla said. "We'll go over and get the bodies. We'll destroy them."

"And how are we going to do that?" Grover asked.

"Simple," Cilla said. "We'll just walk over there, like we're going to see the bodies, and then we'll steal them."

"How?" Grover asked. "He'll see us coming over. And we're unarmed."

"That's no problem," Cilla said. "Because we have our weapons hidden by the reflecting pool. Right, Beogoat?"

Beogoat nodded.

"What weapons?" Grover asked.

"The weapons we brought with us," Cilla said. "Beogoat hid them around the reflecting pool."

"Oh yeah," Grover said. "Now I remember. But I still don't think we will . . ."

"Come on," Cilla said. "We have to catch up with those envoys."

Treachery at Home
and Abroad

The reflecting pool stood empty. Hans could see the rippling pool through the various marble columns from where he hid behind a statue of a long-dead prince. The last time he stood here he had been waiting for Phillip of Wunderkinde to arrive so he could kill him. So much had happened since then that it seemed like another lifetime. Since then, Phillip and Voss had died, come back to life, he had lost Winona and had to retreat back to his own principality, lost the support of his allies and gained them back, and now he was back where he wanted to be, with the armies of Sousterhoven behind him, but with Phillip still opposing him even after death. But that would change. Soon Phillip and Voss would die a second, and hopefully more permanent, death. But as he thought that, he had a strange vision of himself, years from now, waiting to kill the fourth and fifth versions of Phillip and Voss. He shook the vision from his head. It was only a matter of time before Grover and Cilla, as they were called, would arrive with the envoy and he would kill them. Just like he had killed Phillip and Voss.

When he first saw that it was the impostors of Phillip and Voss coming with the envoy he thought his plan had failed. That the Westerhoven alliance would never learn the truth. And then he realized it was the opportunity of a lifetime. He could kill them and it would be the same as informing the alliance they were dead. He never thought why they were coming over. Their intentions didn't matter. Only that they arrived.

He thought he saw some movement and noticed that the two representatives he had sent as the envoy were walking into the enclosure that housed the reflecting pool. The Reichton envoy walked in first and looked back as the Astertov envoy entered. Then they both waited and looked back. Looking, presumably, for Phillip and Voss.

Hans pulled out his sword from its sheath. In a few moments Grover and Cilla would be walking into the reflecting pool looking for him and would see the tarp covering the two bodies. When they discovered the bodies, he would make his entrance.

Hans stared at the spot between two columns where he thought they would walk through. He kept on staring. A few moments later he was wondering what took them so long.

"Where are they?" Hans muttered.

Behind him Byron coughed. "Maybe they got lost."

"But they were being guided," Hans said.

Byron shrugged. "Well, maybe they changed their minds."

"Maybe," Hans said, and kept on looking. The two members of the envoy went over to one of the columns and looked back in the direction they had come. They conferred for a little bit and shook their heads.

Hans waited a stretch of time more and then sheathed his blade. "They're not coming. We'll move to plan two."

"Send the bodies over," Byron said.

"Send the bodies over," Hans agreed.

The darkness of the forest enveloped them and cut off the steady breeze. Deflected by the heavy foliage, it whistled through the treetops, making a sound like waves on the beach, as the leaves were made to constantly vibrate. Looking up, Grover could see the various colors of the leaves, as they had changed. There were reds, yellows, oranges, and purples. And mixed in were a few green leaves that just refused to change color at all. But the leaves that were beneath their feet were primarily the dead color of brown. They crunched beneath his boots.

Grover was busy gazing up at the foliage and didn't even notice Cilla had stopped right in front of him.

"What the . . ." Grover said, looking down to see Cilla spilled on the ground with a dazed expression. "What's up?"

"Not me," Cilla said, struggling to her feet. "Can't you even watch where you're going?"

"Why'd you stop?" Grover asked. "Those guys are going to lose us."

"Good," Cilla said, pulling a few leaves out of her hair. "Let them get far ahead of us."

"I don't get it," Grover said. "I thought we were going to get the bodies."

Cilla shook her head. "I've been thinking it over. We should leave."

"Leave?" Grover said. "But that was my idea. I thought . . ."

"Sorry," Cilla interjected, "but this is stupid. Hans has got us this time. We won't be able to get those bodies. I don't know what I was thinking."

"But you said . . ."

"Forget what I said," Cilla said. "I was wrong."

"You were what?" Grover asked.

"Wrong," Cilla said.

"Wrong," Grover said. "Did you say wrong? As in you were incorrect? As in not right? As in mistaken, inaccurate, false, amiss, etc., etc. Like maybe you didn't know what you were doing for once and your companion was right all along? That you were misguided in your thoughts, false in your premises, and faulty in your thinking? Is that what you're saying? Or have I misinterpreted what you said, and misrepresented your intentions in any way?"

"No," Cilla said. "You got the general idea."

"Then I was right?" Grover said. "Correct, accurate, true, on target?"

"Stop gloating," Cilla said. "It's bad for your complexion."

Grover kept smiling anyway. "I'm glad you've come around to my thinking."

"No, *my* thinking has finally . . . no, your thinking has . . . Just shut up, Grover." And she hit him for good measure.

Grover winced but kept on smiling. He turned around and started to walk his way out of the forest and back to their own encampment. Cilla followed closely behind.

In the Westerhoven encampment, Ivan was saying, "I didn't even know Beogoat was a person. I really thought he was just a goat," when Lord Richard walked in with a small, pudgy man in tow. All the Lords stopped what they were saying and looked up. Richard stopped at the edge of the circle and was beaming from ear to ear.

"We were just talking about Beogoat returning," Dianna said.

Richard nodded. He looked hastily around the circle of Lords. "Where's Phillip?"

"Why, we're waiting for both of you to show up," Sajin said. "We heard there was an envoy."

"He's not here?" Richard asked in surprise. "How about Voss?"

"Why would Voss be here?" Bertrand asked. "You know those two only travel as a pair."

Richard looked flustered. The man behind him fidgeted.

"Is there something wrong?" Dianna asked.

"Yes, plenty," Richard said. And he looked back to the man and gestured for him to come forward. "I'd like you all to meet

Brother Benjamin. He used to be known as Beoweasel, and was Beogoat's assistant in evil. He has an interesting story to tell."

"Stories?" Kirk asked. "What's this about?"

"Just listen," Richard said. And he turned to Brother Benjamin. "Tell it to them just like you told it to me."

Brother Benjamin came forward and tentatively began to recount his strange and fabulous tale.

On the silent battlements of the ancient city of Hoven, Erich tugged on his red scarf. The wind blew hard and he was cold from being up where there was no protection from the elements. Beside him Prince Thorn also shivered. They had stood side by side all morning watching the movements of both armies. They had watched as the Sousterhoven envoy went over to the Westerhoven camp, and saw the familiar shapes of Phillip and Voss walking into the *Still Standing Forest*. They had been waiting for the right time to launch their surprise attack. And with the primary leader of the Westerhoven forces gone to possibly confer with the primary leader of the Sousterhoven forces, it seemed like the right time to move. "It's time," Erich simply said.

"Attack just the Westerhoven forces?" Thorn asked.

"No," Erich said. "I want you to attack the flanks of both the Westerhoven and the Sousterhoven forces."

"But they outnumber us," Thorn pointed out.

"It's time," Erich said. "I feel it." And he reached into the pouch that never left his side and pulled out the pearl-white sphere with a green streak running through it.

It was only the second time Thorn had seen the *Stone* and it took his breath away. The air in their immediate vicinity seemed to vibrate and tingle with its very presence.

"Can I touch it?" Thorn asked in awe.

"No," Erich said, and pulled the *Stone* out of reach.

Thorn withdrew his hand. "I'll attack on your signal."

"Attack now," Erich said, "before Phillip and Hans have a chance to come to an agreement."

Thorn nodded his head and withdrew. He did not signal the trumpeters to alert the troops. The nature of the assault was to be silent and sudden so that they could create an atmosphere of chaos among the two armies, so that before the Sousterhoven or Westerhoven armies could reorganize to meet their assault, they would be put upon by another threat, the power of the *Sacred Stone*.

First, the Wind Will Stop

Grover and Cilla emerged from the forest and started to trod down into the great field that lay between the three armies. The sky was dark and overcast and the armies on either hill seemed like great black tumors on the earth, pulsing with a vibrant malignancy. The ancient city of Hoven stood stark and silent on the hill, no sign of the forces within except for the banners that stood taut in the breeze.

"So what changed your mind?" Grover asked.

"It didn't make sense," Cilla said. "I've been pushing this thing too far. It's better to get out while we can still cut our losses. We've done pretty good so far. We've held the alliance together for longer than it would have lasted. But Hans knows the game is up and can prove it. There's no point in struggling now. I was doing everything on impulse, and when I had some time to think about it, I didn't see any way we could pull it off."

Grover nodded his head. "We did do pretty good, though, didn't we?"

"Yeah," Cilla said, clapping him on the back. "We did do pretty good."

Grover smiled. "You were great too. Involved in all those plots."

"I know," Cilla said. "I was pretty great. But I was just being myself."

"Me too," Grover said. "But at least I was a guy."

"What are you saying?" Cilla accused. "I bet I was a better guy than you could ever be."

"Well, I bet I could be a better woman," Grover said.

"Hah, that's a laugh," Cilla said. "You wouldn't last a minute."

"You think so?" Grover cried.

"Yeah," Cilla said.

Grover turned to say something else when he noticed a change in the air and he thought he saw something flash out of the corner of his eye on the walls of the ancient city of Hoven.

"Did you see that?" Grover asked. "That light?"

"Yeah," Cilla said. And then she noticed that the banners on the castle had fallen limp. "That's weird."

"What?" Grover asked.

"Don't you feel it?" Cilla asked. "The wind has stopped."

Grover sniffed the air for a moment and raised his hand up but the former steady breeze had halted. "You're right. But why would it stop?"

"I don't know," Cilla said, shaking her head.

Grover looked at the ancient city of Hoven, at the limp banners, and turned to Cilla. "Let's get out of here." And started to move faster to the Westerhoven lines.

In the Sousterhoven camp, Hans raised his head and felt a change in the air. The cold biting wind seemed to lapse for a moment. His mind went back to the bodies which were being brought forth and placed in a wagon, where they could be pulled over and displayed to the Westerhoven forces.

Hans wouldn't have noticed the wind lapse if he hadn't been wearing such warm clothing. He grew hot immediately in the heavy fabrics. He pulled the cloak away from his neck and noticed that the banners all along the lines were lying limp against their poles.

"Strange," Hans said, and he felt a chill run through him. His gaze went to the walls of the ancient city of Hoven and hovered there. He felt an expectancy in the air. Something was about to happen.

"The bodies are almost ready," Byron informed him.

"Good," Hans said absently. "Did you notice the lapse in the breeze?"

"I hadn't noticed," Byron said. "Do you want me to bring the bodies over myself?"

Hans nodded absently. Byron took this as an affirmative and departed to lead the wagon over to the Westerhoven side.

Hans turned to an aide who stood beside him. "Did you notice the lapse in the breeze?"

"Yes, Lord Hans," the aide said. "It's very strange."

Hans nodded. "Notify the other Lords. Ready everyone for battle."

The aide departed and soon calls were going up and down the line to all the troops. But the calls fell dead in the overbearing stillness of the air.

On the opposite hill, the Westerhoven Lords had moved to the battle lines where they watched the return of Phillip and Voss.

"You see," Ivan said. "They have returned. There is no betrayal."

"It's your word against theirs," Dianna said. "And I don't like this Brother Benjamin character."

"All we need is Beogoat to corroborate the story," Richard explained.

"Are you sure this had nothing to do with your dislike of Beogoat?" Dianna asked.

"I'm surprised you would think I would have such petty vendettas," Richard said. "This is beyond all that. I wouldn't make charges unless I thought they were true."

Dianna nodded grimly and said, "We will see."

It was then that the wind lapsed. Sajin was the first to notice it, since the wind had been especially hard on his face. The lapse came as a welcome relief and he breathed easier. And then he noticed that the wind did not resume and the air seemed to grow stale and stagnant. The banners that had been standing taut now fell limp. Sajin loosened his collar around his cloak and looked to the other Lords to see if they noticed.

"The wind," Sajin finally said. "It has stopped."

"Stopped," Dianna said almost in puzzlement, and then she too noticed the banners. "I hadn't noticed. I guess it's a good thing because we would have had it in our faces during the whole battle."

"Winds just don't stop," Bertrand said.

And all along the line, soldiers and knights raised their heads and looked around, feeling the absence of the wind.

"What was that?" Kirk asked, pointing to the ancient city of Hoven.

Everyone looked at the dark walls of the city and noticed a bright flash of light, like a piece of the sun reflected in a mirror.

"I don't know," Dianna said.

Cilla and Grover were about two-thirds across the field now when Cilla put out a hand to stop Grover.

"There it is again," Cilla said. "That flash. You saw it, didn't you?"

"I didn't . . ." Grover started to say, and then turned to look at the ancient city of Hoven again. He saw the flash, and it was brighter this time. "What the . . . what is it?"

Cilla shook her head. "Hopefully we won't be around long enough to find out."

Grover saw the flash again. "It looks like . . . like it's a signal of some kind. You know?"

"A signal," Cilla said. "But who could Erich be signaling?"

Grover shook his head. "I don't know, but I think maybe we should adjust our pace to a run."

Byron looked at the wooden wagon with the bodies of Phillip and Voss prominently displayed on the riding bench. They had been strapped in for security and maximum visibility. Unfortunately the wagon had to be pulled by human power instead of horse power, since they hadn't been able to bring horses over to the island.

"Okay," Byron said to the six soldiers who were assigned to pull the wagon. "We're going now."

And the four soldiers in front started to pull the wagon out of the forest while the two soldiers behind pushed on the back.

Byron walked ahead to make sure the path was clear.

Hans and his fellow leaders all along the line also noticed the flash of light that looked like a signal.

"What does this mean, Hans?" asked Bertold, who had come up from his reserve forces. "You didn't tell us about this."

"He has neglected to tell us many things," said Luke, who had also come up to confer with Hans.

Hans just kept silent and stared at the city.

"You see," Romeo was saying, "I don't get it. Why would Phillip order us to guard the ground on the other side of the river? Nobody is going to steal it."

Beogoat nodded. He had walked back into camp to wait for Grover and Cilla's return only to stumble into Romeo and Bill, who had just lately arrived.

"Exactly," Bill said. "I mean how can we write any epic poems if we can't live the experience, of man fighting against man, in a great battle of ideas and honor? We need to see it and feel it to write it. You understand?"

"Then why don't you participate in the battle?" Beogoat asked, puffing on his pipe.

"Hey, whoa," Romeo said with an appropriate hair toss. "Let's not get carried away here. We meant—watch from a safe distance. We're artists. If we die who's going to record the experience almost as if you were there?"

"Why should the experience be reported?" Beogoat asked.

"So people will know and learn from the events," Bill answered.

"Learn what?" Beogoat asked.

"Learn what happened, dude," Romeo said.

"But you don't write it like it happened," Beogoat said. "So what will they learn?"

"That we're great poets," Bill explained.

"Yeah," Romeo said, and he looked closely at the pipe Beogoat was smoking. "Do you have any more of that stuff?"

"No, I . . ." And then Beogoat noticed the absence of the wind. "The wind stopped."

"So what?" Romeo asked. "That's good."

Beogoat shook his head. "No. No, this means something. I know it means something." And he rubbed his forehead.

"It means it's not windy anymore," Romeo said.

"No, that's not it," Beogoat said, and promptly stood up and started to pace to decrease his agitation and increase his memory.

"Yes, it does," Romeo said. "Doesn't it, Bill?"

"Sure," Bill said. "Maybe we should write a poem about it."

Beogoat ignored Romeo and Bill and looked out to see the ancient city of Hoven silhouetted against the sky. Then he saw the bright flash of light like signals. And it knocked something in his memory. "By damn. By goddamn," he said, whipping the pipe out of his mouth. "I know this means something. First the wind stops. Then there are bright flashes of light. W then F. God, it's right at the tip of my tongue."

Romeo strummed a chord on the lute. "The wind was cold and brisk . . . and then it stopped." Romeo looked up. "I don't know, Bill, the song really doesn't flow."

"Try again," Bill said.

Beogoat shook his head, stomped his feet, and then put the pipe back in his mouth again but the answer he was looking for still eluded him. "Damn it. Damn it. Damn it. I know this means something. Something bad. Something very bad. Something very bad is going to happen."

Grover and Cilla looked up the hill and noticed that the Lords of Westerhoven had gathered and were watching their progress.

"Look," Grover said, nudging Cilla. "They're waiting for us."

Cilla nodded. "I see them. What do you want me to do about it?"

"Should we just ignore them?" Grover said. "Pretend we don't see them?"

"I don't think they'll buy that," Cilla said. "I guess we'll just have to talk to them. Get it over with and then get out of here."

"You mean *I* have to talk to them," Grover said. "That's what you mean."

Cilla nodded. "It's only one more time."

"Well . . ." Grover started, and then he looked to the ancient city of Hoven. He was about to turn away when he noticed that the gates were wide open now and troops were beginning to gush out, like blood from a serious wound. They did not walk out but came out at a trot. There were knights wearing the black colors of Erich and there were knights wearing the white and red colors of Hoenecker.

"Oh shit," Grover said. "They're attacking."

"What?" Cilla shouted, and then saw that what Grover said was true. "What an idiot. He'll be slaughtered." And then she laughed.

"Please tell me what's funny," Grover said, "because those troops are going to be attacking our lines."

"They're not our lines anymore," Cilla said. "Don't you understand?"

"But I don't think Erich knows that," Grover said.

Cilla shrugged. "Better keep running, then." And started running straight toward the Lords of Westerhoven.

"They're attacking," Hans said, watching the troops emerge from the gates of Hoven. Dark shapes, carrying swords and spears. White-and-red-colored knights heavily armored but still moving swiftly. All of them running forward. And then dividing, the two forces splitting to go straight for the flanks of both armies.

"He's attacking both of us," Hans said aloud. And he looked to his aide who stood beside him. "I don't believe it."

"Do you have orders?" the aide asked.

"Yes," Hans said. "Tell David to repulse only." David of Gustavus's armies were the ones being attacked on the exposed flank. "And tell him not to advance until I order it. Tell Calvin the same. Bertold should just hold. And tell Luke to wait until I give further orders."

The aide nodded and left to give out the orders.

"I don't like this," Hans said. "This doesn't make sense."

The orders were sent to various runners who sped swiftly down along the crest of the hill to report to each leader. David, who was already in the midst of repulsing the forces on his flank, scowled when he heard the orders but decided to stand fast until Hans ordered otherwise. He didn't know that Hans's order was given partly in an attempt to have him killed in battle, and had he known he couldn't have acted much differently. Calvin, who was the next closest to the battle, also agreed to the orders. Bertold had no problem with his but worried that he might have to be called into battle after all. Everyone agreed with the orders to stand fast except Luke.

"What?" Luke cried at the runner.

"Those are the orders," the runner said.

"Go," Luke ordered him. And the runner departed. Luke, who was on the other extreme flank, far away from any immediate danger, looked grimly at the battlefield where Sousterhoven knights fought sword-to-sword with the knights of Hoenecker and Erich and felt stymied. He had come here to wage war, not to wait for orders. Now was the perfect time to attack the Westerhoven forces on the other flank when they were being distracted by the attack of Erich and Prince Thorn's forces. Hans just couldn't see the opportunity. He was still hoping the Westerhoven leadership would collapse when they saw the bodies of Phillip and Voss. But that would never happen. The best way to defeat them was to attack when they least expected it. Like now.

Luke turned to his aide. "Order the troops forward. We're attacking."

"Very good," the aide said, and eagerly departed to give the message.

But back along the line Hans was unaware of the defection of one of his allies. He stood on the hill, looking gloomily on, as the Gustavan line buckled in under the onslaught. That wouldn't last long. Soon the forces of Erich and Thorn would wear thin and they would stumble and be repulsed. And then, when the time was right, he would attack the Westerhoven line. He just had to give more time so that the wagon could get across.

Second,
the Earth Will Shake

If seen from above, the deployment of all the forces in action made an equilateral triangle. At the top of the triangle was the ancient city of Hoven holding the army of Erich and Prince Thorn, and at the bottom left of the triangle was the army of Westerhoven, and at the bottom right was the army of Sousterhoven. And in the space between these three points was the great field before the city.

Now, when the armies of Erich and Prince Thorn left the city gates, they divided and went separate paths. Half of the forces went along one line of the triangle to the Sousterhoven army, hitting the extreme flank held by the Gustavans, and the other half of the force went down to the Westerhoven army and hit their extreme flank, which was held by the Ubbergammus.

In this sort of situation, where a small force was attacking an extreme flank, all the commander of the larger force would have to do is send out other forces to envelop and surround the attacking force and eventually pacify it. Which is what Hans would have eventually done, had not Luke of Astertov decided to pull out from the consolidated force, and move his army, along the bottom line of the triangle, straight for the other unprotected flank of the Westerhoven army. Which put the Westerhoven army in the position of defending two extreme flanks at once.

Grover and Cilla reached the front of the Westerhoven line just as the Astertov forces pulled free of the Sousterhoven line and started to descend their hill onto the great field.

"We're being attacked on two flanks," Sajin said. "And you wish to put up with this foolishness." Sajin looked down the line where his troops would bear the initial brunt of Erich's assault. Just now the troops were beginning to engage in combat, and Sajin had sent a runner to his other commanders telling them to hold fast.

"It's necessary," Richard said. "How can we trust him in battle?"

Grover and Cilla stopped running when they reached the assembled Lords. It was then that they noticed that Beoweasel was standing there and not meeting their gaze at all.

The Lords had formed a semicircle in which Grover and Cilla were at the head.

"Uh-oh," Cilla said, nudging Grover and nodding in the direction of Beoweasel.

Grover's eyes opened wide, and he noticed that the Lords were scrutinizing them.

"They look like them to me," Ivan said, rubbing his protruding stomach. He still supported Phillip as long as everyone else did.

"Hello, Lord Phillip, or should I say Grover?" Lord Richard asked. He did not say this with any malice, but with contempt for who they were.

Grover looked at Cilla with a worried expression.

"And greetings to you too, Voss, or should I say Cilla?" Richard asked.

Cilla glanced over at Grover, and gave him the eye about Beoweasel.

"What?" Grover asked the Lords. "What are you talking about?"

"Why did you meet with the envoy without consulting us?" Dianna asked. She took the position of clearing up the matter. She seemed to be saying, I'm not part of this nonsense, but somebody has to take charge.

"Because it was for me," Grover lied easily.

"Let's forget that nonsense," Richard said. "We know who you are. If you value your souls then you'll confess."

"I don't understand," Grover said, who understood all too well. "We're being attacked. We should be coordinating a plan."

"But what did you see Hans about?" Bertrand asked. Like all businessmen he drove to the heart of the matter.

"He's right," said Sajin, whose only concern was for the battle at hand. "This is all nonsense, and I'm sorry I was a part of it. I'm going to my troops."

"Wait," Richard said.

Sajin shook his head. "I'm leaving. And you all would do well to return to your forces as well."

"Lord Sajin," Dianna pleaded, because she knew she was losing an ally in this argument.

But Lord Sajin was hurrying down the line to meet the thrust of Erich's attack.

"Forget him," Richard said to Dianna.

Some runners from the Wunderkinde came up and broke in to speak to Phillip.

"Lord Phillip, what are your orders?"

Grover turned to Cilla, and Cilla said, "Stand the ground."

Grover turned to the runner. "Stand the ground."

"You see," Richard exclaimed. "It's just like Benjamin said. He refers to the other one because she is the leader."

"She?" Kirk said. "That is obviously not a woman." He pointed straight at Cilla. Kirk, who only knew that he owed Phillip and Wunderkinde a debt, wasn't able to understand the issue at hand.

Grover turned to Young Dianna and tried to pretend he didn't know what they were talking about. "I don't understand what's going on here."

"Neither do I," Dianna said. "But Lord Richard claims that you are an impostor."

"Impostor!" Grover exclaimed. "I'm not an impostor. I'm exactly who I am and no less."

"Yes, you are," Beoweasel said. "He lies. He's really a hired hero."

Grover looked shocked. "How dare he?"

Lord Richard looked at Grover. "A member of the Brotherhood would not lie."

"That's true," Dianna said with some puzzlement. "I have never heard one that lies."

"I still think it's false," Kirk said. "How could this not be Lord Phillip and Voss?"

"Maybe there's some test we could give to verify," Bertrand said. "Something that only he knows."

"That's easy enough," Richard said.

"Are you saying we are not who we say we are?" Cilla asked. "I don't believe this. You have insulted us both."

"Have we?" Richard asked. "If you are Voss and Lord Phillip I apologize, but what I see tells me that I'm not wrong."

Grover reached down his side reflexively for his rapier but found it wasn't there.

"Though you do look remarkably like him," Richard said.

Grover's hand leaped to his blond beard and he appealed to Cilla for help with his eyes, but Cilla just shrugged.

"But you don't look much like a man at all," Richard said, looking solely at Cilla. "I don't know why I never saw it before."

Cilla scowled and tried to sound indignant. "Are you saying I'm not a man?"

Richard grinned slightly. "Come, can't you all see that they are impostors?"

Bertrand looked closely. "Nope."

Dianna shook her head.

Kirk and Ivan didn't think they could see it either.

"It's because of the magic," Richard said. "I told you we should have banned all wizards. But you'll see soon enough." And he turned to address Grover and Cilla. "Answer me this, Lord Phillip, and all doubts will be cast aside. This is a simple question that everyone should know who is from this land. What was the name of the predecessor of each nation of Westerhoven?"

Grover blanched and he looked to Cilla.

"You see, he does not know the answer," Richard said.

"My God," Bertrand said, squinting and rubbing his eyes. "They don't look like them at all."

"Let's go," Cilla hissed to Grover.

Grover turned to go.

And then the earth shook.

All across the island of Hoven the tremor was felt. Along the crests of both hills the armies of the West and South swayed, some soldiers and knights falling to their knees, tents falling toward the ground, banners also making a downward journey. The combatants along both fronts stumbled and lost their balance. All halted temporarily while they waited for the earth to stop moving.

In the middle of the great field the Astertov army stumbled and came to a halt. The banners dipped and fell. Knights and soldiers grabbed onto each other to stop from falling, while a few threw down their weapons and turned to run.

In the forest surrounding the reflecting pool the trees swayed back and forth, and the soldiers pulling the wagon lost their grip. Byron grabbed hold of the wagon and looked up at the treetops. Leaves tumbled all about him in a great rain of foliage. "Don't worry," Byron said to the soldiers, "this isn't supposed to be happening."

"What the . . ." Romeo cried out, feeling the earth sway beneath his feet. "Is this your doing?" he asked Beogoat. "Hold on to me," he told Bill. Bill grabbed Romeo so that he wouldn't fall.

Beogoat stood with his legs spread wide to absorb the shock of the trembling earth. He pulled out his pipe and a light sprang up in his eyes. "By God, that's it. I knew I would figure out the answer." And he laughed and danced around, losing his balance and falling to the ground.

"I told you he was smoking something in that pipe," Romeo said.

"He's mad," Bill said. "He has all the classic signs. Unexplainable mood swings and unpredictable behavior."

Beogoat looked up at the two cringing sycophants. "I'm not mad." And then the joy disappeared from his face. "Oh shit, Erich or Thorn must have gotten the *Stone*." He tried to get up but fell down again. "Oh no, this is worse than I thought. Not the *Stone*. The *Stone* has been found."

"You see, he's talking about getting stoned," Romeo said to Bill.

"I still think he's mad. He's not making any sense. Mad people never do."

"Neither do people when they're really wasted," Romeo said. "I think he's into some really heavy stuff."

"I'm still in favor of madness as an explanation," Bill said.

The earth finally came to a halt and Beogoat stood up. "I have to warn them. I have to warn them." And he ran off, leaving his pipe behind him.

"Freak out," Romeo said, and then bent down to pick up the pipe, sniffing the smoke. "I knew it," he said, and took a puff. He then offered the pipe to Bill.

"No thanks," Bill said. "I never found drugs a stimulus to creativity."

"I'm not offering it to get creative," Romeo said. "I'm offering it to blow your mind. So you won't be able to do anything comprehensible or useful for the next couple of hours."

"You mean, go mad," Bill said.

"You can call it whatever you want, dude," Romeo said. "Either way you get messed up."

"In that case," Bill said, grabbing the pipe, "okay."

No More Compromises

One of the Astertov knights helped Luke up from the ground. Everywhere, the knights and soldiers were getting up from their knees and turning to one another to ask what happened. Luke didn't even think to halt the attack. Even if he had thought about it, he would never have turned back once committing his forces. That would be a great loss of face. And it would show that he had been wrong to attack when he did. But he didn't feel he was wrong. The Westerhoven line lay open before him, not even ready yet to repulse him. He still had the chance to crush them. And once Hans and the others saw the opportunity they would follow also. "Forward," Luke ordered, and the Astertov forces, nine thousand strong, marched forward, their banners raised and their weapons drawn.

"Damn it," Hans swore when he saw that the Astertov forces were already halfway across the field. He had sent runners to order them back, but the runners weren't even allowed to see Luke. Now there was a gap along his line. Luke had forced him into a decision he wasn't ready to make. He had wanted to attack the Westerhoven forces when they were weak and disoriented. But they still believed that Grover was their Lord Phillip and they would be a strong united force. Erich and Thorn were doing much better than he expected against David of Gustavus. He had to commit some of Calvin's forces to the fray, and now his battle line was all over the place. Everything was falling apart just when he needed it to stay together. And the earth shaking had come as a surprise also. He had no idea where that came from, but it worried him. So thinking quickly, Hans ordered Bertold to take the place of the Astertov forces along the front line. And he would wait to see how Luke fared before committing any forces. He wasn't going to present a disorganized battle line.

Bertold received the orders to proceed forward to take the place of the Astertov troops. He had suspected something like this would happen all along. They all had said he would be held in reserve, but he knew in the end that they had been lying. They were all liars. Because here was the order to proceed forward. He knew Hans had ordered Luke forward to attack just to goad him into battle. Well, he, Bertold of Teuton, wasn't going to leave his position. Not for a moment. Not until he was attacked.

On the wall of the city, Erich stood poised against the dark sky. He could easily see that the surprise attack had worked better than he had thought. His forces were actually succeeding in their attacks on the flanks of both armies, taken unawares. For a moment, he almost thought he could win it just with his forces alone. But he was wise enough to know that his forces would eventually lose if they didn't have any support. So he kept on using the *Stone*.

It pulsed beneath his hand, glowing bright. He wasn't even sure how to use the *Stone*, but one didn't really need to know how. The *Stone* knew how. And Erich had read enough to know what to expect next. He cast his eyes skyward.

The alliance fell apart right after the earth moved. The disguises which stood so long under the power of belief wavered under the onslaught of doubt.

"You see," Richard said with conviction. "We have been deceived all along." He pointed straight at Grover and Cilla, who actually appeared as Grover and Cilla to the Lords of Westerhoven.

"Well, then," Bertrand said gruffly, "that means my alliance to Wunderkinde is invalid. And I no longer have to stay here and get slaughtered."

"Bertrand," Dianna pleaded.

"That goes for me too," Kirk said, shaking his head. "My father's alliance was with the *real* Phillip of Wunderkinde."

Ivan, seeing that everyone else was denouncing Phillip, joined in. "I knew it all along. But I didn't have any proof."

"All our alliances are invalid," Richard said. "And we have been fooled into an all-out war by a scheming wizard and his two accomplices."

"Hey," Cilla said. "We were just doing our job. We didn't mean for this to happen."

"Yeah," Grover said, but not too aggressively because he expected Richard to kill him. "I was just supposed to come here to marry Winona in Phillip's place to legitimize the heir. To help you. But everything got fouled up."

"Do you know the penalty for such treason?" Richard asked. He pointed at Grover.

Grover gulped.

Just then a runner from the Ubbergammus came in. He bowed to the Lords and then swiftly said, "Lord Sajin requests help. His forces are being pushed back."

No one said anything. The runner looked around. "Won't anyone lend us aid?"

"Ivan is closest," Cilla said evenly.

"You have no right to talk," Richard said without malice. "This has nothing to do with you."

The runner looked confused. He turned to Ivan of Dresdel. "Should I tell Lord Sajin that you will be sending troops?"

Ivan looked past the runner. "My alliance was to Lord Phillip also. I have no alliance with Lord Sajin."

"And neither do I," Bertrand said. "And as far as I'm concerned this ends our partnership." He then turned his back and walked off.

The runner turned to Grover. "Lord Phillip, what is this?"

"He's not Lord Phillip," Richard said. "He is an impostor. You have been deceived."

The runner looked confused. "Not Lord Phillip?"

Grover shook his head. And he looked at Richard and Dianna. "We were leaving anyway."

Cilla nodded. "We were on our way out."

"You're leaving, Lord Phillip?" the runner asked. "But . . . but what about your promise to Lord Sajin?"

"Well," Grover said, "I'm sure the real Lord Phillip would have kept his promise."

"I don't understand," the runner said.

Cilla turned to Grover. "We have to find Beogoat. And get out of here."

"The alliance is shattered," Dianna said to the runner.

The runner looked stunned.

"I will send my troops to help Sajin," Dianna said with conviction. And she looked at Richard when she said this.

"As you wish," Richard said. "But I'm withdrawing also."

"And to think we were betrayed by our own side," Cilla said. And she walked out of the group, with Grover following. "I don't think we ever had a chance in the first place."

Lord Richard turned back to Dianna. "You see, I was right."

"Congratulations," Dianna said coolly, and she walked away also.

Kirk then withdrew, as did Ivan, until only Richard and
Beoweasel stood together. Beoweasel said nothing. Richard
turned to order that his troops withdraw.

Byron emerged from the dense foliage first, plucking leaves from
his hair. The six soldiers were still trying to pull the wagon up the
last incline and onto the ridge. The wagon had caught on some
underbrush and they were having some difficulty dislodging it.
Byron called back to ask about their progress.

"Just a few moments," one of the soldiers said.

They had survived the earth shaking, and Byron had pushed on
to complete his task. The soldiers had been worried, but when the
earth did not shake anymore, Byron said there was nothing more
to fear. The earth moving was not such an unlikely event that
people had cause to fear.

And so they were almost out into the great field, and soon they
would deliver the bodies to watch the Westerhoven alliance fall.
Byron was satisfied. It was then that he moved up further and
looked out on the field.

All he saw were troops everywhere. Troops running across the
field, troops engaged in combat, troops falling to the ground dead
or wounded, troops running away from the battle, banners being
boldly brought forward, and banners being boldly picked up when
a soldier fell. There were Erich's troops, Prince Thorn's troops,
and Astertov troops. The war had already started.

"We got it free," one of the soldiers said.

Byron shook his head and yelled back, "Forget it. The war has
already started without us."

"Son of a bitch," one of the soldiers said, and they let the
wagon slide back down the hill. "That doesn't mean we have to
fight, does it?"

Sometimes Miscommunication Helps

The Astertov forces stampeded the Westerhoven flank, falling hard upon the troops of Wunderkinde and Kurtonburg. The Kurtonburg troops, unaware that the alliance had fallen, had started volleys of arrows as Astertov approached, but there weren't enough archers to hold back a force that large. The arrows, which usually were good at holding a force at bay, did nothing to deter the speed and the mass of the Astertov troops as they stormed up the hill. And neither did the fact they were charging uphill against a rooted force. By all accounts Astertov troops should have been repulsed, but instead they were able to break through the enemy lines with little difficulty, throwing the Westerhoven line into confusion. Luke's gamble seemed to be working. But he thought it was due to surprise, when it was really due to the fact that there were no leaders behind the armies.

And now the Westerhoven line was in danger of collapsing along both flanks, because the middle forces, made up of Bertrand's, Ivan's, and Richard's troops, were making no move to help reinforce their endangered allies. In fact, they were getting ready to pull out.

Luke found that development wholly invigorating and it only seemed to prove his point that he should have attacked in the first place. But even though he was doing so well, and the Westerhoven troops were breaking wherever he attacked, he was still worried that he was out there all alone. He expected Hans to send the Reichton troops in support, but instead they remained frozen on the opposing hill. Luke sent off runners to request aid from Hans, but his runners were rebuffed as he had rebuffed Hans's runners. It was almost as if Hans wanted him to fail.

Grover and Cilla moved quickly behind the lines to the Wunderkinde camp. They passed through abandoned encampments, some of the fires still burning where meals had been cooking. They heard the shouts and cries of men engaged in battle, the sound of sword on armor, of sword on sword, and of sword on flesh. But they were the distant background noises to their movement. It wasn't part of their problem anymore.

It was along the way they saw Beogoat running toward them.

"Good," Cilla said. "We're ready to leave."

Beogoat looked genuinely surprised to see them. "Then you've destroyed the bodies already."

"No," Grover said. "We changed our minds. We decided to leave."

"The alliance has fallen apart," Cilla said. "Beoweasel spilled the beans. All the Lords know who we are."

Beogoat looked shocked. "And you did all this in the past hour?"

"Apparently," Cilla said. "They know you're involved too."

"This is dreadful," Beogoat said. "Dreadful for my future employment prospects."

"Yeah, dreadful for everybody," Grover said. "You're just lucky they didn't kill us or we'd be pissed with you too."

"Yeah," Cilla said. "So zap us back."

"You can't leave now," Beogoat said. "Erich or Prince Thorn has the *Sacred Stone* and they're going to destroy us all."

"More reason to leave," Grover said. "Come on. Zap us now. We're not kidding."

Beogoat sighed and looked from Cilla to Grover. "I'm sorry it had to end like this. Are you sure?"

"Yeah, yeah," Cilla said. "Just do the magic trick."

Beogoat thrust his fingers to his temples in concentration.

But just then Dianna of Helmutov ran up, almost out of breath. "Wait, wait," she cried.

Grover turned, expecting to see that the Lords had changed their minds and were coming at them with torches and hand axes.

"It's Dianna," Cilla said.

Beogoat dropped his hands to his sides and waited.

"Don't stop," Cilla said.

Beogoat went back to concentrating, tightly closing his eyes.

Dianna ran until she was only a few yards from them and then stopped. "Wait."

"Stay back," Cilla said. "We don't want to hear it."

Dianna caught her breath. "I'm not here to condemn you."

"You're not?" Grover said. "Are you here to say good-bye, then?"

"Forget it," Cilla said to Grover. "You're not going to get her address. Intercultural dating never works. Besides, she's too smart for you."

"Hey," Grover protested.

Beogoat opened his eyes. "Do you want me to transport you or not?"

"Don't leave," Dianna said. "Stay a moment, and hear me out."

"Okay," Cilla said, shrugging. "I guess we can spare a moment."

Dianna walked closer. "I know that you two aren't the real Lord Phillip and Voss. But your army doesn't know that. It doesn't matter that we know the truth. If you leave, we'll be destroyed. But if you lead the armies, we'll win. Bertrand and Richard think they can just withdraw, but they'll be destroyed also. If you really meant to help us, then help us now. Don't leave. Stay and fight."

"Nice speech," Cilla said. "What do you think, Grover?"

"It was well done, impassioned, with a sense of urgency about it. I give it an eight and a half."

"I agree," Cilla said. "But I think she could have sounded a little more desperate. I give her an eight."

"What are you saying?" Dianna asked.

"We're not swayed by speeches," Cilla said.

"Well, I was sort of swept away with the moment," Grover said. "But I'm not motivated to do anything."

"Then you will not help?" Dianna asked.

"No," Cilla said.

Grover shook his head.

"Then you really have betrayed us." Dianna swore.

"Ouch," Grover said. "That hurts. Did you hear the way she said that?"

"Yeah," Cilla said. "She's a real pro. A real martyr for the cause." She turned to Beogoat. "Take us away, Beogoat."

Beogoat began to concentrate again. And then he opened his eyes.

"What is it?" Cilla asked.

"There's some sort of interference," Beogoat said.

"Stop fooling around," Cilla said, "and take us back."

"I'm not kidding," Beogoat said. "It must be the power of the *Sacred Stone*. It must be causing interference."

"You mean you're getting faulty reception?" Grover asked.

"Something like that," Beogoat said.

"Shit," Grover said. "Now what do we do?"

Dianna was still standing there and she spoke. "It is a sign that you can't leave. You're meant to help us."

"It's a no-exit sign," Cilla agreed. "But I don't believe in fate. We'll just sit this one out, until the *Stone* stops interfering."

"But didn't you say the *Stone* spells doom for us all?" Grover asked.

Beogoat nodded.

"This is not good," Grover said. "This is your fault, Cilla."

Just then, a runner of the Wunderkinde forces ran up. "There you are, Lord Phillip. Our forces are being pushed back."

"You see?" Dianna said, indicating that the runner couldn't tell if he was the real Phillip or not.

Grover turned to Cilla. "What do you say?"

"Well," Cilla said, "if we're stuck here, we might as well kick some butt."

"We're on our way," Grover told the runner. "Tell them not to worry."

"Then you will stay?" Dianna asked.

"For the moment," Grover said. "But we'll still probably get slaughtered."

"I told you the men will follow you," Dianna said. "I'm here. Sajin is here. And I'm sure the rest will follow if you lead them."

"You think so?" Cilla asked.

Dianna nodded.

"You're suffering from serious delusions, babe," Cilla said.

"You don't understand how popular Lord Phillip is," Dianna said.

"You're right," Cilla replied. "I don't."

Last, the Army Will Come

The soldiers and knights cheered when Grover and Cilla arrived in the Wunderkinde camp. In some instances the enemy had made it to some of the campsites and had set fire to tents and supplies, and there already was a haze of smoke in the air. But Phillip's tent was undamaged and it was there that Grover, Cilla, and Beogoat stumbled into Romeo and Bill.

"Whoa," Romeo said, lying on Phillip's cot.

"Yeah, what he said," Bill said. They lay there with glazed eyes.

Grover picked up Phillip's chain-mail shirt and with help from Cilla lowered it over his body. "So this *Sacred Stone* is supposed to be pretty bad stuff?"

"The worst," Beogoat said. "It was the power of the old Hoven kings."

"And Erich or Thorn has it?" Grover asked.

Beogoat nodded.

Grover felt the weight of the armor on him and grabbed his mighty sword, *Biff*.

"And what should we do about it?" Cilla asked. She went to pick up her club.

"There's nothing you can do unless you get the *Stone* before it's used."

Cilla shrugged. "Well, I guess we can try. What do you say, Grover?"

"I say I want to wear a helmet this time," he said.

"Grover, who's Grover?" Romeo asked, lifting his head.

"Shut up," Cilla said, waving her club.

"Okay," Romeo said, and fell back onto the cot.

Grover looked back and forth and found the helmet. "The hell with Phillip. I'm going to be protected." He placed the helmet firmly on his head. "I'm ready."

"Okay, then," Cilla said, and they exited the tent.

Once they rejoined the Wunderkinde troops, the troops had a focal point to rally around. Just the presence of Phillip made the Dude

Knights fight harder and better. Where they had once been pushed back, now they were doing the pushing. Where there had once been chaos, there was now order. And where there was once a rout, now there was an advance. All around, Grover heard the cheers of the knights and soldiers. The cheers of victory.

Luke of Astertov wasn't sure what was happening. One moment, his forces were breaking through all along the line. Some had even penetrated as far as the camps. Reports of success had not even gotten boring and then suddenly he was being pushed back by a tidal wave of knights. His green and white banners which had pushed forward almost out of sight, over the crest of the hill, were now rushing back at him. The green and white triangles chased the backs of knights and soldiers. And behind them came the Dude Knights whooping and cheering. Thousands of knights. Not just the Wunderkinde troops either, but the Kurtonburg troops were also pouring down the hill like the waters from a broken dam. Where one moment he had been able to touch and fondle victory, it now declared it had a headache and he was left on his own.

Not too far away, Hans watched with complacency as the Astertov troops were pushed back. He knew the attack had been unwise so he hadn't supported it. But now he saw the Westerhoven line was breaking apart. The Wunderkinde and Kurtonburg troops were pulling forward, but the rest—the Vagners, Meistertonnes, and Dresdels—were holding firm. It was akin to a limb that hangs on only by a small thread of flesh and muscle. It wasn't very strong and was soon to fall apart. This could just have been because they were being held in reserve. Even so, a gap was building between the two Westerhoven forces, between those who were pursuing the Astertov troops and those who were staying behind. It was the perfect time to attack. While the lines were broken apart, his forces could easily drive a wedge between the two and divide their strength, so they wouldn't be able to reinforce each other.

Hans was going to give the order to march when he noticed that Bertold was still holding ground. Why wasn't he advancing? He sent another runner, but the runner only returned to say that Bertold was having difficulty organizing the move and would be up when he could.

The Gustavan line had re-formed and the forces of Erich and Thorn were finally being pushed back, albeit slowly. That left

Calvin's and Hans's own forces free for the moment. It felt like the perfect time to strike. He knew it was. He never felt surer in his life.

So he gave the order.

Slowly his forces and Calvin's forces descended the field. Together they were about twenty thousand strong. They were about two-thirds the size of the entire Westerhoven force, but they weren't attacking the entire Westerhoven force. They were driving a wedge between the Kurtonburgs and the Vagners, acting as the knife that would sever the limb from the rest of the body. And as everyone knew, once the limb was severed from the body it was dead.

The day may not have gone as planned, but it seemed as if he would be victorious after all.

Dianna, true to her word, did the difficult maneuver of pulling her troops out of line, and bypassing the Dresdel troops which remained stationary, all in an effort to help Sajin. She felt as if she were the surgeon who could sew the damaged body back together. But the wounds were too many, and like the surgeon who has too much to do with limited resources she only ended up doing more harm than help. By the time she had pulled her troops from the line and scattered them, Sajin had already begun to repulse the troops of Erich and Prince Thorn, killing Thorn in the process. So now she was of little help to anybody.

Sajin might have appreciated her gesture, but he was too involved in the battle to notice that some of his allies were not taking part. It was this sort of concentration that had enabled him to repulse the attack of Thorn and Erich in the first place. But his concentration was also a hindrance. He had been trying to isolate Thorn so he could force him to surrender. Thorn's death had come by accident, or Sajin would have been able to prevent it. A stray spear had taken him down. But now Thorn's troops were pulling back, milling around without any central thrust, or attack. Sajin decided to move forward then, of his own accord, still operating under the theory that he was being backed up by his allies. Had he acted differently it is possible to assume everyone would have been destroyed that day. Instead, his faithfulness helped save the day.

Prince Thorn wasn't alone in death. Luke of Astertov joined him in hell shortly after his army's rout. He didn't even live long enough to see that Hans and Calvin were coming down to support him. His death came quickly, and suddenly, as he fell to the ground, his pleas for help ignored. Luke only had himself to blame for his death. Because that day he had decided not to dress in any outstanding uniform, not desiring to be signaled out for any archer's arrows, and was thus mistaken for just another soldier. And was thus trampled to death just like any soldier. Only his aides noticed his absence. Even without him, his troops pulled back to rally, and stood their ground as the Kurtonburg and Wunderkinde troops came down the hill.

Grover, posing as Phillip, led the way swinging his two-handed great sword to great effect, to his surprise and to the surprise of those that he killed. Cilla followed in his wake, braining with her club those who had survived Grover's initial onslaught. Acting as a team, they formed a fighting unit, driving into the Astertov lines, killing any hapless soldier or knight who came into their path. It seemed they were going to take the field that day. You could feel it in the air, and see it in the faces of the knights fighting beside them. The evidence of their victory was all around them, as soldier after soldier fell to the ground or fled in terror.

And then someone cried out that the rest of the Sousterhoven troops were making a move.

Grover had just flung off his helmet, claiming it made his head sweaty, when he heard the cry. He looked above the heads of the other soldiers and knights, since he towered above them, and clearly saw the twenty thousand troops coming down, like a massive wall of steel. It was a tidal wave of human flesh, unstoppable and unrelenting, and it was coming for them.

Grover quickly appraised the situation. "Better retreat."

Cilla nodded in agreement, and then brained another fellow with her club.

The Sousterhoven wall came sweeping down like a giant broom, manipulated by a muscular giant. It came down hard and swift and didn't waver in its path. Any stray matter in its path, such as a Westerhoven soldier, was immediately moved out of the way. In this manner they swept down into the center of the great field unopposed. Hans led the way, going for the gap—that weak piece of hanging flesh. The Astertov troops saw them sweep down and, taking heart at this moment, renewed their attack. But since they had no central leader, their attack was not concentrated, and wasn't successful. But they didn't lose ground either, so you could say it was successful in halting the advance of the Wunderkinde and Kurtonburg troops.

It was at that moment that all fighting ceased. It was like a hush that comes over a room, suddenly and for no reason, and in that silence, one person usually speaks out loud, saying something about his underwear. It was in this silence that everyone heard one sound. It was a rippling wave, like thunder; muffled, but rhythmic. It made the air vibrate and pulse around them. Soldiers and knights let their weapons fall to their sides and cast their gaze upward. Up at the gray sky. But the sky was no longer gray, except right above them, where it resembled a pupil. Because all around that pupil there was a blackness. And as the blackness swirled in closer, everyone could see the darkness was not uniform, but made up of separate entities. Birds. Millions of them.

Looking up, Grover said, "I bet this has something to do with the *Stone*."

Survival Tips
for the Apocalypse

Grover and Cilla weren't the only ones with eyes to see and ears to hear. All over the field the leaders of the various armies cast their gaze upward. Richard looked up and wondered if this was the apocalypse. Ivan just thought it was a hallucination on his part. Bertrand, who was already starting to withdraw, decided that he should hurry to that stone cottage that lay just ahead. Dianna, busy trying to coordinate her troops, didn't have time to be concerned with birds. Sajin had halted his advance against the troops of Erich and Thorn and wondered what this strange occurrence could mean. And Kirk of Kurtonburg, who had watched his troops advance forward without him, had an inkling that this wasn't just an example of fall migration.

On the Sousterhoven field Bertold saw the birds, took it as an omen that worse things were going to happen, and ordered his troops to exit off the island. David saw the birds but did not connect them with any imminent apocalypse. Unlike Richard of Meistertonne, he had never read the Scriptures, so he just ignored the occurrence, and ordered his forces to keep pushing forward against his old enemy, the Hoeneckers. Calvin saw the birds and felt uneasy. But leaving the field now meant betraying his allies, which he knew he would pay for later, so he also did nothing. And last of all, Hans saw the birds, and remembered part of the three omens that would prevent him from becoming ruler of all of Hoven. *When the earth shall move against you* . . .

The birds, who had no idea they were part of prophecy or the pawns of the *Sacred Stone,* flew in a wide circle until the entire sky turned black with their bodies. Below them the day turned to dusk, and a whirling breeze started to pound down on the people below. The paralysis that had halted the movement of the troops on all sides was now gone. But in the mind of each soldier, of each knight, they felt that they were trapped.

"What should we do?" Grover asked Cilla.

"Push toward the castle," Cilla said, "before it's too late."

The troops of Erich and Thorn knew what was to come and started to withdraw toward the ancient city of Hoven. They dropped their weapons, threw off their helmets, and ignored the pleas of wounded and fallen comrades in their haste to reach the city gates. Behind them, the dual forces of Sajin of Ubbergammu and David of Gustavus closed on them like a vice, pursuing them to the gates, cutting them down as they fled. Some of the soldiers of Erich, seeing that they were pursued, closed the gates quickly, trapping hundreds, thousands of their comrades on the other side of the gates to be cut down mercilessly.

Grover and Cilla renewed the attack of the Wunderkinde forces and started to hack their way into the Astertov troops. They tried to cut a path toward the ancient city of Hoven, which might have been easier had not the forces of Calvin and Hans lain between them.

Hans took the opportunity to further his efforts in severing the remaining flesh between the limb and the body by urging his forces faster into the gap between the Kurtonburg and the Vagner forces. Calvin's forces followed suit, and soon they were engaged in a battle. The movement succeeded in uniting the forces of Astertov, Reichton, and Auschwitz to form an unbroken offensive line. A diagonal line that stretched across from the middle of the field to the top of the hill where Bertrand of Vagner's forces were retreating. The advance was so strong that it severed that tenuous bond between the two Westerhoven forces. The Kurtonburgs and the Wunderkindes were cut free, to be isolated, flanked on two sides. Meanwhile Calvin of Auschwitz's soldiers were engaged with the main body, chasing the retreating Vagners and engaging the Meistertonne knights who were still holding their ground.

"This is victory," Hans said.

"This is a disaster," Grover said. "I thought Dianna said everyone was going to follow us."

"You see what happens when you fall for a pretty face," Cilla said.

They were still pushing into the disorganized Astertov forces, but their initial drive was becoming stymied. Soon they found themselves cut off from the other troops and surrounded by Astertov soldiers on all sides. And they weren't looking for

autographs. All around them knights with green and white plumes
attacked their knights and sought their heads as trophies.

"I thought we were supposed to win," Grover said, hacking
with his sword.

"Me too," Cilla said, bludgeoning someone with her club.

"If something doesn't happen fast, we're doomed," Grover
said.

"Like what?" Cilla asked.

It was then that something happened fast. The birds who had been
circling suddenly began to drop out of the sky. They fell like
missiles. Claws extended, beaks forward, they pecked and picked
at any soldier they saw. It was a rain of birds. They circled and
then dropped. Circled and then dropped. A gap began to appear in
the sky above them. Everywhere soldiers and knights were
stopping their fight to push off birds, and to save their faces. But
if they tried to push them off their faces their hands were clawed.
And not just by one bird, but by several. One couldn't even look
up to see them coming down, since they were so many. You
couldn't breathe for the feathers. Grover and Cilla covered their
heads and took refuge under the dead bodies of other knights. All
around them they heard the cries of soldiers and knights as they
were torn apart. No one who was left out in the open remained
unscathed. Hans also hid under the bodies of dead soldiers. Calvin
found refuge under a supply wagon, because his troops had penetrated as far as the camps. Bertrand of Vagner, who had been
eyeing that stone cottage for safety, didn't make it. Richard found
that the birds stayed away from smoke and fire, and so fanned
away the birds with flaming brands and survived. Others were not
so lucky, nor so intelligent. Ivan was caught out in the open,
where the birds flocked all over him. Sajin took refuge by the
walls of the city, where the birds either slammed into the walls or
landed too short to attack him. Dianna was covered over by her
faithful knights who wished to protect her. She survived, but was
covered in blood by the knights who didn't. Beogoat survived by
finding shelter in an old barn. Romeo and Bill hid under their cots
in Phillip's tent.

On the Sousterhoven side Bertold was too far away to be
affected by most of the birds and managed to live, though many of
the soldiers on the fringes were wounded. David of Gustavus was
not so lucky and was killed out in the open as he refused to give
up the fight. Many soldiers and knights also died, but more were
wounded than dead.

And just as soon as the barrage began, it was over and the remainder of the birds were flying off. All along the field lay the corpses of millions of birds, some still fluttering, some wounded, some still attacking, some trying to fly away, but most just dead. The whole field had been leveled. No soldier or knight stood up. All were either lying on the ground or were on their hands and knees.

Erich looked out on the field and was pleased.

Grover and Cilla pushed off the corpses that had saved them. All around they saw the littered field.

"Are they all dead?" Grover asked.

But as he asked that, soldiers began to cry out in pain. Knights helped their friends to their feet. Everywhere people began to pick themselves up. From the ground the armies rose up again. But not as many, and not with the same desire for killing they had just a short time before. They were much diminished armies. Shaken armies. Thousands of their comrades lay on the ground either wounded, dying, or dead. Of those who stood, only a few could say they had no injury. They looked around them and called out their friends' names, but many names went unanswered. Many bodies did not move. They picked up their weapons and looked at their neighbor who was their enemy. And they did not feel the same anger.

The possibility for peace, or at least a truce, seemed imminent. In the wake of this sort of destruction who could keep on fighting?

Grover and Cilla saw that everyone seemed uncertain of what to do. But beyond the soldiers they also saw the light above the city walls of Hoven. The bright light was still flashing, still casting out its signal.

"Come on," Cilla said, nudging Grover. "We have a chance to cross the field now."

"What?" Grover cried, and then he saw that indeed the path was clear for them to reach the city. Erich's destruction had served to help them as well as hurt them, because no great force stood between them.

So together Cilla and Grover stood up and gathered a few Dude Knights with them and ran across the field for the city.

They weren't alone in this endeavor. Hans, who had pulled himself free from the dead bodies that had protected him, also saw that there was a flashing light emitting from the city. And he knew what it meant now. It was the *Sacred Stone,* and it was calling for the trees. First come the birds, then the trees, and what need does any Hoven king have for an army of men, especially since you don't have to pay the birds and trees? It was all part of the second omen, which spelled out the failure of his securing the throne of Hoven. But that was only if he didn't reach the *Stone* first and prevent Erich—because he knew it was Erich now who had the *Stone*—from using it. So like Grover and Cilla, he called a few of his knights and made for the city, pushing past the wounded and dazed soldiers.

Erich had no fear. He stood on the city walls with the *Stone* pulsing in his hands like a living heart. He had felt the power of the birds and that had been good. The destruction had been powerful and even beautiful. They had all denied him and had suffered for their obstinacy. Looking at all the wounded, at the milling soldiers, he wondered if it was enough. Should he stop now? He could be acknowledged leader of the Westerhoven forces and begin his kingdom here. But looking out, he realized he had the chance to destroy the Sousterhoven armies now. All he had to do was let the *Stone* keep working. He felt it calling out to the trees. He felt their roots pull up from the ground. He felt them break free of the earth and move forward. He felt the second wave of his army heeding his call.

Byron, and the six soldiers who accompanied him, watched from beneath the wagon as the trees began to sway. At first, Byron thought it was another movement of the earth. But the earth did not tremble as before. The tremors were more localized, centered, and short.

"Should we not worry this time too?" a soldier asked.

"I'm not sure," Byron said.

It was then that he saw the first tree rip out of the earth. It then bent over and picked up a boulder. All around them, the deep roots of trees popped out of the earth. Dirt went flying into the air. The branches of trees moved and bent like the limbs of a man as they stooped and picked up boulders. And they marched like soldiers as they walked up the hill.

"Well, maybe you can worry," Byron finally said, when he could speak.

"Is that an order?" a soldier asked.

"No, merely a suggestion," Byron said, who covered his eyes, and hoped the trees would ignore him.

• • •

Even though David of Gustavus was dead, his soldiers had managed to break down the gates to the city. They hadn't been securely barred, and the weight of many soldiers, plus the previous tremors of the earth, had weakened the mortar around the gates, so that they crashed to the earth under the brute force. The enmity of the Hoenecker and Gustavan forces went way back, so they did not pause in their fighting at all, but pressed onward an inward into the city.

Sajin saw this and led his forces through also. And behind them came Hans and his seven knights, and Grover and Cilla and their five knights. They didn't see that behind them the forest of trees was marching onto the field, causing great chaos among the soldiers, who thought they had already seen the apocalypse.

Inside the city there was massive fighting. It was Erich's Avengers and Thorn's Hoeneckers against the combined forces of Sajin's Ubbergammus and David's Gustavans. And it was also Ubbergammu against Gustavan as well. It wasn't the sort of battle that could be directed. It was a giant melee acted out in front of the gates on both sides, and within the first few streets of the city. It even extended up the stairs of the walls as soldiers fled to the battlements. So even though Prince Thorn was dead and David of Gustavus was dead, their forces no longer needed them. All they needed for their motivation was their hate. They were fighting for their lives, in a battle of no quarter.

And into this melee came Hans with his knights, and he was able to gather some of the Gustavan knights about him and form a formidable fighting wedge. With this force he was able to fight his way to the stairs. On the stairs the black-garbed Avengers were the thickest. It was an uphill battle. There were two sets of stairs up to the walls and the Avengers held both of them. Hans took the stairs on the left side of the gate and pressed forward.

Grover and Cilla, who didn't want to be left out, also entered the fray and met up with Sajin of Ubbergammu.

"What are you doing here?" Sajin asked in surprise when he saw them. He looked back for their troops. "Where is your army?"

"Back on the field," Grover said. "We've come to get Erich."

"I can handle him," Sajin said. "Phillip, you should really return to your troops."

"It doesn't matter anymore," Cilla said. "Unless we get the *Stone* from Erich we're probably all doomed."

"The what?" Sajin asked.

"The *Sacred Stone*," Cilla said. "This battle doesn't matter as long as Erich has it."

"How come no one came to support me?" Sajin asked.

"We have no time to discuss your persecution complex," Grover said.

"My what?" Sajin asked.

"We need your help," Cilla clarified.

Sajin nodded. Together they formed a fierce battle unit and fought through the Hoenecker and Gustavan troops to gain the right-hand stairs. But just like the left-hand stairs there were the troops of Erich's Avengers. As soon as they were spotted, the Avengers cried out for Phillip's death, so it didn't seem likely they were going to surrender, and much to Grover's and Cilla's disappointment, they found their advance slowed.

Outside of the city the trees came up to the crest of the hill and surrounded the forces on the field. Those who had managed to withdraw, such as Bertold of Teuton's army, Bertrand of Vagner's army, and some of the Dresdel army, found themselves out of danger. But for the rest of the Westerhoven and Sousterhoven armies, they found themselves facing another danger. Soldiers who tried to run through the wall of trees were caught in a web of branches and torn apart. The only option for those on the field was to retreat and pray for a forest fire.

In the city, it was a blind contest to see who would reach Erich first. Neither participant knew the other was competing, but each had his own reasons for reaching the top and so pushed harder and faster. Hans, knowing that his prophecy hung in the balance, sacrificed his knights without remorse just to gain a step or two. Since his conscience was more flexible, he was able to accept huge losses of life as long as he made the greater progress on the steps.

Cilla and Grover were just as much in a hurry to get to Erich, but their consciences were less flexible and they weren't as willing to risk their own lives, or the lives of those who fought with them. Only one knight at a time could fight on the stairs, and they didn't sacrifice knights just to gain a few steps. So they were not the first to arrive at the top of the wall.

It was Hans who first reached the top of the wall. Behind him trailed his own Reichton knights. The Gustavan knights had all fallen in his pursuit to the top. A slew of bodies lay in his wake. Only a few of the Avenger's men stood between him and Erich.

He advanced on these quickly. There was more space up on the battlements and he and his knights were able to fight side by side. It didn't take long to clear a space, because their rapid advance only gave the Avengers two choices: a swan dive off the wall or evisceration without anesthesia.

Erich wasn't deaf. He heard the screams all about him and knew that they meant fighting was going on in the city, but he also knew he couldn't stop the control of the trees. He had to make sure they surrounded all the forces on the field and none escaped. It was the only way he would win. He was too close to lose. And because he was too close, he couldn't see what lay directly in front of him. Or in this case, behind him. Which gave Hans all the opportunity in the world to do his worst.

Grover and Cilla reached the top of the wall just in time to see that Hans was there.

"How did he get here so quick?" Grover asked.

Cilla shrugged. "Maybe he knew a shortcut."

They watched as Hans advanced on Erich. Erich stood facing the field with a beatific glow on his face. In his hands he held the pulsing living *Stone*. It flashed brightly, almost blindingly. They watched as Hans raised his sword to strike Erich.

"I guess this saves us the trouble," Grover said.

But the blade didn't land. It turned bright red, as it increased in temperature. In a moment it was white-hot. Hans immediately dropped the blade. Erich did not turn or wince, or make any sign he saw what was happening. The blade lay on the walkway, burning into the stone.

"Well, I'm glad he tried that first," Cilla said.

But Hans was not done. He stepped past the blade and reached out with his hands to Erich. His hands found either side of his red scarf, and he pulled the ends tight. Erich's face jerked back as the scarf was pulled tight as a noose.

"That's what I would have done," Grover said.

"No, you wouldn't have," Cilla said, and punched him in the arm.

Erich fell to his knees, his face growing red. One hand left the *Stone* to grab at the scarf, but Hans wasn't letting go. He pulled even tighter on the ends of the scarf, only relaxing his grip to change his hand position. Erich fell to his knees, the finger of one hand digging beneath the scarf, trying to pry it free.

"If I was Erich," Grover said, "I would try to use both hands to pry that scarf off."

"But he doesn't want to lose the *Stone*," Cilla said. "You have to understand how the psychotic mind works."

"Oh yeah," Grover said, nodding. "But I still would have used both hands.

Hans hugged Erich close to his body so that he could better use his strength. Erich struggled with his one free hand, but to no avail. His struggle grew weaker. He fell backward onto the pavement. The *Stone* rolled out of his grip and onto the walkway. And it kept on rolling, toward Cilla and Grover, until it lay halfway between them and Hans.

Hans pulled the scarf tighter once more and then let go. The body of Erich sagged to the ground. His lifeless blue eyes stared up at the gray sky.

Cilla clapped her hands. "Very good."

It was then that Hans looked over to see both of them standing there. His two inconvenient impostors. The incarnation of his first omen. And in between them lay the *Sacred Stone*, all white, and not glowing at all.

How to Fulfill a Prophecy

"Hans," Cilla warned, "don't even think about going for that little *Stone*." She stepped forward.

Hans stood up then. "So we finally meet face-to-face."

"Don't let it overwhelm you," Cilla said. "It wasn't intentional."

Hans's eyes went down to his sword, still simmering on the walkway. He then looked to one of his knights and nodded toward the knight's sword.

Cilla darted forward quickly and grabbed the *Stone*. It was cold and lifeless in her hands.

Hans took the sword from the Reichton knight and turned back to Cilla and Grover. "All this trouble caused by just a man a woman."

"Excuse me," Cilla said. "Not just any man and woman. We're professional heroes."

Behind Grover, Sajin had come up. "What's this about a man and a woman?"

Grover shrugged. "I think Hans is losing it."

"Why is *Voss* challenging Hans?" Sajin asked.

"You don't think *I'm* going to challenge him?" Grover asked in surprise. "I could get killed."

"He is the enemy," Sajin said. "If you will not fight him, I will. But I will not watch as your swordbearer gets cut down." Sajin made to pass by Grover. Grover held out his arm to bar his way.

"Don't spoil the moment," Grover said.

Meanwhile Hans and Cilla were facing off.

"Professional heroes," Hans remarked.

"You got it," Cilla said. She held the *Stone* in one hand and the club in the other.

"Give me the *Stone*," Hans said.

"I don't think so," Cilla said. "I don't think you would use it wisely. You seem to have a very violent nature, and this *Stone* isn't a toy. You can hurt people with it."

Hans hefted the sword in both hands. "If you give me the *Stone* I will make you a king."

"I don't think you're telling the truth," Cilla said.

"You're right," Hans said. "But if you give me the *Stone* I will let you live."

"You're still lying," Cilla said. "And besides I don't think you could kill me."

"You don't?" Hans asked in surprise. "I am a master swordsman."

"Well, my partner is a master duelist," Cilla said. "And he always gets his butt kicked. So I don't think this adjective 'master' means what you guys think it means."

"Hey," Grover cried out.

"What is he talking about?" Sajin asked.

Cilla turned to address Grover. "It's true, you do get your butt kicked."

"Well, you don't have to tell everybody," Grover yelled back.

"Why not?" Cilla asked. "Nobody knows you here."

Hans spoke. "Then I guess you'll have to find out."

Cilla backed up a step. "A great sword against a club isn't a very fair fight. Especially when I have to hold the *Stone* in one of my hands."

"Then give me the *Stone*," Hans said.

"Ah, you don't give up, do you?" Cilla said. "But you know, I have a better solution." She tossed the *Stone* up in the air and whacked it with the club. The *Stone* cracked when the metal-shod end of the club hit it, and sailed into the city, hitting the wall of a building and bouncing to the floor, where it shattered.

Hans's eyes widened with surprise.

"There," Cilla said. "Now both of my hands are free and we can have a fair fight."

Hans readjusted himself. He held the sword out. He looked back to his knights and nodded to them, indicating they should attack. So together, Hans and his knights advanced on Grover, Cilla, and Sajin.

Cilla, seeing she was outnumbered, retreated toward Grover.

"Good going," Grover said. "You had to piss him off."

"And I suppose you would have done better?" Cilla shot back.

"Yeah," Grover said. "And you destroyed the *Stone*."

"He might have gotten it," Cilla said.

"I bet it was irreplaceable," Grover said. "If we don't get paid for this mission because of this, it's your fault."

"Shut up," Cilla said, "and fight."

Sajin looked over. "What is this talk of missions?"

"Later," Grover said. And he raised his sword to meet Hans's blade. "Hans," he said. "Meet my sword, *Biff*."

Grover killed Hans. So much for the prophecy. He was just as surprised as Hans was. Hans had come down with his knights full of anger toward these two impostors who had upset his plans for the domination of Hoven, and had signaled out Grover for a one-on-one fight. Grover had improved since his battle with Erich during the wedding. He knew how to maneuver and fight with the blade. But he was far away from being a pro. Yet he was able to counter every blow by Hans. And Hans was very good. He seemed like he had two swords instead of one. But Grover was able to block them all, and with ever-increasing accuracy he landed blow after blow on Hans, beating him back. Suddenly he took the final battle—a winning, life-destroying blow—and cut off Hans's head. The head sailed through the air and into the city, where it didn't even phase the heated members of the great melee.

Romeo and Bill wrote a song about that moment that went something like this:

> The fight went on for nigh a year
> Long enough to drink one's beer
> And Hans was tough, there was no doubt
> But his game was over, he was out.
>
> With a wayward swing of the mighty *Biff*
> And the sweet sound of a lute riff
> Hans's head was soon set free to sail
> Going faster than our modern express mail.
>
> O joyous moment, O raptured bliss
> It was a sight few could afford to miss.
> The head went sailing far and wide
> And oh yes, of course Hans died.

The song never really caught on. But for Grover it was a moment to treasure forever.

"Ha," Hans cried as Grover fell back. There was a huge gash along Grover's head where he wasn't able to stop Hans's sword. Blood covered his face. Grover lost his balance and fell back, hitting his head on the rough stone of the wall, and immediately went unconscious.

Cilla saw this all in one of those suspended instants in time. Everything was clear and vivid. Grover's cry as he was struck with Hans's blade. Grover's hand as he reached up to the wound. The blood covering his face. The look of disbelief. Grover losing balance and falling backward. She was operating in a different time frame. She was aware of everything. She was never surer of herself than now.

Before Hans could even recover she was swinging with her club, hitting Hans on his outstretched arm and breaking the bone. She remembered the feeling as the club hit his arm. The shock of the wood hitting a solid object, and then that audible *crack*. That satisfying *crack*. She remembered watching the blade drop from Hans's numb hands. The blade fell to the side. There was the sound of steel hitting stone. A scraping kind of sound. And then she was hitting Hans again. Hans hadn't even recovered from the first blow. He hadn't even cried out in pain. Everything was happening too quick. Before Hans even noticed his arm was broken she was swinging again. This time her club went into his stomach, like she was chopping a tree. Hans instantly doubled over. As his head dipped to waist level, Cilla knew what to do and struck again, this time hitting him on the back of the head. There was a clanging sound as she hit the helmet, but there was also a *crack* as Hans's skull split. Hans collapsed to his knees. Cilla didn't even think as she struck him on the head again. This time his head twitched to the side as his neck snapped. It seemed as if they were the only two people left in the world. Just Hans and her. Hans fell slowly to the ground. Too slowly, because Cilla didn't even wait until he stopped falling before she hit his head again. She kept striking his head until blood seeped out of the helmet and Hans's body stopped quivering. That seemed to be about the right time to stop. So she did. Her job was complete.

When she looked up, still in a daze, she saw that everyone was staring at her with a look of total amazement: the Reichton knights, Sajin, and the Ubbergammu knights behind him.

Ignoring them all, she let her club drop to the pavement and went to see if her partner was all right.

Epilogue

Most of the Black Avenger's men weren't killed, but were able to hide in the city and later flee. The Hoenecker forces, without a leader, eventually stopped fighting the Gustavan forces in the city. By nightfall the battle was over, and everyone had withdrawn to their camps, looking warily at the trees which now surrounded the field. They stayed at their opposite camps that night, and in the morning both sides waited for what was to happen. But nothing did occur. The surviving leaders of the Westerhoven Lords—Dianna, Kirk, Richard, and Sajin—conferred and sent over an envoy to the Sousterhoven side. Calvin responded by saying he had no further intentions of battle. So a few days later after taking care of the dead and wounded, both sides withdrew from the island.

PHILLIP and VOSS: Their bodies were eventually found sitting in a wagon. They were interred in the crypts beneath the Castle Wunderkinde as was their due. But their death date is given as the day of the great battle and not when they were killed by Hans. No mention is made anywhere of the impostors, and Phillip is given credit for winning the battle. Voss is given credit for being a faithful servant. Go figure.

OLD LORD PHILLIP: He was really the only one to benefit from the battle, resuming the Lordship in Wunderkinde that he had once abdicated in favor of his son Phillip. But regretting his son's death, he later signed a treaty with Kirk and Dianna giving the rights to his kingdom over to them upon his death.

RICHARD: He went on to live a long and prosperous life, and until his death claimed that Phillip and Voss were really impostors. But he was never able to get any other Lords to concur with his claim, and thus was seen as a fool to the end of his days.

BEOWEASEL: He later rose in the Brotherhood, and since he was knowledgeable in magic and the ways of wizards, he headed the inquisition against known users of magic in the backlash against wizardry that resulted after Beogoat's intervention into politics. Later he was to become so versed in the arcane arts that he started an investigation against himself which resulted in his own execution.

KIRK and DIANNA: Both eventually succeeded to the thrones of their principalities and later married. Their nations were officially joined. They met with other leaders both West and South, and are working to bring Hoven under one ruler someday.

SAJIN: He didn't live very long after the battle. He suffered from a bout of pneumonia and died. His questions about hired heroes, and what really happened to Phillip and Voss, were never quite adequately answered.

BERTOLD: Retreated to his country where he started an isolationist policy. He grew fearful of all birds and trees and began a great deforestation project around his capital. He later choked to death on a piece of parsley when he saw a bluebird on his windowsill.

CALVIN: He kept to himself and didn't involve himself in any more great battles, even when the successors of both Luke and Hans called for them. He devoted himself to keeping peace within Sousterhoven, and opened up ties with Kirk and Dianna, becoming the first Sousterhoven Lord to be truly welcome in Westerhoven.

BYRON: Survived the day and went on to write a book about Hans's life called *The Three Omens of Hans and the Curse of Doom*. It was put down by critics and didn't do very well. Still, he went on to have a successful literary career after that.

ROMEO and BILL: Went on to become a great songwriting team, and were guests in courts all over Hoven. But their time in the limelight was to be short. Drugs and ego took their toll, and now they can be found on the oldies circuit, putting out solo work which no one thinks is really that good.

BEOGOAT: Found that he was no longer welcome in any principality of Hoven during the anti-wizard sentiment that sprang up after the great battle. He went back to his job agency and worked with the Wizard Collectors for a while. Later he got a break, and is now working in the Kingdoms of the West with Belgarion. He still hasn't finished his memoirs.

THE BLACK AVENGERS: They later went on to form the backbone of various other subversive movements. But in a unanimous vote they ditched the black uniforms in favor of something more distinctive.

GROVER and CILLA: They returned to Heroes, Inc., to find that Gallin had been fired for mismanagement and Sallu had been hired as his replacement. Grover and Cilla, finally successful, were offered multitudes of great adventures and huge offers from weapons companies, and higher pay and benefits from hero and villain companies alike. They were never able to cash in on their success and decided to split up. The nature of the final dispute isn't well documented, but it was believed to be over who actually killed off Hans. Cilla's citing that Grover was an incorrigible prick was the last straw. Published reports later said it was over "irreconcilable differences."